ROGUE FLAMINGO

L A Kent

Published by WillowOrchard Publishing

www.lakent.co.uk

Rogue Flamingo

First published in Great Britain in 2014 by WillowOrchard Publishing

Published by WillowOrchard Publishing.

A CIP catalogue record for this book is available from the British Library

ISBN 978-0-9575109-2-0

www.lakent.co.uk

info@willoworchard.co.uk

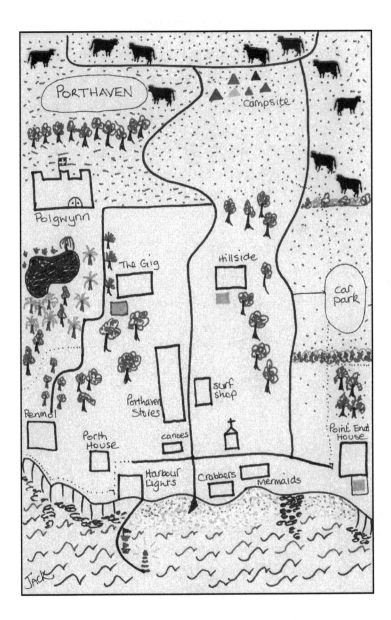

*'Porthaven has a sheltered sandy beach offering safe
bathing protected by a stone quay, with properties
clustered along the steep narrow streets of a wooded valley
and stretching along the cliffs to east and west. Excellent
scenic cliff walks for the intrepid. There are facilities,
toilets and a large car park 300 yards from the beach.
Found on narrow minor roads with passing places south of
Truro. A traditional, peaceful anchorage.'*

Cornish Cove Guide

But not that July morning.

18 July 06:00

As Marianne Temple walked down the lane past the closed surf shop and Porthaven Stores at 6:00 that Sunday morning, she hummed softly to herself: Vaughan Williams' Fantasia on a Theme by Thomas Tallis. She loved the village at this time of day at this time of year; too early for visitors, too early for most locals. She crossed the road that ran parallel to the shore, passed Crabbers café, and stepped onto the dimpled sand at the top of the beach where the tide does not usually reach. Flashes of sunlight were reflecting off the wave-tops like hundreds of signal lamps. Breathing deeply she gazed at the sea which was rolling gently over the few pebbles and strands of seaweed strewn along the waterline.

'OK my beauties,' she said quietly, unleashing two greyhounds who raced off to the west towards the quay. Since her husband's death she had assumed the task of walking the rescue greyhounds Shadow and Max, and what she had once thought would be a terrible chore had become a cherished opportunity for solitude.

Marianne turned and headed east, strolling along the length of the beach on the hard damp sand left by the falling tide. Above her to her left she could see the blank windows and deserted terraces and gardens of the large houses which skirted the cliff edge curving off towards Point End. The sky was the palest of blues, tinged primrose at the horizon and the only sound other than the sea was the occasional cry of a gull. Perfect.

Ahead of her at the far end of the beach she could see a shape on the sand. At first she thought it was some lost sail washed in and abandoned by the tide, but as she got closer it took on the unmistakable shape of the human form. Someone was lying, spread-eagled on the beach. Sod it. Simultaneously surprised and annoyed, she braced herself for an encounter with some summer visitor sleeping it off.

Before retirement Marianne Temple had been a paediatrician at The London Hospital, and whilst not overly familiar with adult patients she was aware that something about this individual looked wrong. As she closed upon the prone figure she saw a naked man with a black bag over his head. He was lying with arms and legs outstretched, all four limbs tied by some kind of coloured cord to the summer-laid mooring ropes which stretched into the sea to anchor the lane marker buoys which separated swimmers from boat users.

Marianne ran towards him calling out 'hello' but already convinced there would be no answer. Kneeling in the damp sand she reached out to take a pulse. He was icy cold and very dead. She pulled back her hand and covered her mouth gasping, then stood, pulled out her mobile, and dialled 999.

'Police please, no, no ambulance will be needed, just the coroner's undertaker.'

As the dogs raced towards her, she knelt again calling them and much to their disgust reattached their leads.

One week earlier.

10 July 11:45

'For Christ's sake Jack, pick up your feet, you're wasting valuable drinking time!' said Oliver Osborne QC to his fourteen year old son as he marched him into the White Café in Gatwick Airport's North Terminal departure lounge. Jack shuffled along behind in his overlong baggy jeans and trailing behind him came David Cavendish and his son Robin aged fifteen, neither paying much attention as they were discussing cricket.

At thirty eight, Oliver Osborne was the youngest and most successful barrister in his Chambers and he was en route to Cornwall with second wife Julia, his son Jack and old Etonian chum David and his family. Off to Sardinia was the norm for the Osbornes at this time of year; lazing by the pool for Oliver and a little light shopping for Julia. Presumably Jack did something, but Oliver would be hard pressed to say what that might be. The norm at this time of year for the Cavendishes would be off to Hampshire for a week with Helen's best friend from childhood, but this year Oliver wanted David's company and what Oliver wants, Oliver gets.

The White Café was half full with people drinking alcohol earlier than they would at home. All but one rather anxious young man sitting alone at the end of the bar facing the mirror nursing a coke, and repeatedly glancing at the entrance as if waiting for someone.

'Welcome, how can I help you?' said the smiling girl behind the bar in a South African accent as Oliver drummed his fingers on the counter.

'Your best Chablis, a large one for me. Davy what do you want?' said Oliver.

3

'Just a bottle of Becks for me thanks Oliver, and the boys would like grapefruit juice.' The two boys walked over and sat at a table by the window.

'I'm sorry sir, we're really low on white wine at the moment I'm expecting a delivery. We do have two Australian Chardonnays however, please do try both before you commit'.

'My God, we are less than fifty miles from the centre of the city which formed the hub of the world's largest empire, and you only have Australian Chardonnay, that evil piss?'

Oliver's mobile phone rang. 'What Julia? For Christ's sake I told you the White Café. Julia, I know they limit the liquid contents to 100ml in hand luggage but they don't mean you have to put your brain fluid in the hold! If you would only listen woman! Yes, the White Café, surely Helen can find it,' Oliver snorted.

People turned to stare at the red-shirted man with the loud obnoxious voice.

'Oliver, stop it, please. We're blocking the queue. Why don't you have a red?' David was, as ever, calming and conciliatory.

'Fine, whatever, OK I'll have the Merlot, a large one, no sod it, give me a glass and a bottle. What? Anything else? Oh yes, a bottle of Stella and two juices, orange will do.'

As Oliver and David moved over to the window with the drinks, David grinned at Jack who wore his normal vacant expression and tried to engage him in a conversation about England's recent batting exploits.

'Do you know Robbie that at Eton whilst I was opening for the house your father was twelfth man carrying on the lemon squash? Couldn't carry a bat but was a little master with the lemon squash heh, what?' Oliver snorted

4

a laugh, a sound that echoed across the centuries; the snort of the horses on the Russian Steppes, herded by his forebears, obviously not then known as Osborne. Oliver's ancestors had been horse traders and bandits.

On the lower floor shopping concourse Helen Cavendish was wearing a pair of five year old hand made clogs bought from a man in Lymington in Hampshire close to her childhood home. Dressed for comfort and travelling, she was forced to walk slowly because Julia Osborne was wearing a pair of Alexander McQueen blue stiletto pumps, dressed, as always, to please Oliver.

Julia spoke in a pleading tone. 'Helen, can we go in here please? Ollie says I need to look more girlie, I was thinking, maybe pink pearly lipstick just for now and maybes some Botox when we get back. I know I can't get that here but I know a little man who says it's wonderful and that actress who got it wrong and puffed up horridly? Well he says she obviously went to the wrong people. And I do so want to look good for Christmas when we go to Daddy's.'

The Honourable Julia Jocelyne Honor had grown up at Netherholt House in leafy Buckinghamshire. She had met Oliver Osborne at a shooting party in Oxfordshire, and David and Helen Cavendish through him. At the time she was working as a receptionist in a London art gallery and engaged to Tim Petherbridge-Brown of the Guards who was sweet and gentle and softly spoken like David. Oliver was loud and boorish. But Daddy had liked Oliver. Oliver could ride to hounds, Oliver could shoot and above all Oliver could write very large cheques which didn't bounce. For that alone Viscount Netherholt could overlook any number of dubious ancestors.

Helen sighed deeply. Being with Julia was exhausting, but being her must be perpetual hell. To Helen, Julia was of a type where you were thick and it didn't matter because you were rich. But Helen loved David, David was Oliver's oldest friend, and Julia was Oliver's wife, so she tolerated Julia, consoling herself with the thought that Julia's innate stupidity meant that she was oblivious to Oliver's petty cruelty.

Helen had always loathed Oliver. In a way she held a deep seated relish that Oliver had ended up with someone so truly dense, but mostly she just felt sorry for the poor cow. And poor Jack. The sad creature was the progeny of a loud ugly man descended from horse thieves and a dead, drowned mother who had been replaced by a blonde bimbo who could trace her lineage back beyond Hereward the Wake.

Helen sighed again and said. 'Julia, I think it would be really good to join the boys. Aren't you thirsty? I'm sure there will be Champagne.'

Julia looked at Helen with the eyes of a dog that's had a hard day, and not for the first time. 'I know where they are, obviously I know that, you heard Ollie, everyone heard Ollie, but do you think we might go to that sushi bar just for one drink? I know we could have Champagne there and it's ever so close. I know it's wrong to leave Jack, but David and Robin are there and they'll look out for him.'

Jamie, the solitary young man at the White Café bar, had always been a quiet, self-contained, observant individual and he was watching the window table intently. So *that* was Oliver Osborne in the flesh. He didn't look much like his pictures but those head and shoulder shots didn't show that he was scarcely five foot six and wedge shaped, broad shouldered and narrow hipped.

Oliver was getting drunk. 'For Christ's sake Davy, Ian Bell is totally unreliable. Bring on the lemon squash twelfth man, bring on the squash!' With a negligent flourish he swept his arm across the table, knocking over the empty wine bottle and sending it spinning towards the side of Jack's head just then laying on the table turned away from his father.

As Jamie watched fascinated, David Cavendish reached out to catch the bottle, looked up, raising a hand and smiled at an attractive woman entering the bar holding onto another woman whose heels seemed to be too high. Jamie blushed to the roots of his hair. Helen Cavendish, his beloved Helen, and with her presumably, Julia Osborne. The two women crossed to the table.

'Air Southwest flight SZ105 to Newquay now boarding at gate 57'.

'For God's sake David is he drunk already?' hissed Helen. 'They won't let him on the plane and then what do we do, we're NOT missing the flight. He is such a selfish bastard.'

'Don't worry, you know him of old, by the time we get to the steps he'll be as sober as the judge he intends to be.' David grinned sheepishly at his wife and ran his hand down her arm. Helen tutted and rounded up the boys and their small rucksacks, pulling the earphones from Jack's ears. 'Come on then guys, I can hear the sea calling.' And with that, the Cavendish and Osborne party headed for the departure gate unaware of the slight dark young man following at a discreet distance.

The flight was uneventful, mainly because Oliver snored throughout not even waking when they landed briefly at Plymouth.

Jamie was seated at the back on the right with a window seat. He followed the coastline, stealing the odd surreptitious glance at Helen Cavendish who was across the aisle ahead of him reading a paperback, occasionally leaning across to check on the boys opposite her. Jamie gazed out as they crossed the Tamar with its twin bridges and continued deeper into Cornwall passing over rivers branching in from the sea with houses lining their banks. When they finally turned inland from the sea they crossed a strange moonscape with deep green pools and white man-made hills of China clay spill: the Cornish Alps. Soon Jamie could see the runway stretching away into the distance seemingly endless, and they banked and started their descent.

When they landed and disembarked Oliver was in the foul mood of the recently woken, slightly hung-over.

'Fuck me, it's like the third world,' Oliver had never been to a small regional airport in the UK. Newquay Airport sits on an RAF base in open countryside along the coast from the town in north Cornwall. There were no landing gates and walkways, just a few ground staff marshalling passengers. As they walked across the tarmac they could hear cows and the occasional passing car, no aircraft engines; no tannoys, no trucks. They entered a small baggage reclaim area where their cases were already waiting. Helen silently raised her eyes to heaven and thanked God.

'Right, let's get the car, boys you load the bags onto a trolley, David you bring Oliver and those guitars, Julia come with me.' Helen was a primary school teacher and often, even on holiday, it showed.

They emerged into a small vestibule with two desks, a group of welcoming people, some with makeshift name boards, and a parking ticket machine. The glass walled room overlooked open fields to distant hills with slow moving wind turbines and through the open doors they could smell the white belted black cows twenty yards away across the road.

Helen realised that with all the luggage and Oliver it would be a nightmare for the others to lurk around whilst she filled in the forms, even on fast-track.

'David, you and Oliver take the boys outside and wait for Julia and me. It's warm and sunny and it will get too crowded in here for all of us.' She gave him a meaningful look and he nodded.

'Come on guys, let the women do the work and we'll sit in the sun. You know this airport has one of the longest runways in the country. They needed it to land heavy long range US bombers in transit during the Second World War,' he winked at Helen who smiled back knowingly. His first comment was aimed at appeasing Oliver and it worked.

With the males despatched, Helen and Julia waited in line at the desk with their driving licences. In the end it was all very efficient and speedy and in no time at all they emerged into the sun with the keys to a Black Sapphire BMW MX6.

They collected the men and boys who had been sitting talking on a bench seat outside the nearby departures entrance and headed towards the car park where they spotted the car in a lay-by with a young man holding the driver's door open. Having gone through the usual checks with Helen, who was to be the main driver, he handed her a pack of maps and brochures and walked away leaving the Cavendishes and Osbornes alone at the start of their first Cornish holiday. Alone that is but for the slight, dark figure sitting at the wheel of a flower-stickered blue and white VW camper van parked just the other side of the car park barrier with a map spread in front of him and his eyes on the group by the BMW.

As they loaded up the luggage, climbed, squabbling over seats, into the car and drove away, he folded the map and smiled. He had no need to follow; he knew where they were going.

Reflections

She lay on her back, in the cool coarse uncut grass, legs outstretched and feet apart, wearing her favourite skirt, a short blue cotton number which was a present from her mother, and a bright yellow T shirt with 'my dad went to New Orleans and all I got was this bloody T shirt' printed on the front in blue – a gift from her father on his return from a recent business trip to the Big Easy which just happened to require his being there at Mardi Gras. She had taken off her white sun hat and was squinting, eyes scrunched up tightly, to see if she could define the black dots, wheeling high in the light blue spring sky.

One of the dots began to grow in size. It was getting bigger, and bigger, moving quicker and quicker and she thought it would crash into the orchard, but then it disappeared from view behind the tops of the trees, there was a distant splash and the Fish Eagle had caught his lunch. The lake near Casheral village provided plentifully for those that knew how to harvest its riches.

Moments later, still looking skywards still on her back, she heard a strange sound – was it a continuous whoop whoop whooping, or a swishshsh swishshsh swishsshshshing, and a peculiar honking sound - getting louder and louder. Suddenly, the noises were just overhead, and she saw a mass of long necked pink cartoon birds, striped with black on their wings. She held up her arm to touch them but they were actually well above the stunted lemon trees. They just seemed close enough to touch.

Flying in a wide V there were too many to count, honk honk honk they said, announcing their arrival, swish swish swishshsh went their wings as the birds dipped towards their destination, came even lower and seemed to brush the trees with their wing tips. They disappeared, flying noisily towards the lake, and she giggled gleefully. Then she heard loud gabbling from the birds already there as the new arrivals loped, and long and triple jumped clumsily through the shallow water as they landed, gradually slowing until they were nearly still, then looking round curiously before dipping their bills into the welcome water they had travelled so far to reach yet again.

She turned over, kept low and crawled on hands and knees to the brambles at the edge of the lemon grove, away from the acrid smoke from the freshly lit barbeque, until she saw the glint of light off the water and giggled again with glee at the tall, funny, pink birds pecking in the water just a short distance away. Dropping her shoulders to the ground, her bum in the air revealing bright yellow knickers she giggled again.

It was OK, she was only three, and on the first holiday she would truly remember in detail.

Rolling over onto her back on the grass under the lemon trees, arms flung wide, the back of her right hand touched something cool and sticky. Looking, she saw a shining black roll half an inch across and three inches long, with a bright orange stripe running along the side. It reminded her of the yummy chocolates she had chosen from last week and turning her hand over she grasped it in her palm and bought it to her mouth. It seemed to shrink somehow as she bought it closer before biting greedily into it at one end.

Bitter and sticky, it was NOT chocolate. She held it above her head looking closely and small tentacles appeared, *slowly stretching longer, with small knobs on the end. She began to squeeze, slowly increasing the pressure until black goo was running between her fingers. Opening her palm, it wasn't shrinking now, the tentacles weren't there any more, just a black gooey, dripping, mess. The Greater European Slug may be attractive to limacologists and even look a bit like chocolate to small girls, but they definitely don't taste nice.*

She stood up, wiped her hand over her bright yellow T shirt from New Orleans, looked closely at her hand then wiped it again, thought about going through the gap to look at the funny pink birds, but skipped off towards Jean, Anne and the adults gathering around the smoking coals of the first barbeque of the season.

Porthaven forms part of the original Pentreath estate which had been in the Pentreath family since 1420. But in 1924 it was bought by Yorkshire coal magnates the Hardcastles after David Pentreath, bankrupted, ran off to Bordeaux leaving massive debts and several illegitimate children.

The village originally consisted of a group of fishermen's cottages and estate houses clustered around the stone quay and the sandy beach at the bottom of a narrow lane winding down through a wooded valley to a sheltered bay in a gap in the granite cliffs. Over the course of the nineteen fifties and sixties the village had expanded rapidly with developments of mostly bungalows branching out up the hillside.

The estate houses and cottages in Porthaven are largely holiday accommodation rendered and coated in tasteful pastel shades of cream and green paint with names like 'solace' and 'liniment' and named after seabirds; 'Fulmar', 'Guillemot', 'Cormorant', 'Whimbrel' and so forth.

The independently owned cottages, bungalows and houses have names like Robin Cottage, Sea Holly House, Mermaids, and Last Resort. When John and Gwen Elliot retired from Swindon they had named their house 'Turnstone'. The following summer they soon realised their mistake with numerous people hammering their brass anchor knocker at all times of the day to enquire about vacancies, and the beautiful hand-painted sign was swiftly removed and replaced with a 'Number 21' etched into Delabole slate.

This summer the Cavendish and Osborne families were staying in Porth House, a large Victorian detached house, formerly a sea captain's, at the extreme westerly point of the beach. The house offered: 'luxurious accommodation for up to eight with every luxury you would expect: family room and sitting rooms with large televisions with Sky+, DVD, integrated sound system, WIFI and log burning stoves, fully fitted kitchen and utility room, three double ensuite bedrooms, and a master bedroom with large rolltop Victorian bathtub for luxurious bathing with amazing sea views'.

For once they were doing something which wasn't Oliver's suggestion. The wives having decided on Cornwall at Christmas, Julia had gathered a selection of holiday houses and initially Helen had suggested one in Flushing, imagining that Julia would be drawn by the retail delights of Falmouth just ten minutes away by ferry across the estuary. But much to Helen's surprise, Julia's choice had been the beach house in Porthaven, 'such fun for the boys'; she had prevailed and for once Oliver had agreed without a word. David, as ever, went along with the others.

From Porthaven quayside, the original road climbs up the hill northwards heading out of the village, but just past the slipway it branches towards the east off to the right running along the cliff edge. Here are to be found the larger private houses perched on the cliff top with impossibly steep gardens sloping to oblivion. At the very end, where the unappointed road peters out and the coastal path reappears veering left over a stile into a field inward from the cliff top, stands Point End House with vistas over the sea and across the cove to the east and Penmassick Point. The original Point End House had been a dilapidated Victorian villa acquired by a wealthy property speculator five years previously. He had spent an unknown, but clearly large sum totally refurbishing, extending and renovating the property, installing a large conservatory to the rear facing out towards Penmassick Point to house a swimming pool. The speculator, Kit Brett-Morgan, rarely visited as his wife disliked holidaying in the UK, but throughout the summer the house was full of various offspring and their extended entourage, much to the chagrin of the neighbours who moaned regularly amongst themselves about noise, but rarely complained directly.

In the house this summer there was a group of eight or so in their late teens and early twenties who frequented The Harbour Lights pub and were often to be found hanging around Crabbers beachside café. Amongst them was a stunning girl with long curly red hair and the concomitant pale skin who sat under an umbrella on the beach most days swathed in a green dragon print kimono. It was on one such occasion that Sunday morning, around 11:30, that she was spotted walking back to her usual table on the Crabbers' terrace by Oliver Osborne, who had reluctantly agreed to keep an eye out whilst Jack and Robin paddled a two-man sit-on canoe, hired for the morning. It was the first weekend of the school holidays and with the tide almost out Porthaven beach was filling rapidly with pallid families laden with blankets, cool bags, and inflated lilos. Fathers were struggling with deckchairs and windbreaks whilst small children were dashing whooping into the waves or shovelling sand in attempts to dam the outlet which ran down to the sea from a culvert beside Crabbers' terrace. Teenage girls were posing coyly on outspread towels whilst their male counterparts strode manfully down to the sea lugging inflated inner-tubes.

Oliver watched the red-headed girl intently, then strolled onto the café's seafront terrace and sat at the table next to her. He could not resist beautiful young women. Leaning across towards her he spoke.

'Have you heard of the Pre-Raphaelites? You remind me of Rossetti's wife and model Elizabeth Siddal, only you are far more luminous than she.'

Ellie smiled. 'Yes I have been told before that I look like the lady in the painting of Ophelia.'

'Well it's only partially true, as I say your beauty outshines hers. My name's Oliver by the way and I'm here with family and friends. That's my boy Jack down there on the shoreline with his pal Robin,' Oliver pointed. 'They're the ones in wetsuits with the green two-seater canoe.' He offered his hand.

'Eleanor Constant,' Ellie replied taking Oliver's hand, 'but everyone calls me Ellie'.

Oliver savoured the slim cool hand in his own rather warm damp one. 'Well, amazing. Elizabeth Siddal's second name was Eleanor after her mother,' he said. 'Perhaps your parents knew?'

'Oh no. My mother's favourite Beatles' song was Eleanor Rigby,' Ellie replied. 'Here come your boys'.

Oliver turned from ogling Ellie to scowl towards the two figures running up towards him. Bugger and sod it he thought to himself, but then remembering Ellie's presence, he stood and waved to them smiling.

'Hi chaps how goes it? Ice cream, coke, Red Bull?' He asked ruffling Jack's salty, sticky hair.

The boys stood open-mouthed. Oliver hardly ever spoke to them and never in such casual language and he never offered to buy them anything, let alone Red Bull which was strictly forbidden by Helen.

Robin recovered first. 'Red Bull for me please Oliver, Jack?' Jack shook his head to remove his father's hand and stepped away closer to Robin. 'Coke please,' he mumbled.

'Right you are. Sit yourselves down and talk to my new friend, the lovely Ellie.'

Ellie smiled at the two boys. 'Hi, I'm Ellie, you must be Jack and Robin.'

'I'm Robin, he's Jack, pleased to meet you,' said Robin smiling and brushing sand from his face.

'Hi,' said Jack looking at his feet.

Oliver returned with a coke and a Red Bull, handing the coke to Robin and the Red Bull to Jack who swapped without a word.

'Well Ellie, what brings you to Porthaven?' asked Oliver pulling his chair closer to hers.

'I'm staying with friends for the summer, this is our third week,' she said.

'Oh this is our first week,' said Robin 'we're staying at Porth House over there,' he pointed to the house set back from the beach at the furthest most westerly point of the bay.

'Well, we must be as far apart as possible,' said Ellie laughing. 'I'm staying at the Brett-Morgans' place, Point End House.' She pointed in the other direction. 'You can't quite see the house from here, it's right at the end of the road overlooking the bay and Penmassick Cove.'

'Wow!' exclaimed Robin. 'You mean that huge white place with the conservatory, right on the end at the edge of the cliff? We saw it from the canoe. It's got a beach with nobody on it. It's awesome.'

Ellie laughed. 'Yes it is rather splendid. The beach is private, reached by some steps at the bottom of the garden. You must come along and see it. Toby, that's Toby Brett-Morgan, he won't mind, he's very laid back. Bring some swimming gear, there's a great indoor pool and a terrace overlooking the cove.

'We'd love to,' said Oliver almost purring.

'Oh right, of course,' said Ellie taken aback as she had only meant to invite the boys, 'you must all come, and bring your wife, and your parents Robin.'

'J J won't come,' said Jack, 'she don't swim.'

'She doesn't swim,' corrected Oliver cuffing Jack's head, rather hard Ellie thought, seeing the boy flinch.

'Well, I'm sure she'd enjoy the view from the terrace, come later on this afternoon if you'd like. I'll be there but Toby and the others are off to the nudist beach round the headland and well, with my skin obviously that's not on for me. Do come, I'd enjoy the company.'

'We'd love to. Say about four?' said Oliver knowing what the boys didn't; that with him in charge for once, Helen, Julia and David had decided to go over to Padstow for the day and wouldn't be back until supper. 'And as we are to be your guests may I introduce us formally? I am Oliver Osborne, this is my son Jack and this is Robin Cavendish, son of my oldest and dearest friend, David.'

'Well, I am Eleanor Pansy Constant, and I look forward to welcoming you to Point End House, and now I really must go meet the others at the pub. See you later.' Ellie stood, tying her kimono, donning an enormous straw hat and gathering her belongings into a large soft wicker basket; sunglasses, towel, a Garnier Flammarion edition of Madame Bovary, a Le Robert & Collins dictionary, two bottles of Evian, a pencil case and reporters' notebook. So, Oliver thought, she's studying French.

'Right you two back to the house for lunch,' he commanded. The three of them rose and followed behind Ellie until she turned left down towards The Harbour Lights and they carried on along the path towards the cliff and the gate to Porth House.

Jean and Anne were giggling together and poking at each other as usual, and most of the adults were chatting and drinking wine and beer. Uncle David was walking carefully from the kitchen across the patio carrying a chopping board on which she could see a glass of red wine, full nearly to the top. It was sloshing from side to side with each step and occasionally splashing over. She could see in his frowning face, which was trying to see where his feet were going while balancing and watching the glass, his concern that the wine might be splashing onto whatever else was on the board.

Eventually he made it to the table at the side of the barbeque and gently put the board down. She walked over to it intrigued, and standing on tip toes, gripping the edge of the table with her fingertips she saw the big prawns that had been carefully selected and packed in ice that morning by the fishmonger. There were flowery paper napkins on the table.

The prawn shells were gleaming, and some near to the glass were spotted with wine. Uncle David smiled, he didn't seem worried anymore. He picked up his glass, took a sip, then picked up a napkin and daintily dabbed the spots of wine that had jumped from the glass onto the prawns. He shrugged his shoulders, smiled at the others then turned and walked back to the kitchen.

He reappeared almost straight away carrying a big round red plate with a cover on top. It was white and looked like a small umbrella without a handle. He took it over to the table and put it down next to the prawns, then sat down next to Aunt Julie, hazy cigarette smoke drifting between them.

She saw Caroline, who lived down the lane in the village with Robert her husband, stand up and walk over to a large bag. Reaching down Caroline took out a tall bottle filled with something orange, and two cups with handles. Placing the cups on the patio some orange liquid was poured into each, before two lids were retrieved from the bag and placed on the cups which were picked up, one in each hand. Caroline walked over to Jean and Anne who stopped giggling and waited, looking expectantly from their bouncing cradles, before reaching out greedily and grabbing their cups. Caroline went back to sit down next to Robert, who was hungrily eyeing the table with the prawns, the big red plate with the umbrella, and the barbeque.

She walked towards the barbeque, feeling her face getting warmer and warmer as she got closer and closer and as she got very close she held her hands out towards it and they felt even warmer, hot in fact.

She turned and walked to the spare seat next to a big flower pot, clambered up onto it then stood so she could look into the barbeque. It didn't look hot, the flames had stopped and she could see they were grey, but she could still feel the heat even though she was at least six feet away.

Uncle David eventually took the hint, smiled, stood up and walked to the table with the prawns and the big red plate with the umbrella. He picked up a brush, dabbed it into a white bowl then brushed the grill. The liquid coated the bars and some of it fell onto the coals and little fires flared up. He then picked up the prawns one at a time and put them quickly on top of the grill. There were lots and they covered the whole grill.

Suddenly Uncle David smacked his forehead with his right hand and ran to the kitchen from where he reappeared a few seconds later with some white plates in one hand and a large white bowl in the other. He placed them on the table the adults were sitting around.

Some of the prawns were dropping liquid onto the coals and there were flames, but not many, and some were sizzling. It wasn't long before Uncle David used a big fork to turn the prawns over. They had gone from being quite pale to bright red and there was a strong pleasant smell she was noticing for the first time; later she would know it was the combination of caramelisation, of seafood beginning to char, and roasting garlic.

The prawns were put onto the plates which were handed out to the adults, with one left over with two prawns on it and Uncle David picked up a prawn from the one left over. She was fascinated and walked to the table and saw him hold the prawn with one hand then hold its head with the other and pull it off and drop it in the bowl. Then he pulled off the tail and it followed the head into the bowl. Using both hands he then held it and used his thumbs to pull the shell right off before dropping it into the bowl. Later she would know the shell had already been opened using a sharp knife to remove the black intestinal tract she had not noticed at the fishmonger and that his thumbs had simply prised the slit shell apart.

Uncle David picked up a napkin, wrapped it around the prawn about half way down so that the head end was sticking out and held it out to her. She grasped it and examined it closely, smelled it, licked it then nibbled it and smiled. She sat cross legged on her red blanket on the

patio and carried on nibbling until she had chewed down to the napkin, when she removed it, held the prawn tail in her hand and finished it off. She walked back to the table where the second prawn on the spare plate had been wrapped in a napkin. She noticed the bowl was piled high with bits of prawn, red and pink, and lots of heads with long spikes sticking out and round black eyes. She picked up a head with meat still attached at the end without the spikes, put it in her mouth and sucked the meat away before putting the head back in the bowl. Then she picked up the prawn wrapped in the napkin, went back to her red blanket, sat down, and nibbled away until it had all gone. She licked her fingers one by one then dried them on her bright yellow T shirt from New Orleans.
Ma and Pa would be where they were going now. She wondered if they had seen any elephants yet, or lions....or giraffes.

Stirring from her day dream she noticed the tang of cooking meat on the air and walked back to the adults. Uncle David was using the big fork to take pieces of meat from the barbeque, putting them on plates on which salad leaves had already been piled, before handing them to the others. The umbrella was upside down on the table.

One of the plates on the table was bright blue and made of plastic. She saw Uncle David cut the piece of meat on it into strips. There was also a big piece of bread on the plate and some red sauce. Uncle David passed her the bright blue plate and she took it back to her red blanket.

She was enjoying dipping the strips of meat into the sauce, which she would learn later was made with real tomatoes, olive oil, onions, garlic, chillies and oregano and took ages to cook, when a big fly with yellow and black stripes, which she would soon learn was a wasp landed on her plate. It walked slowly to the sauce, seemed to sniff it, then walked to a piece of meat. It climbed up onto it, its wings stopped fluttering, and using a knife like thing sticking out of its mouth it began sawing. She was intrigued and couldn't take her eyes off it. After a minute it made a careful turn and continued sawing, at the end of the cut it had already made but at a right angle to it. She was still, barely breathing, and couldn't hear the adults guffawing over a funny story, or the big funny pink birds gabbling away not far away on the other side of the bushes.

Then it made another careful turn and began sawing again, then a final turn which made the cuts into a square. It looked as if it was using pincers stretching from its mouth, lifted the chunk of meat, and unsteadily took off carrying it. She was amazed, and watched it flying unsteadily and slowly away.

She carried on, picking up strips of meat and dipping them into the sauce, occasionally putting the bread into her mouth, ripping a small chunk off and chewing it. Then the big yellow and black striped fly was back and did the same thing all over again. This time when it flew unsteadily and slowly away she put down her plate, stood up, and ran after it through the lemon trees to the corner of the garden where it disappeared into a pile of logs underneath the brambles.

24

In the kitchen Oliver rustled up cheese and onion sandwiches whilst the boys hosed down their wetsuits and hung them over the washing line in the walled garden. He opened a tub of potato salad, one of coleslaw and a bag of washed leaves which he tipped onto a dinner plate. The garden door opened and the boys fell through it laughing.

'Where's J J?' asked Jack sensing his stepmother's absence as he always did. They may not have been kin but in their fear of Oliver they were decidedly kith.

'You know I completely forgot to tell you. When I was appointed babysitter, your stepmother, Davy and Helen, all buggered off to Padstow for the day. Your stepmother was suffering from retail withdrawal, Helen wanted to look for places of cultural and historical significance and Davy fancied Rick Stein's fish and chips. They threatened to bring back a takeaway for us but Christ knows what it'll be like after the car journey. Still the gulls will like them.'

'You're not supposed to feed the gulls, it encourages them to raid bins,' said Robin who in many ways took after his mother.

'Really?' asked Oliver listening to the gulls which were circling, screaming and squabbling over the harbour outside the kitchen window, 'how about poisoning the buggers? Christ it's like a fucking Hitchcock film!'

He dumped two sandwiches and a bottle of Sol beer on a plate and turned towards the kitchen door. 'Help yourselves then amuse yourselves without bothering me. We leave for Point End House later this afternoon. Be ready with your swimming kit.' With that he went through to the family room where his laptop was already online.

'OK Gustave Flaubert, speak to me of Emma Bovary,' he whispered.

The Harbour Lights public house was built into the cliff face at the end of the quay where it continued to repel all boarders trying to buy it up for holiday lets or a 'gloriously located' second home. It was actually owned by the Pentreath estate, but managed by a former rugby star and his third wife.

Ellie spotted her friends at a large bench table outside under an enormous umbrella installed when the smoking ban came in.

Toby Brett-Morgan was nowhere to be seen, but the brothers Tom and Nick Haldane, Asif Iqbal, Jane Masterson and Harriet 'Harry' Jordan were sprawling across the table, smoking and drinking beer from plastic glasses.

'Hey gal,' cried Nick Haldane, the first to spot Ellie approaching.

'Hi all,' she said, dumping her bag and hat and flopping down in a wooden chair. 'God it's hot, I'm going to change. Where's Tobes?'

'Where he always is, chatting to the delightful Amélie behind the bar,' said Jane gloomily. She idolised Toby unbeknownst to him.

Ellie picked up her bag and strolled through the open pub door, pushing her sunglasses back on top of her head as the dimness temporarily blinded her, turning everything green. The pub's interior was always dark. Dark grey flagstone floors and black wood wainscoting with walls artfully painted the colour of nicotine stain. Toby was indeed lounging against the bar laughing and pushing his blond Hugh Grant locks back with his left hand whilst he held a large glass of clear liquid in his right. The object of his attention, the barmaid Amélie, was a small curvaceous girl with closely cropped black hair and enormous liquid green eyes. From his first sighting of her Toby had been smitten, much to the amusement of his friends with the obvious exception of Jane.

Ellie smiled and went through to the ladies unnoticed. She pulled a pair of cream linen shorts and a faded denim shirt from the bag, removed her kimono and swimsuit and dressed. Putting the swimsuit inside her towel with the kimono into the bag, she tied her hair back with a green silk scarf and walked out to the bar.

Amélie saw her approach and smiled. Amélie and Ellie both knew they were beautiful, recognised the quality in each other and shared the mixed feelings that beauty brought. They also had France in common as Ellie had spent many family holidays there.

'Hello, Ellie what will you 'ave?' asked Amélie in a soft, lilting French accent.

'Do you know, I would absolutely love a Pimms if it's not too much trouble?' Ellie replied.

'Sure. Do you like all the fruit and green things?'

'Please,' said Ellie, turning to Toby as Amélie moved away to make the drink.

'Hello my angel,' said Toby with a slight slur and a goofy smile.

Ellie picked up his glass and took a sip: very strong vodka and tonic.

'Oh Tobes,' she said, 'it's only 12:30 how many have you had, when did you get here?'

Toby's smile faded.

'Christ don't you start, you sound just like Jane.'

'It's only because I care about you Tobes. You can't drink like this and then go swimming and boarding. What on earth is Amélie thinking, letting you drink so much?'

'She's only just come on shift, she doesn't know. I just had to get away from the others for a while. They were doing my head in. You know what they're like sometimes, so I came over early about quarter to eleven. Please don't say anything Ellebelle, Amélie hasn't noticed, I'll just finish this one verrry slooowly.'

'OK, but with at least another tonic in that glass.'

Amélie returned with a Stella Artois pint glass brimming with red liquid, ice, sliced strawberry, orange, mint, cucumber and a twirly straw.

'Voilà, Madame,' she said passing the glass across the bar with a flourish.

'My shout,' said Toby, 'and a cold tonic to go in there fair wench.'

'Good idea,' said Amélie raising her eyebrows to Ellie and accepting the ten pound note.

Amélie poured all the tonic into Toby's glass and handed him his change and a packet of dry roasted peanuts. 'On the 'ouse,' she said and then moved along the bar to serve a bunch of locals who had just walked in to take their usual table in the window, eyeing the visitors with their usual cold stares.

'Tobes, I hope you don't mind, I met some people at Crabbers and invited them up for a swim this afternoon as you're all going over to Long Beach.'

'No problem Ellebelle, but I'm not going to Long Beach now as I'm sure you'll be pleased to hear. But I'll keep out of the way'.

'Don't be silly it's just two couples and their two teenage sons. The boys saw the house from their canoe and were so impressed, I felt obliged really.'

'Ma maison, ta maison,' said Toby smiling dreamily.

Ellie laughed. 'That's what they say in Spanish you idiot not in French, mi casa su casa, but I appreciate the sentiment and thanks. Now come on, outside. Amélie is getting busy and you'll be a distraction. Plus you are the host remember and you know you love them all really.'

At that moment there was a whooping from outside and the light from the doorway was blocked as a very tall, very broad, young black man walked in.

'Yo! 'It's Benjamite. Ben mah man howzit hangin?' cried Toby in a corny mock American accent.

Ben walked across, unblocking the light as he reached them in about four strides. He beamed at Toby, dropping an enormous rucksack and enfolding Toby in a huge bear hug. He stood six foot six and must have weighed sixteen stone. When Toby resurfaced, grinning he said. 'Ellebelle, meet Benjamin Dexter III of Boston US and Oxford UK, Rhodes scholar and main man. Ben, meet my best girl Ellie Constant of Edinburgh Scotland.'

Ben stuck out an enormous hand with the pinkest palm and engulfed Ellie's delicate white freckled one. 'Hi Ellie, charmed I'm sure,' he said in a deep, sonorous American East Coast accent, with a look that implied he truly was.

Ellie was instantly in love. Clearing her throat she squeaked, 'Hello Ben, likewise.'

Toby was still grinning. 'You made it, excellent and from the noise just now I gather you saw the others. Now a drink, a beer no doubt. Best bitter or that fizzy muck you normally drink?'

'Well now, I always say 'when in Rome', so what's good and local?'

At that point Amélie reappeared and stood smiling at Ben, who turned from Toby and returned her gaze, rapt.

Toby, oblivious to the static in the air, said 'Pint of Betty Stoggs for my man please wench'. But Ellie caught the atmosphere instantly and frowned. It was clear that Ben was entranced. As Detective Sergeant Scott was to comment to Detective Inspector Treloar later that week, where female friendship is concerned it is the love of men not the love of money that is the root of all evil.

Drinks in hand the three left the bar and joined the others on the terrace. Ben, who was bringing up the rear, turned stooping in the doorway to look back at the bar where Amélie remained smiling, impervious to the shouts for service at the other end of the bar.

The next hour passed in laughter and conversation until the main party clambered out of their seats, grabbed their bags and headed off to Long Beach.

And so with the sun at its hottest, a six foot six African American, a six foot one bronzed blond Englishman and a five foot seven pale red-headed Scots girl climbed Chapel Hill heading for Point End House whilst a five foot six swarthy Englishman of Russian descent sat in a darkened room, Googling Gustave Flaubert and dreaming of seduction. At the same time, three miles uphill away from the sea, a lone Irishman turned his Honda Gull Wing into a campsite car park and drew up next to a battered blue and white VW camper with peeling flower stickers.

Back again with David and Julie, she was five now and she was happy. Ma and Pa would be where they were going now, and she would make the most of the freedom she knew she had. David had picked her up from the airport yesterday, and now he was in the house, Julie was in the kitchen, she didn't know about Jean and Anne. The twins had been dropped off earlier. Julie had told her they were staying for a few days while Caroline and Robert went away for a break. It was two years since her first Easter holiday here, and this one would be even better.

She was wearing blue denim shorts, a bright red T shirt with 'My Dad went all the way to Rio and all I got was this stinking T shirt' printed on the front, red sandals with no socks, and her hair was tied back in a shoulder length pony tail with a red scrunchy. The new T shirt was a gift from her father who had recently been to Brazil on a business trip, selling what he sold, at Carnival time.

She raced over to her favourite part of the garden, the gap in the brambles from where she could watch the flamingos doing their funny dance and dipping their heads in the water. The sun was glinting brightly off the surface and she turned and looked up as she heard the familiar swishshsh swishshsh swishsshshshing, and honking getting louder. More birds joining their friends gabbling, dancing and dipping their heads underwater. Just as she remembered.

She laughed as she saw the new arrivals struggling to stop as they landed noisily in the water, gangly legs pawing and wings flapping until they were still, then looking slowly and jerkily around, as if to make sure they were in the right place. While some were still looking around, others dipped their heads into the water then, straightening their long pink necks, turning their heads to look back and down at their fluffy pink bodies, then bending their necks sideways she watched them stroke through their feathers with their big black beaks that looked like hooks. There were a few fluffy clouds in the light blue sky, the sun was bright, and it was sparkling in the distance off the water.

Walking towards the patio she heard a bright chirrupping up in one of the lemon trees. She stopped and looked for the bird, saw some big yellow lemons, some smaller green lemons, and a few white flowers but couldn't see the bird, so carried on walking. On the patio the barbeque was still there, so was the big flower pot and the chairs and tables. The big flower pot was still empty. The kitchen door was open and she heard Aunt Julie humming and the clatter of plates being taken out of a cupboard and put on the table. She knew lunch was being prepared using the bread and ham that they had stopped to buy on the way through the village.

The sound of a bell being tinged and a drum being bashed was coming from an open upstairs window. The noises stopped, she looked up and her fluffy red felt elephant with big orange eyes flew from the window and landed at her feet. She looked back at the window then at Elephant, walked two paces thoughtfully then turned and kicked it. It flew into the big flower pot that had been empty. She turned, turned again and carried on.

Walking in front of the kitchen she went round the corner and along the path towards the front of the house and a wasp buzzed in front of her face before turning and flying on, down to the ground, and disappeared into a hole in the bottom of the wall. A second later two wasps appeared from the hole, standing for a second just outside before taking off and flying over her head, then turning towards the front of the house. As she lay down on the path with her head not far from the hole, another wasp landed close to the hole and as it walked into the hole she could see its wings clearly and its body bobbing up and down. Then another landed close behind and followed it in.

She stood up, looking towards the front of the house, the direction the wasps were flying from, and another flew towards her face. It turned before hitting her and where its wings should have been she could see a silvery blur on each side. As it flew by, beginning to drop towards the hole she heard it buzzing. Another was getting close on its way to the hole, she raised her left hand to her face and grabbed it and then she could feel it wriggling between her finger and thumb. Bringing it close to her eyes she could see little black tentacles that she knew were actually called antennae, moving forwards than back again. It had round black eyes that looked like small balls and seemed too big for its face, and she could hear it buzzing; she thought it sounded angry. With a black claw coming from each side of its mouth it was clinging onto a piece of something red. She could feel its yellow and black body squirming, trying to escape. Two wings, one big one small were held by her finger against it's body and two were jerkily moving, stuck out above her thumb and she could see through them. Thin black lines made it look like small see-through leaves. She knew she shouldn't touch the tail because last year when she had smacked a wasp on Ma's arm, it had put a black sting in Ma's skin before flying off and Ma had screamed in pain and her arm went red after the sting had been pulled out with tweezers and it had hurt for ages.

She squeezed her finger and thumb together, there was a

*soft crunch, and a sticky dark goo squirted onto her hand
and the buzzing stopped. She stared at the squashed insect
for a while then wiped the remains onto the wall, and
poking her tongue from her lips she tasted the goo on her
finger. It was bitter and she curled her lips and spat, then
wiped her hand on her T shirt twice and carried on
walking underneath what she could now see was a steady
flow of wasps towards the front of the house.*

*She walked past the big red car parked on the drive, out of
the gate and into the red dusty lane, turned right and went
towards the village. After a minute the wasps were lower,
and she could see that some were flying down onto a
grassy bridge that crossed a small stream towards
something orangey brown, and some were flying away
from it and back over her head. As she got nearer she
could see it looked a bit like a dog, with a long fluffy tail
with white at the end, and it wasn't moving. The wasps
were flying into and out of a red patch at the top of a front
leg that a white stick was poking out of. She stood and
watched for a few minutes and turned and ran and skipped
back to the back of the house, following then passing the
steady stream of what some would call Paravespula
germanicae workers or German Yellow Jackets taking food
for the grubs in their nest.*

Jamie Deverell had lived a solitary childhood. He had grown up the only child of a single mother who was the housekeeper to the recluse Edward Meacher at Linton Crucis Abbey in the New Forest. Linton Crucis was a 13th century abbey which had become a private house with the Dissolution of the Monasteries under Henry VIII.

As there was no sign of a father, Jamie's paternity was the subject of much speculation in the neighbouring hamlets but nothing was ever confirmed. However, when Edward Meacher had died five years previously leaving Linton Crucis Abbey and his entire estate of some twelve million pounds to Jamie Deverell there were many *told you so's* to be heard in the local hostelries and shops and when Jamie's mother died of cancer two years later many said it was of a broken heart.

Growing up the lone child in an enormous house Jamie had led a sheltered, over-protected existence. Consequently, when he appeared at Hindhurst Primary School at the age of five, a small, delicate silent child, he was bullied mercilessly. So when a spirited trainee teacher Miss Helen Everleigh arrived for the summer term of his third year, took him under her wing and vanquished his persecutors, Jamie thought she must be an angel and worshiped her utterly.

With her departure at the end of term Jamie was devastated and he spent the summer torturing himself with the thought that come the autumn his enemies would return to smite him with a vengeance, fuelled with pent-up resentment at their perceived unjust suffering at the hands of his protector. But that autumn a new boy arrived in his class: Alisdair Frobisher, whose father was a big-shot computer man transferred from Scotland, and inexplicably

Alisdair, who was tall, extremely smart and extremely popular, took an instant shine to Jamie becoming his new champion for the rest of their primary schooling. Under his protection Jamie flourished academically and the two boys went on to Winchester College together, only parting when Alisdair went off to Cambridge to read Mathematics and Jamie stayed home to be with his ailing mother.

Alisdair now spent most Easter and summer vacations at Linton Crucis as his father had been promoted again to corporate headquarters in the US. They spent their time messing with software and communications technology using Alisdair's computing acumen, inherited from his father and honed at Cambridge, and Jamie's unlimited funds. This summer Alisdair was with his parents in New York but the two friends still communicated in one way or another virtually every day.

Since his mother's death Jamie had become obsessed with discovering everything he could about the only other woman in his life that had cared for him in his view: Helen Everleigh, now Cavendish. In this endeavour he had enlisted the aid of Alisdair and it was at Easter whilst conducting various searches of doubtful legality that Alisdair had uncovered in the Oxford Police records a statement made by Helen in connection with a housemate's rape complaint against Oliver Osborne. The complaint had been dismissed. Jamie now had a mission: to mete out the punishment that Oliver Osborne had evaded. He had tracked Helen's life for three years and he could not understand why she allowed the Osbornes so much of her time; joint holidays, opera visits, dinners in town.

The previous week Jamie had been down to Cornwall to reconnoitre the area. He had discovered the booking at Porth House and the flight details through hacking Julia Osborne and Helen's credit card records. Taking a train to

Bristol he had purchased the camper van at a car auction for cash and driven down to stay at a campsite further along the coast near Trengissey. Armed with a large holdall containing a bucket and several chamois leather cloths he had caught a bus to Porthaven and posing as a window cleaner had gained access to the garden of Porth House and got a good look, albeit from outside, at the downstairs interior. He had even talked his way into the kitchen for some hot water to rinse out his cloths. He had been very pleased with himself. Now he knew where they would be, when they would be there and what the house was like. But today had been fruitless. Oliver had been inside the house, on the beach with the boys or chatting up some girl at the café. His beloved had left early with her husband and Julia and wasn't back when he felt too obvious still sitting on a bench outside the house at 3:30. So he had started back hot, tired and frustrated.

It was uphill all the way with the pavement running out after the first mile. The road was narrow with several blind bends and hedges overgrown with brambles, rosehip and blackthorn which pricked at his skin when he was forced in to avoid a passing car.

At last he reached the top, turned right and in two minutes turned right again into the campsite. His bad mood turned to anger. He had lugged his holdall with the binoculars, cameras and a change of clothes uphill for over two miles and now to cap it all someone had parked a bloody great flash motorbike in his quiet corner next to the camper van, and was sitting cross-legged on the ground beside it smoking.

It was quite dark and she was in bed. She could see through the white curtains the outline of the window and the shadow that could only have been made by the big tree at the side of the house. It had been showing only a few shadow branches at the edge of the window when the light was switched off and now shadow branches were all across the curtains.

Wearing her Ma's plain dark blue T shirt, which came down to her knees she had finally gone to bed and been tucked in by Julie what seemed like hours ago. She kept hearing the crunch of the wasp, seeing the wasps' air path just over her head and wondered about the white stick coming out of the dog creature. She wondered if wasps slept at night, were they tucked up by big wasps, did they have beds, if they did what could they be like, did they carry on buzzing when they were asleep, did they eat anything apart from meat?

She got out of bed, walked to the window, pulled back one of the curtains, and looking up she could see that the sky was full of stars. Even standing on tiptoes and pulling herself up with her fingertips she could still only see the tops of the branches, and stars, and the big round bright moon through the branches. Wanting to see the lagoon she went out to the landing and as she walked quietly past the twins' room she couldn't hear them, a nice change. She heard snoring from David and Julie's room, and went to the end of the landing where the window was, and pulled back the curtain but could still only see stars. There was nothing to stand on. She wondered about getting the chair from the bedroom, dragging it out and along the landing, but not for long because she had tried moving it before and knew it was too heavy.

She listened carefully, her head leaning to one side and she could hear only the snoring, it was loud. She quietly opened the door at the side of the window, crept into the bedroom and was amazed to see, in the shadows, that it was Julie doing the snoring. Julie's mouth was open, she wore a white T shirt and the blankets were raggedly around her ankles, she was on her back with her legs apart. One knee was raised and had a black stripe across it which stood out against the white skin and she could see a black shape at the bottom of Julie's tummy. Fascinated, she walked round the end of the bed went closer and leaned over to look at it and even in the shadows could see it was short curly hair and it sparkled in the moonlight as she moved her head from side to side. A fishy smell got stronger as she got closer, she wondered what made it. It was a narrow triangle with the arrow end pointing towards what she had learned from Ma before they had both laughed at the funny name, the pussy, which had no hair. Not like Ma's, which had brown hair all over. She reached over and touched it, covering it with the palm of her left hand, it felt just like her own but hotter and it was sticky. Julie snorted then carried on snoring. Wondering why there was no hair, she took away her hand, put the first finger slowly to her lips and quietly went sshh, and smiled. Ma had told her that pussies shouldn't be talked about to other people and when they talked about pussies to each other they always giggled and put their fingers to their lips. Then she wondered if Ma had seen any kangaroos yet.

She could see Julie's lips shaking as she snored, it was so loud she wondered why she didn't wake up. She looked at David, he was on his side, facing Julie, also in a white T shirt, and the blanket on his side of the bed was down to his tummy. He was still and very quiet. She looked again at Julie's bare pussy for a few seconds, and then crept quietly out of the room and gently closed the door.

It was the second time today she had seen Julie lying down. In the afternoon the clattering of plates in the kitchen had only been the beginning of the adult noisiness. Later there had been glass smashing noises and bottle dropping into the bin on top of other bottle noises until quite late in the afternoon. Then it went quiet apart from the twins stumbling around the garden and screeching at each other. Julie had disappeared after bashing her leg on a chair on the patio when carrying two glasses of wine from the kitchen and dropping them. David had laughed and she had stomped back into the kitchen, limping. Later she had seen Julie lying down on a sofa, looking asleep but humming. A glass on the table was half full of red wine and there was an empty wine bottle lying on the floor.

The lagoon and the wasps were too loud in her head to ignore and she went downstairs.

Walking through the kitchen on the cold tiles towards the back door she saw something moving on the floor, it was small and dark, highlighted against the tiles that looked white but which she knew were yellow. It was moving slowly and she walked over to look at it. With the moonlight coming in from the side window she could see as it walked between the shadow branches that it was not quite round, about an inch long, and had lots of legs. It was close to the floor and didn't have a head.

She knelt down to look at it closely, then her left hand darted out and she picked it up between the thumb and first finger of her left hand. As she moved her hand close to her eyes, even in the moonlight she could see that it was black, its legs were waving madly, and that it had two antennae that were waving madly as well. She squeezed her thumb and finger together but they wouldn't move. She squeezed harder and they still wouldn't move. The legs and antennae were waving more now but she couldn't squash it. She stood up and could see at eye level on the kitchen counter one of Julie's cigarette packets. She leaned against the counter, stood on tip toes and reached out to pull it towards her with her other hand, flipped the top open, turned it upside down and the cigarettes fell out. Then she dropped the thing that she would later know was a cockroach into it.

She could hear it scrabbling about. She shook the packet and it sounded a bit like one of the twins rattles being shaken. She put the cigarette packet back on the counter, at the edge, and went outside. Going first to the gap in the brambles she could see the moon glinting on the water, and hear no noise from the flamingos. They were standing still in the water, on one leg, and even though she knew they were pink they looked white in the moonlight and they had their heads turned back along their backs, hiding their beaks under their wings. They looked like funny stumpy tables with curved tops.

Something made her jump, something up high that she saw moving out the corner of her eye. She looked to her left and could see a big bird on the top of the old stable in the corner of the garden. It was turning its head from side to side. She walked closer until it was just a big black shape with the moon behind it, with a short black stick on each side of its head at the top. Later, she would remember it and know it was a Eurasian Eagle Owl, that it was nearly as tall as she was and that it was hunting for mice and rats for its hungry babies. Its head stopped turning and she watched it watching her.

After a few minutes she went through the gap and walked quietly towards the flamingos, pebbles sticking painfully to her feet. She had to stop every few paces to wipe them off on the sandy grass. As she got closer she could see their tabley backs were as high as her head but she wasn't frightened. The nearest opened an eye and it shone in the moonlight. It looked at her for a while, then closed its eye and went back to sleep. She watched them, still and making no noise for a while then walked back through into the garden and to the wasp hole at the side of the house.

There were no wasps near the hole. She could see it clearly in the moonlight, the shadow trunk of the tree was just to the right of it. She lay down with her head close to the hole and she heard a soft buzzing sound. It was a quiet, low tone, almost like Julie's humming. So they did buzz in their sleep. Because she would never study Entomology or meet a Hymenopterist she would never know that the soft humming sound was made by the few worker wasps whose job it was to guard the nest at night and keep the queen safe.

As she stood and turned, her foot trod on something soft and squashed it. Lifting her foot she could see a long black gooey shape on the path glistening in the moonlight. She stepped onto the grass at the side of the path and wiped her foot to get the goo off it. She looked down again and could see another long black shape in the bright moonlight, slowly moving across the path. She knew it wouldn't taste of chocolate but reached down to pick it up. It got shorter and fatter as she moved it close to her face. She could see what she knew were antennae and what she now knew was a slug was slowly wiggling its antennae forwards then backwards.

If she had been facing the big bright moon, anyone looking at her face would have seen her eyes suddenly sparkle as an idea came into her head.

She walked back to the kitchen, opening then closing the door quietly then went to the counter, put the slug down on it, picked up the cigarette packet and lifted its lid, then picked up the slug and stuffed it down inside the packet before closing it again. She shook it and could hear only a small sound as if one of the twins rattles had stopped working properly or it was wrapped up in a cloth.

She went back upstairs and could not hear the snoring anymore. The twins were still quiet. The only sound was a very slight scrabbling inside the cigarette packet. In her bedroom she opened a draw, put the packet under some T shirts, and clambered back into bed. As she dropped off to sleep the slight scrabbling was still there, very faintly, and she wondered what it was that was in the box with the slug. She could still feel its sharp edges that had left marks that she hadn't seen in the dark and would be gone by morning, as they had pressed into her finger and thumb.

'Boys, boys time to go!'

Oliver was freshly showered and dressed in shabby chic black linen shorts and a fine blue striped shirt, sleeves rolled to the elbow. He had seriously considered sneaking out alone, but on reflection decided this would seem odd to the delicious Ellie and put her on her guard.

With a thundering of steps and slamming doors Robin and Jack tumbled down the stairs dragging assorted towels and swimming shorts, snorkels and flippers.

'Christ aren't you two ready? I told you we were leaving at quarter to four,' (which he hadn't).

'We're ready, just need to shove this in our rucksacks, one minute,' said Robin in the conciliatory tone he had learned from his father. 'Where's your kit?'

'Oh, I'm not swimming, just coming along to watch over you two.'

'There's no need we'll be fine,' said Jack.

'Jack. I was abandoned here by your stepmother with the express mission of keeping an eye on you. To that end I have spent a totally wasted day and I am not going to compound that injury with accusations of neglect. I am going with you. No debate.'

Jack shrugged, stuffing his rucksack and followed Robin out of the front door.

They walked along the lane passing the slipway and Crabbers café and started to climb Chapel Hill towards Point End House. Oliver had to stop frequently to catch his breath as the boys strolled on ahead bearing right along the cliff road. *Christ*, Oliver thought, *I'm getting old. No puff and this bloody headache. Too much sun.*

Other than his lack of condition Oliver was feeling rather pleased with himself. He had spent a fruitful, if tedious, afternoon researching the life and works of Gustave Flaubert and was now confident that he could engage the delightful Ellie in a reasonable conversation on the subject. If the boys had not already made themselves scarce when they arrived at the house, down to the private beach or off to the swimming pool, he was sure that a literary discussion would drive them away. That would leave him alone with the lustrous Ellie. Perfect. The boys were some way ahead and Oliver thought it best for them to arrive first with him trailing behind, the reluctant dutiful adult, so he did not shout for them to wait.

At the end of the cliff road the coastal path veered left over a stile and onwards to Penmassick Point and beyond. The entrance to Point End House was a wide gap in a wild hedge marked with a simple slate sign and whilst Oliver could appreciate the fabulous location he started to wonder about the state of the property. The boys were hesitating at the top of the drive.

'Go on. Get down there, I'm coming. Go ring the bell'.

As they disappeared around the bend in the drive Oliver adjusted his crotch, smoothed back his hair and sauntered after them.

Around the curve hidden from the road the drive was paved in simple brick sweeping down to splay out in front of a substantial Victorian detached house rendered in off-white with duck egg blue wooden window frames surrounding sash windows. *Mmm very nice, very nice indeed,* thought Oliver. Standing in an open porch littered with flip-flops, snorkels, flippers, old wellington boots and discarded socks stood Ellie and the boys, all laughing. Hearing Oliver approach Ellie looked up and smiled.

'Hello, welcome to Point End House. Do come through'.

She stood back against the open front door her arm held out pointing down the hallway as the boys hurried in.

'Straight through to the back,' she cried after them. Oliver walked in brushing unnecessarily close to Ellie, as they followed the boys. The long hallway had several doors leading off, all closed. The walls were lined with simply framed black and white photographs of smiling people and seascapes. The light was dim other than the bright sunlight flooding in from the open door at the end of the hallway. Oliver was reminded of descriptions of near death experiences. He smiled as he walked slowly along seemingly admiring the photographs, but really staring at Ellie's rear as the light filtering through her light cotton dress revealed her shape beneath. He could hear the excited voices of the boys but then his face fell, as a loud deep laugh rang out ahead. Another man. *Shit, shit, shit.* His plans were foiled; no tête à tête, no intimate talk of Flaubert, no tales of travels through France, no seduction.

The door at the end of the hallway opened into an enormous sun room built at the back of the house. Ceiling to floor glass at the far side looked out into a conservatory with a flagged floor where a large expanse of blue water reflected the sunlight: the swimming pool. Beyond through further glass doors a bricked terrace bordered lawns sweeping down to overlook the sea and beyond to Penmassick Point.

Sitting at a wooden table on the terrace were two young men, one blond haired, tanned and willowy, the other enormous and black. Jack and Robin were flopped on an elongated wicker chaise longue with bright yellow cushions, laughing out loud, even Jack. Ellie strolled through onto the terrace and smiled, coyly Oliver thought, at the black youth.

'Guys, I see you've met Robin and Jack. This is Jack's father Oliver. Oliver this is Toby Brett-Morgan, the master of the house and his good friend Ben Dexter of Boston Massachusetts.' The black man stood up holding out his huge hand. Oliver was annoyed and he had been guzzling beer whilst Googling Flaubert, but as a highly successful barrister, he was used to thinking on his feet, and now was a time to shelve his plans for Ellie, now was a time for innocent charm.

'Delighted to meet you both,' he said smiling broadly advancing with his hand extended in greeting.

'Welcome to our seaside retreat,' said Toby still seated at the table, but leaning across to shake Oliver's hand, 'would you like a beverage?' He pointed to an ice bucket on the table. 'Ellie's on the Chablis, but there's beer or Coke and stuff if you prefer. Hey guys, Coke or juice for you?' he drawled turning to Robin and Jack.

He's pissed, Oliver thought. 'Chablis would be delightful,' he said as the boys both asked for Coke.

'I'll go,' said Ellie turning back into the conservatory.

'Splendid house,' Oliver stated 'and what a marvellous view.'

'Sure is,' said Ben in a rich deep tone. Oliver hated him instantly. He was strikingly handsome and clearly very fit, but worst of all, Ellie was obviously smitten and this was a major setback.

Ellie walked back onto the terrace with a tray of glasses, beer and coke bottles, which Ben moved swiftly to take from her.

'Allow me Ma'am,' he said. *Christ a true bloody gentleman,* thought Oliver as Ellie blushed and whispered thanks.

'You're welcome to use the pool,' said Toby to the boys 'or if you want there's the beach. It's down there,' he pointed giggling at the sea.

'Tobes,' Ellie said sharply 'don't be a jerk.' She turned to the boys. 'You can get down to the beach via some steps over in that corner of the garden,' she continued pointing to her left. 'I'll show you. Come along Ben, you might as well come and see where the steps are. Oh I'm sorry Oliver did you want to go down to the beach as well?'

The boys were already on their feet and Oliver took their place on the chaise longue.

'Christ no,' he exclaimed, then, thinking about the impression he was making, 'unless of course the boys want to go down. Then of course I'll go down to keep an eye on them.'

'No need Sir,' said Ben 'I'd be glad to watch them. If that's OK with you'all?'

'Boys?' asked Oliver stretching out his legs, hands behind his head.

'Great!' said Robin as Jack shrugged.

'Allons y,' said Ellie rounding up the boys and leading the way across the lawn.

Ben stood picking up a towel from the ground beside him and tossing it over his shoulders. He strode off after Ellie and the boys leaving Oliver with Toby on the terrace. *Fucking marvellous,* thought Oliver, *I'm left with the Hugh Grant lookalike inebriate,* but as he turned back from watching the group descending the lawn, he was relieved to see Toby Brett-Morgan with his head on the table snoring gently.

She woke up suddenly, with an idea in her head from a dream, went to the drawer and took out the blue cigarette packet and listened for the scrabbling sound. She couldn't hear it. She shook it and it still sounded like a broken rattle. Then she heard the scrabbling sound. She was smiling as she went quietly down the stairs, hair only half in the pony tail, the scrunchy had slipped, wearing her mum's blue T shirt that came down to her knees and with bare feet. There had been no snoring and the twins were still quiet as she had walked along the landing.

She kicked at the cigarettes that were still on the kitchen floor where she had dropped them, one got squashed and one slid to the middle of the floor. She went to the door, opened it and stepped outside, turned left and walked round the corner to see if the wasps were up yet. They were.

Already on their air path crossing the road to and from the dead dog creature, they were buzzing in and out of the hole at the bottom of the wall in two lines. She walked slowly towards the line coming towards her bringing her left hand up towards her head. Then when her head was level with the wasps her left hand darted out suddenly and was holding a wasp between her thumb and first finger. She felt it wriggling and could see its tail wagging. With the thumb of her right hand she flipped the packet open, dropped the wasp in, and quickly closed it again. She could hear it buzzing angrily as she held the packet up to her ear. She heard the scrabbling as well. She shook it and it still made a sound a bit like a broken rattle. The wasps on the air path carried on their way.

She walked towards the old stable in the corner of the

garden and went round the back, walking between the side and the brambles.   She went to the hole she had found the last time, stood on the two bricks she had put there the last time, put her left hand through it feeling for the treasure she had put in the old box inside and lifted out a cigarette. The brown stuff inside was sliding out onto the grass and by the time she had it level it looked like a white tube that was only half full. She threw it into the brambles.

Then she put her right hand through the hole and put the packet down.   Then moving her hand to the left she touched, picked up, and bought out Julie's pink lighter that she had put there the last time. She remembered David laughing when she had been trying to find it - under the cushions on the sofa, in the drawers in the kitchen, in her handbag, even under the car. She tilted it and could see the liquid inside sloshing about. She smiled. She pressed the small black button and a yellow flame spurted out straightaway. She giggled, took her finger off the button, and the flame went out. She put the lighter through the hole and back on the box next to the cigarettes before going back to the kitchen to see what was for breakfast just as it started to rain.

That morning Julia woke and looked out of the window into nothingness. For a moment she was totally disoriented. Gently she pushed open the window so as not to wake Oliver who was lying on his back snoring. She was greeted by a warm wet mist which was obscuring everything, clinging to the air in tiny water droplets and dripping from the ends of the palm tree leaves in the front garden.

Julia smiled, leaning out. Instantly she was transported back to her childhood. Staying in Africa with friends of her father, she was walking along the path to overlook Victoria Falls feeling the warm spray on her face, totally drenched, hearing the thundering water.

'Fuck what time is it? Shut that bloody window and pull the curtains I'm knackered,' groaned Oliver. The previous evening David, Helen and Julia had returned from Padstow to find the boys watching a DVD and Oliver nowhere to be found. They had got out of the boys that Oliver was still up at some big house with some students they had met on the beach. They had all been up there that afternoon and the boys had been swimming on some brilliant private beach with a terrific guy called Ben who was American and had crewed in the America's Cup trials and was a Rhodes scholar at Oxford and was huge and black and was a brilliant swimmer and a qualified lifeguard and everything. He had clearly made a very favourable impression. Oliver has sent the boys home at seven for supper with the message that he was staying on and not to worry about him. They hadn't.

Julia did as she was told and pulling on a dressing gown, left the room.

Downstairs she found Helen and David sitting at the kitchen table drinking coffee and munching toast.

'What happened to the sun?' Julia asked.

'It's only sea fret', Helen replied 'it'll be gone by lunchtime.'

Julia poured herself a cup of coffee and yawning wandered out of the kitchen and into the Family Room where Jack and Robin were playing a Wii tennis game. 'Hi boys,' she said sitting on a faux leather sofa, curling her feet underneath her and cradling the coffee cup in both hands. The boys stopped playing and Robin smiled at Julia and walked out. Jack plugged in his iPod headphones and lay on the floor.

On the phone, Zac from home had asked Robin how he put up with Jack, but he wasn't so bad. Jack could always get money and that was worth a lot to Robin. Jack's parents would pay him to go away when he engaged with them. Robin's would want to bond with him in some ghastly family pursuit, especially Mum. No, Jack wasn't so bad, not once Robin had made it very clear that he didn't want Jack to suck him off in return for his company. The poor sod must have a terrible life at school. Robin could put up with him for the holiday.

Around 11:30 Helen brought a tray of coffee and a glass of coke into the Family Room. Jack was still lying on the floor on a rag rug in front of the wood-burning stove, writing in an old battered A5 notebook, Julia was now sitting in a large Lloyd Loom style wicker chair reading Saturday's edition of the Daily Mail. She looked up.

'It's almost cleared now,' said Helen, 'just a drift over the sea. David and Robin have gone up to the surf shop for a look around and I'm not sure where Oliver is.'

'I don't care where Oliver is,' said Julia bitterly.

'Right,' said Helen not knowing what else to add.

'You heard about Tim Petherbridge-Brown?'

'No,' said Helen then 'oh no, not…?'

'Yes. Yes killed in action three weeks ago somewhere in Helmand. I felt it physically when I heard, like a kick from a horse. I wrote to his mother of course, but what could I say? He was her only child you know and he never married, not after.' Julia wiped her eye with a tissue.

'Oh Julia I am so very sorry. I know how fond of him you were'.

'Do you know what Oliver said?' demanded Julia.

'No,' she replied, thinking, *but I can well imagine.*

'I was crying when Oliver walked in and asked 'Who's dead?' and when I explained he snorted 'Oh that plonker, hardly a devastating loss to the nation.'

'I am sorry, Julia, truly,' Helen scoured her mind for something to change the subject. 'What's that you're writing Jack?' she asked gently.

'Oh, that's Jack's poetry, said Julia brightening. 'He loves poetry, especially nonsense like *The Owl and the Pussycat* and rhyming stuff, oh and Rudyard Kipling's *Smuggler's Song.* You'll know it Helen:

'Them that ask no questions isn't told a lie.
Watch the wall, my darling, while the Gentlemen go by!'

'Yes of course! We did it last term. The children loved it, we had some doing actions to go with the words,' Helen laughed, remembering. 'Do please show me Jack. I won't tell anyone else about it, not even Robin, promise.'

Jack looked up at his stepmother who nodded. He handed Helen the scruffy open notebook and she read aloud:

Ruby is a clever cat
Hardly ever wears a hat
And she knows just where it's at
Just like Lily Allen

'That's brilliant Jack and what a great metre, the way it builds from line to line. It's a quatrain like William Blake's *Tyger*:

"Tyger! Tyger burning bright"'

Helen spoke with genuine enthusiasm, beaming at Jack and handing the book back. Turning to Julia she said. 'Is Ruby a real cat, I didn't know you had pets?'

'Oliver wouldn't agree to a dog; too dependent, too noisy, too much trouble. Sometimes I think he feels like that about Jack and maybe that's why the boy's so quiet. God I hope that's all it is. Anyway, Oliver actually likes cats. He admires their savagery, their untamed quality, so we have Ruby.' Helen was quiet. That was probably the most articulate, coherent sentence she had ever heard come out of Julia's mouth. Helen watched as Julia stood to stamp on a large spider scuttling across the wooden floor. Horrified, she looked up.

'Oliver hates spiders,' said Julia without emotion.

The mood in the room had darkened and Helen shivered. 'Right!' she said leaping to her feet. 'Come on you two what we need is exercise. When I can't sleep and I haven't taken a pill, I get up and go for a walk whatever time of night. Exercise is a recognised remedy for gloomy moods.'

Jack ignored her but Julia stood up throwing the newspaper to the floor and prodded Jack with her foot. 'Jack, now,' was all she said and the boy was on his feet.

She woke up suddenly from a dream about horses and bulls, and water. She couldn't remember exactly what the dream was about but the horses were white and looked like the ones she had seen yesterday being ridden on the beach when they had been driving back through the rain which had gone on all day.

It had rained all day without stopping, and the day before, when David had been painting walls, Julie had cooked cakes and cleaned out the freezer, and the twins had crayoned in books, shrieked and cried a lot, watched the telly and tinged their bell and bashed their drum.

Yesterday they had driven to everyone's favourite chocolate shop. There was an amazing dress there, a whole chocolate dress, long and reaching right down to the floor, but you could only look at it, you couldn't eat it, at least not yet. It looked like a wedding dress. David and Julie had bought tickets and if their numbers were picked out by the mayor, they would win it, next week. They promised her and Jean and Anne they would all get big pieces before they gave it away to the special children's hospital not far away up in the mountains. She told Julie she wanted a piece from the bottom at the side, it had looked thickest there. There were pink squares on a necklace round the model's neck which looked as if they might be made with strawberries.

After looking at the dress and walking round it for ages she went to look at the people making the chocolates, through a big window. They were dressed all in white, two men and two women. They had white trousers and jackets and funny flat white hats. One of the women was standing by a stove stirring something in a big pot with a long stick that was bashing the side of the pot a lot. The other woman was pouring chocolate over little shapes that were standing on metal bars and one of the men was following her dropping small white circles on top of the wet chocolate and she could see a lot of it was dripping through the bars. The other man looked at her; he smiled and held out his hand with two chocolates on it. One with orange stripes along the sides and top, the other was pink and the same as the ones on the necklace. She smiled back and nodded her head and he walked towards the window. Then the door opened and as he came through she stepped back and could smell the smell of chocolate even more. One of his hands was held up and his first finger was moving forwards and backwards, calling her towards him, the other was holding the two chocolates. She smiled girlishly, later she would know some people would call it coquettishly or flirtatiously, at the man in white, then walked towards him and took a chocolate in each hand. She thanked the man and walked back to look at the dress while she ate the chocolates. He watched as she put the chocolates one by one to her mouth, biting them carefully in half, then he saw the pleasure on her lips and in her eyes as they slowly turned to sweet liquid and she swallowed it a bit at a time. She knew he had seen this, but not that he had noticed she was wearing a short red skirt and plain yellow T shirt or that as he walked away he had shaken his head from side to side and smiled before going back through the door.

The shop sold lots of different sorts of tea as well as chocolate and Julie and David had been looking at them, deciding what to buy while she had been looking at chocolates being made then again at the amazing chocolate dress. She remembered from last time they had told her the shop was very famous for its chocolates and teas. After the teas had been chosen Julie had walked round the shop pointing at six different chocolate shelves and a woman in white, wearing gloves, had slowly picked chocolates from the shelves and put them into black paper bags with a picture of a man in white on the side, then put the bags into a black box with gold stripes and tied a red ribbon round it.

While David ran through the rain to get the car they had sat outside the shop under a shelter and they had looked at people walking by with umbrellas and at the box which was on a table. She didn't know what the twins had been doing while she had been looking at the people making chocolates, but when they had sat down she saw they both had chocolate round their mouths and were very quiet. David got out of the car, opened the doors and they ran to the car and got in before they got too wet. David had carried the box with the red ribbon back to the car then put it carefully in the back.

They drove to the supermarket and while Julie and David had shopped she and the twins had played in the cage with lots of coloured plastic balls and soft springy clowns that she could climb onto but the twins couldn't because they couldn't reach the arms which were held out straight each side to pull themselves right up. They reached up standing at the front of the clowns, held onto the clowns arms then put their feet onto the clowns bent knees and rocked backwards and forwards. The clowns were on big bendy springs and the twins were seeing if they could touch the balls with the backs of their heads while they pushed and pulled to and fro. They couldn't.

Last time she had done the same, and touched the balls with the back of her head from one of the clowns, the smallest one. This time she tried it, it was easy, and she was bored. As she stopped swinging backwards and forwards on the clowns, most adults watching her would have seen she was thinking, wondering what else she could do. She was holding the clown's arms and looking up at its head. Suddenly she swung round so she was riding the clown piggy back, then she pulled herself upwards with her arms, swung her legs up and round to the left. Her left leg was first, it went high and she put it over the clowns left shoulder – then she grasped the clowns head, first with her left hand then right, pulled herself up and put her right leg over the clowns right shoulder. She was suddenly sitting on the clown's shoulders holding onto his head and she laughed.

Jean stopped rocking and looked at her in amazement. Anne fell off her clown, struggled through the balls as she moved towards the door and then out of it before being sick on the trousers of the lady that looked after the children in the cage.

She had tried out all the clowns and was pleased she could sit on all their shoulders and make them swing easily. She had noticed the backs of their necks had different shapes. The first one had been sharp and cut into her between the legs, but the other two felt soft and comfortable and she had smiled and her eyes had widened when she first noticed the difference as she had rocked the clowns a long way forwards and a long way backwards without falling off.

The curtains weren't closed and she could see that the sky was blue. It wasn't raining.

The fret had cleared as they left the house so they took the cliff path along to Long Beach and returned across the cow strewn fields. When they got back fishermen were unloading their catch on the quay and Jack wanted to take a look so he and Julia headed towards the lighthouse as Helen returned to the house to start on lunch. As she walked in the front door David called out from the front Sitting Room and she walked in leaving the door open behind her.

'Hi darling,' she said brightly 'I've been for a walk with Julia and Jack. They've just gone over to the quay but I shouldn't think they'll be long so I'll start lunch.'

'Good walk?' asked David.

'Yes I think so. Julia's rather down this morning. Apparently Tim Petherbridge-Brown was killed in Afghanistan three weeks ago and Oliver was his usual bloody self about it. So watch out, she's looking for a shoulder to cry on.'

At that moment Julia had just entered the hall to fetch her sunglasses and hearing the tail end of the exchange stopped to listen.

'She reminds me of a dog we had when I was a child,' said David. 'Wouldn't leave me alone, slept on my bed, followed me around, dear old thing. When I went to prep school she would sit by the door all day waiting for me to come home. When I went away to Eton she howled for days until my parents got a new puppy which replaced me completely in her affections. It was as if I had never existed,' he laughed.

'Well we can't get Julia a puppy more's the pity. Apparently Oliver can't abide dogs or indeed spiders.' They both laughed.

In the hallway Julia wiped a tear away. *Even you David. You think I'm like an old dog. You're all bastards, all of you.'* Coming on top of Tim's death this betrayal was too much to bear, like stitches being torn from a fresh wound. Silently, she picked up her sunglasses, pulled her mobile phone from her bag on the floor beneath the table and walked out the front door closing it gently behind her.

Julia closed her phone and put it in her pocket as she walked along the quay to join Jack who was watching the fish being lifted into ice-filled plastic trays on the quayside.

'What's that fish there J J?' asked Jack pointing at a red fish.

'No idea J,' Julia replied. When they were alone together she called him J rather than Jack and the boy loved her all the more for it. 'Best ask Helipedia. She knows everything.'

Jack giggled at the reference to Helen who he found to be very bossy and overly friendly for an adult.

'Do you fancy a pasty?' she asked, fully aware that Helen was preparing a nutritious salad of smoked fish and mixed leaves.

'Yeah,' Jack replied with gusto, 'but what about Helen's lunch?'

'Fuck that,' Julia replied putting her arm around Jack's shoulders and leading him back down the quay towards the stores.

She was standing by the barbeque, which David had lit not long ago and she could see orange flames coming from where the white things he had set fire to were covered with coals. Julie was in the kitchen cutting up chunks of meat and David was next to Julie pouring red wine into a bowl and making something she would later know was a marinade. If they had seen her face while she was looking at the flames they would have seen her look around, see no one, then smile as an idea jumped into her mind.

This morning, two minutes after seeing there was blue sky and no rain when she had woken up she was behind the old stable wearing Ma's plain blue T shirt, her feet were wet from the grass but she didn't care, and she was reaching through the hole to pull out the blue cigarette packet. She had held it to her left ear and could hear nothing, no buzzing and no scrabbling. She had shaken it and heard a sound like a very quiet broken rattle. She had listened again and still heard no buzzing. Slowly and carefully she lifted the top of the packet open and looked inside and saw the thing she would later know was a cockroach crawl away from the light and over the remains of the wasp and start to burrow into the black sludge that was the gooey remains of the dead slug. She had smiled and was pleased that now she knew, then closed the packet, stood on the bricks and put it back through the hole.

She walked to the old stable and round the back to the hole, stood on the bricks, reached through the hole and pulled out the packet then walked back to the barbeque and put it into the flames. She smiled when the flames grew bigger as the packet caught fire and laughed as she saw it crinkle up and turn bright red. Then the red colour faded and she could see the black outline of the crinkled packet through the flames and she was still looking at where the packet had been when David came out and put a bowl on the table. She looked then walked to the table and took a stuffed olive from the bowl, put it into her mouth and walked over to the gap in the brambles to look at the flamingos.

Half-hearted bunting and surly service; sullen bar staff knowing they owed these holidaymakers their living and hating them for it. Not that Julia would have noticed thought Helen. Lady of the manor she strode through life serenely unaware of the antagonism around her. Centuries of breeding and dealing with servants had acquired her a carapace.

Wasps, dog turds, dead fish smells, discarded chips and fat ugly women. Mutton dressed as lamb with cheap fake tan and ankle bracelets and short scrawny middle-aged men with sucked in faces from too many fags and too few teeth. Grubby brats dripping ice-cream on garish acrylic T-shirts and the occasional family of blond, lean tastefully clad Teutonics; Dutch perhaps or German, totally out of place like vegetarians in Texas. Hideous smells of unspeakable things done to dead creatures; tanneries, slaughterhouses, fish processing plants. People with no chins or too many; people who shouldn't wear that or expose that but did; men in socks and sandals, and self-respecting swans staying out to sea. People still buying Crocs, queuing for fish & chips, gobbling pasties in the narrow streets and bellowing at each other with their mouths full. Perhaps the place was charming in the winter.

'Does Robert de Niro actually talk Italian?' asked Julia à propos the canned music.

Not unusually, the others ignored her. Oliver and David had stayed back at the house whilst Helen and Julia had brought the boys along the coast to Trengissey. Helen had hoped to get some fresh provisions but the place was full of shops selling candles, jewellery, fudge and fleets of boats in wood, plastic, ceramic and wire. There were no shops selling food bar a tiny all purpose store and newsagent. Julia was delighted, visiting every tiny shop buying bling and rubbish, the boys were happy looking at boats and children catching crabs and Helen was in a seriously bad mood. The holiday was turning into a nightmare and it had been her idea. David was as ever oblivious to the bad atmosphere, but with Oliver out until the small hours every night and Julia silent and brooding, Helen was getting depressed. The previous evening had been dreadful. Oliver had gone to the pub with his new student pals, again. Julia had sat in the garden until it got dark and then gone to bed. She and David had watched DVDs with the boys. What a great holiday this was turning into. That week they had all been very worthy and visited the Eden Project. The next day she had hung around in Truro waiting for Julia who had just had to go shopping, and then yesterday she and David had queued and traipsed their way around the Lost Gardens of Heligan.

Now they were sitting at a window table in a so-called bistro on the harbour side in Trengissey. The walls were lined with mock wood and a garish, threadbare, patterned carpet stuck to both the floor and the soles of her espadrilles. At a nearby table an ugly small boy, totally ignored by his raucous relatives, was playing with a ghastly toy rocket which made an incessant whirring noise. Outside, the harbour water shone like taupe patent leather. There were missing neon letters in the bistro's name on the outside wall and missing bulbs in the recessed lighting in the ceiling, but the boys were hungry, Julia was driving, and Helen needed a drink.

The menu offered chips with everything: chips with curry, lasagne, sandwiches, probably with puddings. The specials' board boasted 'salad garnish' as a constituent of the meals, and the knives and forks were encased in single ply paper napkins, dampened to stay rolled around the cutlery, and consequently useless.

'Right. Who's for the fish and chips apart from me?' Helen asked, snapping out of it.

The boys both agreed with her choice and Julia opted for a prawn and avocado salad. The lunch was surprisingly good and Helen scolded herself for her curmudgeonly attitude. Look on the bright side was to be her new mantra for the rest of the holiday. Tomorrow they were off to Fowey sailing. Helen and Robin loved to sail. It was to be her day at last.

She saw Julie asleep and snoring on the sofa, mouth wide open, her knees were raised and her legs were apart and her silky pink skirt had slid up and she could see small bright red knickers scrunched up on one side of the pussy which looked shiny. Julie's right hand covered the black triangle and a finger with nail varnish the same colour as the knickers was pointing to the top of the pussy. She put a finger to her lips and went schh and smiled. Julie's left arm was flopped off the sofa and the hand was on the floor. There were two bottles of red wine on the floor next to the sofa, one was half full and the other was nearly empty. There was a glass that had fallen over and had dripped red wine onto the white tiles.

Through the open patio door she could hear the twins trying to play hide and seek in the garden and from upstairs she heard music. It sounded strange and she didn't know what it was, later she would remember it, like it, and know that it was David Bowie singing about a spaceman called Major Tom. She went upstairs and heard that the music was coming from Julie and David's bedroom. She slowly opened the door and the music got louder, she walked in and could see David lying on the bed, his eyes were closed and his mouth was moving as if he was singing the song. She went back downstairs, and as she looked at Julie she heard a bird start chirruping outside.

She went through the patio door and could hear that the chirruping was coming from one of the lemon trees. She noticed there were yellow and green lemons on the trees, some small and some big, and white flowers. She ran towards the sound and bashed her foot on a log that someone had moved from the pile under the kitchen

*window and fell, it hurt. As she sat on the grass she saw
that the twins were still trying to play hide and seek. On
her left, Jean was on the patio behind the table and on her
right Anne was going through the gap in the brambles and
looking at the flamingos. When she got through she went a
few paces to the right and stood still. She could see Anne
through the brambles because there were hardly any
leaves yet.*

*She got up and walked two steps towards the chirruping
before she saw the bird that was making it on a branch not
far away and a bit over David's height. The bird was
small, brown, and had a red front and it began chirruping
more quickly and even more noisily. She pushed her lips
together like she had been practising at home, and
squeezed the air from her mouth through them and quickly
moved her lips together then apart again and again. She
made the song. The bird hopped closer and moved down
to a lower branch. Still making the song she turned slowly
and picked up the log with her left hand, turned back and
threw it at the red fronted bird. Later she would know it
was a robin that she had knocked out of the tree.*

*She walked to the bird and picked it up. It was still.
Holding it in the palm of her left hand, with its head
between her thumb and first finger she slowly closed her
hand until she could only see its head. Bringing her hand
slowly to her face she looked closely at the bird for a long
time, and it opened an eye then closed it again quickly.
She smiled. She heard Jean laughing and running towards
the gap in the brambles. She walked away from the sound
towards the old stable, bought the bird's head up close to
her eye again, so close she saw a small bright green insect
run across its beak, and could feel that its body was very*

soft in her hand. She was realising it weighed nothing when she wondered if it was a clever bird and what it was doing here. She turned and walked with it in her hand, which was swinging by her side as she walked, and stopped when she got to the back of the red car on the drive at the front of the house. She opened her hand and looked at the bird again. It was lying still in her palm, then after a minute she closed her fingers around the bird, holding it firmly, then she moved her arm backwards then forwards and upwards, throwing the bird up into the air over the car towards the road. It flapped its wings as soon as it left her hand and flew over the lane and away.

By eight o'clock that morning Porthaven beach had been cordoned off and a small group of people in coveralls and boots were standing outside a tent which covered the body, its entrance flapping gently in the breeze.

The tallest was the senior attending officer Detective Inspector Phil (Félipe) Treloar, a handsome blond blue-eyed man in his mid thirties. Phil Treloar was unmarried and unattached. The previous year he had turned down promotion and a transfer to the Met to stay in his native Cornwall to be near his widowed Spanish mother who was still running the small family farm near Zennor in the far west of the county.

Treloar's career with the Devon & Cornwall Police had not been without incident. Recently relocated to West Cornwall from Plymouth where he had got on the wrong side of the powers that be, namely Chief Superintendent Jennifer Burns, he had avoided any blot on his record largely thanks to his dear departed dad who had given him his old Cornish name and his handsome face which went down so well with the media and consequently the Chief Constable. Burns had been transferred to 'Justice and Professional Standards' at headquarters in Exeter, so all being well there should be no further need for their paths to cross. In the early days he had suffered the taunt of "here comes da law", a supposed pun on his name which some found inordinately funny, but now his skirmish in Plymouth had earned him respect and he seldom heard it.

The Senior Investigating Officer on this case was actually Detective Superintendent Suzanne Winters and Treloar was her deputy, but as everyone knew DS Winters was not one to get her hands or indeed her feet dirty when she could avoid it, and Treloar often found himself acting

Investigating Officer in charge at crime scenes.
as accompanied by Sgt Sam (Samantha) Scott, a
f Bristol University with a degree in History,
.. u the force and being fast-tracked. Despite that she was actually very popular and affectionately nicknamed 'Samba' (Sam B. A.) which she took with her customary good grace and winning smile. Also present were Detective Sergeant Colin Andrews, designated Crime Scene Manager, and Belinda Hanson, Police Photographer.

Sam Scott walked back up the beach to where Sergeant Charlie Hendra, the Neighbourhood Team Leader, a twenty year veteran, was standing guard on the slipway.

'Ello my 'ansome,' said Hendra smiling. Hendra appreciated the female of the species and found Samantha Scott to be a fine example with her shiny dark blond bobbed hair and turquoise eyes; not to mention her athletic physique and five foot nine height. She was indeed a good-looking young woman.

'Hi Charlie. DI Treloar is grumpy and he wants to know where the police doctor is. He seems a bit out of sorts this morning.'

'Well he would be, he don't like deaths by the sea. I can tell ee'

'Oh?'

'That be 'cos of his dad. Drowned. In the sea. In the cove beneath his farm. Body never found. And 'ee who had swum in that cove every day year through. That were a vicious rip tide that day though. Four others drowned up the coast at Sennen. No Phil don't like sea deaths. He used to be a great swimmer himself like, in the sea. Never been in since that day, must be five year now. Given that, I'm surprised Frosty didn't get off her fat ar.., sorry Sam. Doc'll be 'ere dreckly.'

Sam smiled. 'That's Okay Charlie, I take your point. Ah, at last. Here comes the doctor.' A beautiful old golden Mercedes drew to a halt opposite Crabbers and a small rotund balding man with a bushy grey beard, dressed in a crumpled cream linen suit, emerged. He grabbed his bag from the back, clambered into coveralls and overshoes, and waving, walked down to join Sergeants Scott and Hendra at the top of the slipway.

'Wonderful morning Sergeants, well apart from for the poor sod down there,' said Doctor Anthony Tremayne, Police Surgeon.

'Morning doctor,' said Sam.

'Doc,' said Sergeant Hendra.

'Well in the words of the estimable Delia, let's be having you,' said Tremayne sauntering off in the direction of the tent closely followed by Sam.

'Bye Sam,' called Hendra. 'I'll go see Pete at Crabbers 'ee be wanting to open soon, I told 'un to wait on my word 'fore opening.'

Back at the tent Treloar was talking to DS Andrews. 'So, run that by me again Col.'

'Low water was at ten past eleven last night. High water was at seven minutes past five this morning and you can see that was twenty yards past the body, so he would have been covered by several feet of water with this slope. A six metre tide is a fast moving tide so someone must have known their knots and worked quickly to secure him and be sure not to be seen here on the beach. After that, in the dark with no sound and no movement anyone passing the slipway would probably not have noticed anything suspicious what with the flotsam and jetsam and seaweed. His mouth is taped, so why put that bag over his head, and why is it tarred and tied round his neck with rope? The bag has a drawstring. The rope was superfluous. If he wasn't dead when he was tied down, and he was conscious, he wouldn't have known what was happening because he couldn't see. He must have been terrified.' But the tar and the rope? Beats me.'

'Well my, thank you so much for joining us Tony, finishing your breakfast were you?' Treloar called to the pair approaching over the sand.

'Be still Félipe. I understand my dear friend Marianne Temple formally recognised death and John Forbes could have certified death for you at the mortuary so in a sense my presence is a bonus.' Tremayne knelt and felt for a pulse anyway. 'Clearly it's not suicide. Could be accidental, an extreme episode of autoerotic sex caught out by time and tide. Perhaps not. Probably murder, but we need to get him on the slab. Have the SOCO boys finished with their hi-tech cameras and video gear; can we lift that hood affair?'

'Yes. We lifted it up and his mouth is taped, but if you want to, go ahead. I want to get him moved, he's too exposed here, too public, and we need to make a search around the body.'

Tremayne pulled the bag back to reveal the face. As he did so several small green shore crabs scuttled out and headed for the sea. Sam instinctively jumped back with an intake of breath. Above the taped mouth the eyes bulged, one had been picked at by the small crabs that must have been put into the bag before it was secured with the rope. Tremayne stood.

'They make an excellent soup you know, shore crabs. Well, perhaps not those particular ones,' he grinned at Sam's horrified expression.

'Right, I can tell you now that he was thirty eight, circumcised, reputedly in good health and he broke his left femur last year in a skiing accident at Lake Garda.'

Tremayne grinned triumphantly at the stunned faces of his colleagues. 'That my compadres is Oliver Osborne QC'.

She was smiling as she watched the bird with the red front get smaller as it flew away. She turned and was walking back to the back of the house when she heard the twins screeching and that the flamingos' normal gabbling, which everyone was used to, had suddenly turned to a loud squawking and whooping and she could here a lot of splashing and the whooshhh whooshhh noise that a lot of flamingos flapping their wings made.

She ran down the path, underneath the wasps and past the wasp hole at the bottom of the wall, and when she ran onto the grass she could see too many flamingos to count flying away and she ran to the gap in the brambles. She saw even more, making lots of noise and quickly moving their long legs in slow motion and flapping their wings to take and off and follow. Jean and Anne were running at the edge of the water, flapping their arms, throwing pebbles and laughing.

She ran after the twins and by the time she caught up, there were no flamingos in the water but she could still see them as they flew away and had begun turning to the right, then more to the right and then more and then they were flying back towards the sea, in the distance as a pink cloud. She couldn't hear them any more.

The twins looked at her in amazement as she walked into the water without taking her sandals and socks off and walked until the water came up to her knees. She couldn't feel how cold the water was, or the small shrimps under her feet, and she laughed as she turned and looked back to the shore, and waved the twins towards her with her arms and they walked into the water towards her side by side, still wearing their sandals and socks and giggling. They were still giggling when they reached her and she turned round and stood so they were both on her left and they were looking at the empty lake and into the blue sky where the very small pink cloud had nearly disappeared in the distance.

They were both still giggling and she laughed as she moved so that she was standing in the middle of them and put her left hand on the back of Anne's head and her right hand on the back of Jean's head and quickly and very roughly pushed their heads forward and down so their legs gave way then carried on pushing down until their heads were under the water and their bodies were flat on the sand. Would they drink and eat like the flamingos? When the twins started struggling, trying to get their heads up and flapping their arms and legs, she knew that they wouldn't. She pressed down hard on the backs of their heads and it wasn't long before their arms and legs had stopped flapping and splashing about.

She stood up and the twins didn't move. She kicked Jean's head then Anne's and neither moved and she was smiling as she walked out of the water and back towards the gap in the brambles. As she walked through the gap she noticed that her feet were cold. Then she went back through the patio doors and saw that Julie was still asleep but had stopped snoring, her legs were straight now but she could still see the tiny red knickers and the hand covering the black triangle. She went upstairs and could hear nothing from Julie and David's bedroom then went into her bedroom and took off her sandals and socks. She went to the bathroom with the wet socks and put them in the washing basket underneath David's red T shirt and dried her legs and feet on a towel, went back to her bedroom and

75

took some fresh socks from a drawer and put them on. Then she went back downstairs with her sandals in her hand and through the kitchen to the patio where she noticed the empty flower pot was full of dirty water and that the red elephant was floating in it. She put the sandals down side by side on the warm patio next to the warm wall.

Suddenly she heard the whoooshhh whoooshhh whooshhing of the wings and the friendly honking noise she loved as the leading flamingos flew very low, and only just over the house, down towards the lake. She ran to the gap in the brambles to watch the leaders land in their funny gangly way then looked up and saw too many flamingos to count, their wings pink with black stripes, flying just over the lemon trees as they whooosshhed whooosshhed and honked their way home to the water. When they were all back, gabbling, she watched them for a while then went to the kitchen, took the bag of pink chocolates from the box in the cupboard, went to the telly room and carried on reading her Tin Tin book, laughed a lot and ate pink chocolates, slowly.

'Thank you for waiting in Dr Temple.' Treloar and Sam were seated on the patio of Marianne Temple's large dormer bungalow uphill from the beach.

'Actually, it's Mrs not Dr,' Marianne replied.

'Oh sorry, you were a consultant of course.'

'Well that's true, but now I'm retired I just prefer it. I didn't stand on ceremony when I was working either.'

'Could you talk us through what happened this morning?' Treloar asked.

'It was a day like any other. I brought the dogs down to the beach for a run before the crowds. I prefer to be there very early when it's still quiet. I saw no one and no one had been on the beach.'

'How can you be sure?' asked Sam.

'No footprints in the sand,' said Treloar.

'Exactly Inspector. There were no footprints anywhere on the beach let alone near the body. The tide was still going out.'

'I understand you checked the body?' Treloar asked.

'Yes. He was clearly dead; drowned I presumed. I checked the pulse, but otherwise touched nothing. For what it's worth I thought there was a childlike quality in the way the body was, well..., staged I suppose. A cruel and spiteful element I've seen in the acts of disturbed children; a nastiness, a viciousness. It was strange but that was what struck me straightaway. Obviously it couldn't have been a child, the man was too large and heavy, but my first thought was of disturbed children.'

Still sitting on the floor leaning against a chair she was dozy. The book was still across her knees and she wondered what had woken her up until she heard Julie shouting 'Jean……Anne' from the garden. She heard David thumping down the stairs in a hurry and saw him run past the telly room door. She heard the smack of a hand or leg on wood and a loud growl as he bashed into something in the kitchen on his way outside to see what was up with Julie, then she put the book on the floor, got up slowly, and followed him out into the garden. As she walked to the barbeque she saw that Julie was looking worried as she spoke to David, pointing to the old stable then to the front of the house, and then he ran to the path that went by the wasps and to the front of the house. He was shouting ' Jean…..Anne' as he ran and his voice got quieter as he reached the lane and ran from the house still shouting. It had sounded as if he was running towards the village.

Julie wobbled as she ran over to the stable in her bare feet and pulled madly on the door handle twisting it one way then the other. The door didn't move and she bashed it with her right hand, shouting 'Jean……' then 'Anne……' before running into the kitchen where drawers were opened roughly and slammed madly shut with loads of noise. She guessed that Julie was looking for a key.

At the barbeque she picked a piece of charcoal that hadn't been burnt out of the white ashes, walked a few steps towards the lawn then knelt down on the patio feeling the warmth in her knees, bent over putting her right hand on the ground and began to draw with her left hand, concentrating hard on which edge of the charcoal to use and how to hold it to change the thickness of the lines.

Julie stopped being noisy in the kitchen and wobbled outside, waving her right arm from left to right and screeching something she didn't understand, towards the patio. She stopped drawing and looked at Julie as she got closer, then slowly shook her head from side to side and hunched her shoulders.

Julie had turned and walked, wobbling, back towards the stable door, and stopped when she was nearly there, then screamed and pointed to the wooden bar across the top of the door keeping it shut. She had turned back to her drawing by the time Julie had reached up to the bar and pushed it up and out of the brackets that had held it firmly in front of the door. Julie had then pulled on the door handle, opened the door and rushed inside before making lots more noise shouting 'Jean...........Anne' over and over again and moving and knocking over the storage boxes that she knew had been stacked there.

Back at the barbeque, using her left hand to scoop white ash into an ash tray that she had picked up off the table, she saw Julie leave the stable in a wobbly rush and stagger onto the path that went by the wasps and towards the lane, and heard her screeching 'David .... David .... Jean .... Anne' time after time as she went down the lane towards the village where Robert and Caroline's house was. Soon, it was just a noise in the distance.

She dipped the first finger of her left hand into the white ash, which she had splashed with water from Elephant's flower pot and then stirred it in to make a light grey goo, and added a glowing sheen to a wing of the night bird she had drawn, the one that she would later know was a Eurasian Eagle Owl, realised she couldn't hear Julie any more, and smiled. After adding some more sheen lines to the wing then one of the ears, she outlined a moon behind the bird's head, then coloured it in using two fingers held together. Then she stood up, stepped back, and looking at the Owl she smiled, and realised she would have to add the shed roof and the Owl's feet tomorrow because it was getting dark.

As she walked towards the kitchen to find something to eat she could hear lots of voices, from the direction of the village, getting louder and louder shouting 'Jean..........Anne'. She had just gone back to the telly room with a bag of crisps when she heard lots of people shouting from the lane and when she looked out of the window she saw people waving torches and walking quickly along the lane while they shouted. She dropped the bag of crisps on the floor and ran up the stairs to get a better look and when she looked out of the window she could see that the people with torches in the lane were shining them into the ditch then moving along a bit and doing it again, and there were two torches in the distance shining at a barn in the field on the other side of the lane. She saw the door open and the torches disappear inside. Everyone was shouting 'Jean......... Anne.......... Anne..... Jean'.

She heard people come into the house; Julie's crying was easy to make out and she could hear David's voice but not what he was saying. When she went quietly downstairs towards the kitchen she stopped at the lounge door and could see that Julie was laying on the sofa crying loudly and David was using a tea towel to wipe blood off the bottom and sides of her feet which were still bare. She crept to the telly room and picked up her Tin Tin book then went upstairs quietly to her bedroom, turned on the bedside light before getting into bed with her clothes on before opening the book which she really liked even though Thomson and Thomson who were really funny were only in it at the beginning. She thought it was fun reading about the cold when she was so warm, and smiled as she read about Snowy setting off in the snow to get rescuers for Tin Tin before the book fell onto the covers and she fell into a deep, calm, sleep. Later she would be told that there had been people shouting for Jean and Anne up and down the lane all that night and that the police had come in cars with blue lights flashing. It wasn't until it was light that she had woken up, and smiled sleepily before getting out of bed to look out of the window to see what all the fuss was about in the lane.

Three hours after Tremayne's startling pronouncement Jamie woke confused about his feelings. Oliver Osborne must have been dead and that was good, but he, Jamie had not been the one to avenge his beloved and that was bad.

Jamie had been amazed that Oliver could still stand when he had left Point End House. Earlier that evening he had been drunk, loud and obnoxious in the pub, baiting the huge black guy. Jamie was surprised when Oliver left with the others at closing time heading up to Point End House walking arm in arm with the one called Toby, laughing and joking. He had followed them.

Jamie had arrived in the pub at about 10:40 and it was packed. Luckily Oliver and the students were seated at a large table near the bar and Jamie was able to squeeze into a corner where the bar met the wall close enough to hear there conversation, although it was not difficult to make out Oliver's contributions from the entrance.

'Your reckless bankers almost destroyed the entire world economy not just a few tawdry fishermen in some Godforsaken shithole like Venice, Louisiana. And if wasn't for your national obsession with driving bloody great Humvees, BP wouldn't have been drilling in the fucking Gulf of Mexico in the first place,' Oliver snarled.

Ben smiled broadly at Oliver. 'Begging your pardon Sir, but I don't believe your language and tone are appropriate in front of the ladies.'

'Please,' snorted Oliver 'women may appear to love all that courteous, chivalrous crap but in my experience, which is considerably greater than yours, the intelligent ones, like Ellie, soon weary of it and much prefer to be treated as equals in all ways, including language. It's only the dumb ones like my wife who cling to outdated romantic notions of some bygone Jane Austen era.'

'Well thank you for the compliment Oliver,' Ellie said laughing nervously. She was becoming uncomfortable with the atmosphere at the table.

'Americans,' Oliver continued, ignoring her, 'when Thomas Jefferson wrote most of the Declaration of Independence I've always thought that he should have included alongside life, liberty and the pursuit of happiness another unalienable right:' he paused for effect, 'the pursuit of perfect dentition!'

Silence fell across the table and all eyes turned to Ben as Ellie held her breath.

'Ha!' Ben threw back his head and roared with laughter, and the others joined in nervously letting out a communal sigh of relief. 'You sure are a funny guy, Oliver.'

Jamie ordered a beer and his attention was drawn to the landlord and the pretty French barmaid chatting together at the till.

'...tempted to throw that bloke out. If it wasn't for the fact that he spends so much money and that black bloke doesn't seem too bothered. Still if he doesn't keep it down I'll have to speak to him about his language.'

'It's alright, we close soon and he'll be gone. Let it be.'

So when Oliver staggered up the drive of Point End House Jamie was shocked. He had been hiding in the field over the stile where the coastal path veers off across the fields towards Penmassick just at the entrance to the drive down to the house when he heard the unmistakable bellowing of Osborne at about 3.00 am. The man was an absolute boor.

Jamie had been following at some distance as Oliver stumbled along the deserted road belching and grunting when all of a sudden where the road passed a gated entrance at the back of a large unoccupied house overlooking the sea he disappeared and all was silent. Jamie froze. *What the hell? Had he collapsed?* He scurried along the road close to the fences and hedges on his right and moved into the drive just in time to see Oliver's outstretched legs disappearing around the side of the house towards the cliff. Jamie followed keeping tight in to the side of the house.

In the moonlight bathing the garden and reflecting off the sea he could make out a tall black clad figure dragging Osborne towards the cliff edge. *Was he going to throw him over?* Suddenly they both disappeared from view. Jamie could well understand someone tossing Oliver over, but to go with him? He ran softly across the soft springy turf to the last point he had seen them and looked down.

Below him he could make out the incoming tide and winding down the cliff a rough path with steps hewn into the rock leading onto the beach. He waited, watching until at the bottom on the sand he saw the black clad figure emerge dragging Osborne along toward the harbour on what looked like a body board.

The tide was coming in fast at this end of the beach and Jamie judged he could not follow without being caught so he ran back up through the garden onto the road and sprinted left down the road towards the harbour.

As he reached the bottom of Chapel Hill by Crabbers café he stopped, hidden from the beach and took out his night vision binoculars. Everything was still and quiet apart from the sounds of the waves. Slowly he moved round the side of the café onto the terrace and crawled to the edge. He looked out towards the sea.

The black clad figure was crouched next to Osborne's prone spread-eagled body frantically tying something to the extended limbs. Jamie watched fascinated. Next it picked up some type of sack or bag and dragged it over Osborne's frantically tossing head, constantly checking behind it to assess the state of the tide. Finally as the water reached Osborne's shoulders the figure stood, kicked the prone man and started up the beach towards Jamie, who crawled back behind a small wall separating areas of the terrace as the figure ran up the slipway and turned left towards Porth House. Jamie could make out a figure wearing a full wetsuit, boots, and hood. Only the hands shone pale and very white, one of them clutching a dark rucksack. It could have been anyone.

Jamie was torn between following and turning back to see what was happening on the beach. He chose to look back just in time to see the waves covering the writhing figure of Oliver Osborne QC. By the time he reached the top of the slipway and looked left towards Porth House the road was deserted and Oliver Osborne had disappeared beneath the waves. Jamie stowed his binoculars, picked up his bag and trotted back up Chapel Hill towards the stile and the path leading back up across the fields to the campsite.

So it was with mixed emotions that Jamie opened the door of his campervan at 11:03 that morning. The first thing he noticed was that the Gull Wing had gone as had the tent and clutter of his erstwhile neighbour. It had been there when he got back to the van but obviously the man had decided on an early start and must have pushed the bike out onto the road before starting it to avoid waking the campers; Jamie thought he had seemed a considerate pleasant enough fellow after all.

As he walked out of the site entrance he had to pass a number of large rubbish bins and recycling tubs which were emptied mid-morning on a daily basis at the height of the season. Jamie noticed a roll of black material sticking out of the one nearest the road and recognised it at once. Looking around to check that no one was paying him any attention he pulled a wetsuit from the bin and a hood and boots fell to the ground. The wetsuit itself was covered in small nicks and tears as if it had been dragged through broken glass or as if the wearer had been running through a thorny thicket or along a blackthorn hedge.

Jamie bundled the wetsuit up and jogged back with it to the van then retraced his steps and started down the hill to see what was happening. As he jogged along he thought to himself about the biker. Just a coincidence that he should be gone this morning? What had he said his name was that first evening? Trueman, Trueblood, certainly Thomas. Definitely a job for Alisdair.

The chocolate was fantastic, even better than it had looked in the shop. It was bitey but crisp, sweet, and really delicious. She had pushed and shoved, even used her finger nails on the back of the arm of one of the others who wouldn't let her through before kicking the back of the girl's leg to make her fall over, to make sure she was at the front. Wearing Ma's long blue T shirt, and red sandals, she had smiled girlishly at the man from the chocolate shop after he had stopped pushing the trolley, while the children were still cheering loudly and the nurses were clapping. He had noticed and looked surprised before smiling back, then nodded and winked at her.

*The wedding dress, standing high on a stand on the trolley, hadn't been broken anywhere. There were no big pieces missing from it and even the pink squares that looked as if they might be made of strawberries were still there. After winking, the man, who had been wearing his white trousers and jacket and the funny flat white hat, had held up his arms so they were in front of him at the height of his shoulders and flapped his hands up and back then pushed them down a few times and everyone got quieter. Then he stood back and pointed at the chocolate wedding dress and everyone went mad again, cheering and clapping. The man looked angry and put his hands on his hips, though she thought he was just pretending. Then he put the first finger of his right hand slowly to his lips and very loudly went **schhschhschh!!** She tried to stop but she was still laughing when everyone else was very quiet.*

She wasn't really listening, like most of the other children probably, as the man had talked. She heard him say something about a Black Diamond, and the chocolate dress being given to the children by people who had won it with their numbers, but not much else. When he had finished talking the man took a silver hammer from his pocket, held it out at arms length and with the first finger of his other hand called her over. Because she was looking at the hammer, the plate he was holding out, and the dress, she couldn't see everyone else looking very surprised and staring at her. She took the plate, pointed with her left hand to the bottom of the dress at the side, moved the plate underneath the dress and watched with open mouth and with her tongue poking out and held against her bottom lip, as the hammer hit the dress on the thick part and big pieces of chocolate fell onto the plate. She had looked up at the man and smiled again before walking round the back of the trolley, past the picture of the dress on the notice board in the corridor and back to her chair in the room where her bed was and put the plate down. Picking up a big piece of chocolate she carefully broke a small piece off then walked past the other three beds to the window, and looked down through the gaps in the mountains where today she could just see the sea sparkling, a very long way away.

She put the chocolate in her mouth, then looked up at a big bird with its wings outstretched looking as if it was floating in the air, going in circles that were getting higher and higher and moving in her direction. She wondered how it could do that without moving its wings and watched it until it went past the top of the window and she couldn't see it any more. It was brown, and she wondered if flamingos ever floated in the air like that. She walked back to the chair, picked up the plate and sat down with it, bit off pieces of the bitey chocolate and one by one sucked them round her mouth with her tongue, melting them slowly then swallowing the delicious goo. When the chocolate had all gone she sat looking at the rainbow on the blue wall with its fluffy white clouds, and wondered if she would really see Ma and Pa again the next day.

The Force Home Office Registered Pathologist for Devon and Cornwall, Dr John Forbes, was a stick insect of a man in his late forties with a passion for choral singing and an extremely attractive much younger black South African psychiatrist wife called Priscilla. It was for the latter rather than the former, and his famed attention to detail, that he commanded respect amongst his police colleagues.

It was the morning following the discovery of the body of Oliver Osborne and Dr Forbes, Treloar and Scott were sitting in an office in the Pathology Department of Treliske Hospital in Truro.

'Well, I agree with Tony Tremayne, it wasn't accidental,' said Dr Forbes with a grin.

'Yes I gathered that John,' said Treloar. In fact Oliver Osborne had presumably been stripped naked and tied spread-eagled between the mooring ropes with nylon cord with a tarred bag tied over his head and, as it was discovered when the body was moved, a wooden skittle-like object, which turned out to be a belaying pin from a yacht, firmly inserted in his rectum.

'Your man choked on his own vomit, he didn't drown. Blood alcohol level more than three times the legal driving limit and traces of ketamine, often used as a drug for horses but now well, you know better than I what you can get in any town centre. Last meal of Calvados and red wine partially soaked up by a small amount of brie and crab salad I'd guess, definitely crab. Time of death around the time the tide reached him. There is a small amount of salt water in his tubes. I guess he woke up, realised his situation, snorted some seawater as the waves washed over him, and threw up with his mouth taped. He definitely struggled; there are abrasions in the skin of his wrists where he tried desperately to free himself. Very scary, very nasty, and all for nought.'

'All for nought?' said Treloar.

'Well, he would have been dead anyway within months, massive brain tumour.'

'So, somebody could have avoided all this trouble?' asked Sam.

'No, I don't think so, this was extremely personal. Somebody wanted to take the trouble to terrify him; somebody was also making a point: the belaying pin, the rope and tar, the crabs. Just imagine it. You come round to find yourself in the dark, bound and staked out on a beach with small crabs crawling over you face trapped there inside a bag. Somebody really didn't like Oliver Osborne,' said Dr Forbes.

'Well that narrows it down to virtually everyone he ever met from what Tony says,' said Treloar. 'He knew him from Oxford where he was 'a total shit' quote unquote and apparently he saw him again at a fundraiser for Bart's Hospital just before Christmas where he was mauling every woman within reach, pissed and nasty with it. Charming man evidently,' said Treloar. 'Would he have known, about the brain tumour, I mean?'

'Well, he would have been experiencing symptoms so you could check with his doctor, why do you ask?'

'Just wondering if that would have incapacitated him to any degree?'

'Hard to say but with all that booze and the ketamine he'd have been out of it. But he was a fit man; I can't see a woman doing this, well maybe a very fit woman with a wheelbarrow?'

'Or, a boat trailer?' asked Sam.

It was just light and it was cold. She could feel the small round pebbles through the soles of her pink trainers as she stood on the roof wearing the light blue hooded sweat shirt Ma had left the last time she had visited. It had two frothy beer mugs and a filled baguette that she would later learn was a po'boy printed on the front in the middle of 'UNIVERSITY OF BOURBON STREET' in big letters printed in a circle. It was faded and worn thin, especially at the front where Ma's boobs stretched it, and it hung to her thighs now instead of her knees.

The sky was grey. Her breath was steaming white and she was keeping it away from the binoculars to stop them misting up. They were hanging around her neck and bashed against her stomach with every step when she walked which wasn't comfortable. It would be worse with a bra. She'd already sorted the case by making the strap longer and looping it round the side of her neck over her left shoulder, with her right arm through it so it hung by her right thigh. She had been really surprised yesterday when the staff had given her the wrapped box at her birthday party and even more surprised, totally gobsmacked, when she opened it and found them. There was a card that said 'Happy 11th Birthday' that most of the staff and some of the kids had signed.

When she had first stepped outside, the Ring Ouzel was singing the loud and long chirruping song that had amazed her when she had first heard it, and she glanced up at the noisy silhouette at the top of the tall scraggy lemon tree in the big blue pot and smiled. She could hear her mate singing back loudly from the top of other lemon on the roof across the space over the courtyard but she couldn't see it. Then a light came on in the office under the tree on the other side and through one of the windows she recognised the new doctor, Grinn, as he sat down at his desk. She knew he was usually in his office before the other doctors and again wondered why, as she saw him reach down, pull open a drawer, and take something bulky and black from it then put it on his desk.

She reminded herself that she was there to recognise the dots in the sky through the binoculars as the Short Toed Eagles she knew they were, but way before they landed. She wanted to know if they really did fold their wings right in and behind them and dived and only opened them to brake just before landing, or if they just flew down to ground very quickly. Once turned away from the window she could see over the turrets to the side of the roof room that the sea in the distance looked black and the clouds in that direction were dark and that a storm was coming. She loved the Shorties because they looked funny, like cartoons. They were small for eagles and had big heads.

She had brought them their usual rabbit. The butcher was one of her favourite people and he had smiled and she had laughed as he had told her at the party that he had left two bunnies in bags in the walk-in fridge in the kitchen. She knew as soon as she had stepped out from the roof room that she would have to try to call them in from the cliff. The cliff end formed one side of her painting frame of the Cevannes which she could see in the distance and she knew the birds were nesting there near the top. The bottom of the frame was the long row of Eucalyptus trees at the top of the ridge that stretched right across behind the meadows in the distance where the butcher caught his rabbits and his cows grazed. She had smiled as she had realised that the wind was in the right direction to carry the calls.

She lifted the rabbit out of the bag and gently laid it on the stones well away from the lemon tree and still standing, looking towards the cliff, she put her hands to her face either side of her mouth and angled them outwards and called kiiiiiiiiiiiiuuuuuuu, kiiiiuu, kiiiiuu, kiiiiuu. She waited a minute or so before calling again..... kiiiiiiiiiiiiuuuuuuu, kiiiiuu, kiiiiuu, kiiiiuu. She was looking above the cliff as she called, and then put the binoculars to her eyes. Even though she could easily see tree branches moving wildly in the wind at the top of the cliff, ledges where spindly bushes were being pushed back against the cliff face, and foamy spray from the high waterfall blowing off towards the meadow, she could not see any dots above the cliff or any birds at all as she moved the spy glasses from side to side and up and down from cliff to clouds. She walked forward a few steps and called again kiiiiiiiiiiiiuuuuuuu, kiiiiuu, kiiiiuu, kiiiiuu, waited a short while and called again kiiiiiiiiiiiiuuuuuuu, kiiiiuu, kiiiiuu, kiiiiuu, and again put the spy glasses to her eyes to scan the cliff and sky above. Nothing. She walked forward, past the spread polythene with bricks at the corners that the staff asked her to use to keep the blood off the stones, still looking into the sky and calling again, raised the spy glasses and scanned. Looking carefully she could still see the trees and bushes blowing and the waterfall was blowing sideways now, but no eagles. Looking up and around the sky without the spyglasses she could see the fierce clouds rushing towards the Cevannes, but no dark dots that would be eagles.

The clouds were darker now, nearly black, and they were really racing across the sky. Movement in the lit window caught her eye and she looked and saw that someone else was in with the doctor. She knelt down behind a turret and steadied the spyglasses on top, pointing them at the window before looking through them and refocusing. The square blur of light against the wall turned into Grinn and Natalie – one of the older ones she spent time with – standing and talking at the side of his desk. She hadn't seen Natalie dressed up first thing in the morning before and wondered why she was even out of bed before 7.00, never mind showered, made up, and wearing a cut off dark blue T shirt and a short, flared, pink skirt that she had never seen. She couldn't see her shoes.

They walked to the Red corner and Natalie stood on the upturned box and turned round before putting her hands behind her head while the doctor walked backwards a few steps and nodded. She couldn't see Grinn's face, but she could see that Natalie was looking straight at him, with eyebrows raised and eyes wide. Grinn walked towards Natalie, put his left hand in his left trouser pocket, and when he was close to Natalie his other hand pulled the T shirt up over her tits, flicked the left nipple hard, squeezed it then twisted it and pulled it hard, stretching it. Then he pulled a red crocodile clip from his pocket, let go of the nipple and clamped it in the clips jaws. Natalie's eyes had closed and even though her hands were still behind her head one of her elbows swung round to the side of her head before slowly moving back. After she had opened her eyes the doctor took out another clip, flicked the other nipple twice and squeezed it then closed the clips jaws on it. Both Natalie's elbows swung round, and her knees bent, but her hands stayed behind her head. After a minute Natalie had reopened her eyes but not very far, was standing with both hands and elbows behind her head again, her legs were straight, her lips were pressed tightly together, and she was looking straight at Grinn, eyes wide and lips pursed tightly together.

She knew that Natalie was hurting because she had once clamped her little finger with the jaws of a crocodile clip, which she knew was nothing like as sensitive as her nipples, in the electronics lab, just to see how it felt. Then Grinn turned and picked up the black bulky thing from the desk and she could see he was smiling. He turned back to look at Natalie, raised it to his face and she realised it was the camera. There was a flash, then soon afterwards the photo slid from the camera and he put it on the desk. He moved something on the front of the camera, moved closer to Natalie and there was another flash and another one slid out. He put it on the desk next to the first and looked at them before picking them up, turning a key in the middle desk draw then opening it before placing them inside. Natalie got down from the box, hands still behind her head, and walked to the desk then bent over its end, her arms stretching in front, while Grinn walked to the wall, took down a small picture and put it on the floor leaning it against the wall then pressed a round black button that had been behind the picture. He picked up a cane that had been leaning against the wall, walked back to the desk, lifted the back of Natalie's skirt so it was laid on her back and as he was moving the cane back, she could see Natalie brace herself; long lashed eyes wide open staring straight ahead, red painted nails curled slowly into fists, then the eyes clenched shut. Her sight began to blur and she had to take a long blink, before hearing the THWACK.

Startled, she was made to jump, the noise had come from behind her. She turned and sat clumsily against the turret with her legs outstretched. Breathing heavily she realised *all at once that she must have been holding her breath, that she was damp between her legs and that this was all like something out of her wildest dreams. She sat, trying to take in what she was looking at, not really noticing the noisy wind or feeling the big hard blobs of rain on her face. She saw a fat and stunned looking yellowish brown scorpion in a puddle on the polythene, just as she heard and then saw a flurry of wings in a blur over the rabbit turn in slow motion into a wet and scruffy looking Lanner Falcon that glared straight at her through its yellow Lone Ranger mask before bending its head and tearing at its meal.*

Given the high profile of the victim DS Winters had ventured forth on Sunday to inform the family so when Treloar and Scott arrived at Porth House that afternoon they did not face that unenviable task.

Treloar rang the bell with a sombre expression on his face, Scott by his side. The door was opened by a tall dark-haired woman in her thirties. She was barefoot, dressed in a faded cotton sundress, her hair pulled back in a ponytail tied with a polka dot ribbon. 'Helen Cavendish, do come in,' she said looking at their out-held warrant cards.

DS Winters had established earlier that Oliver Osborne had been staying at Porth House with his wife and son and family friends the Cavendishes. They walked through the hallway following Helen Cavendish into a large sitting room facing the sea. The room was unoccupied.

Treloar introduced himself and Sam. 'Would you like tea or coffee officers?' asked Helen.

'Thank you no,' said Treloar as Sam shook her head. 'We are very sorry about Mr Osborne. It must be a terrible shock for you all.'

'Thank you,' said Helen stooping to lift a glass of white wine from the large square coffee table situated between two black calico covered sofas. With her free hand she gestured at the sofa facing the window and sat on the one facing it. Treloar and Scott sat.

'We do need to ask some questions I'm afraid, to understand the recent events in Mr Osborne's life and when he was last seen.'

'Absolutely Inspector. I understand entirely. How can I help?'

'Perhaps you could explain who is staying here and when you arrived to start with.'

'Right. Well staying here are myself, my husband David and son Robin, Julia Osborne and her stepson Jack, and well Oliver of course. We arrived last Saturday having booked the house for a month.'

'Are you good friends with the Osbornes Mrs Cavendish?' asked Sam.

'Oh yes, since Oxford, well since Eton for the men. We holiday with them often. First time in Cornwall though; Julia's idea actually but I thought it would be fun for the boys, being so close to the beach. It made a change to put them first. We found this place on the Internet.'

'You don't normally put your sons first?' asked Treloar.

'Lord no Inspector. Normally it's Oliver Osborne über alles. Oliver is a very dominating man, what he says, goes. I was amazed he agreed to this to be honest. I never did find out why. I suppose I never will now.'

'Who else knew you were coming to Cornwall and to Porthaven in particular?'

'Well it wasn't a secret. My father, David's mother, Robin's schoolfriends, our neighbours. Various colleagues. The people at the holiday letting company. As for the Osborne's entourage, well Julia's father for sure, maybe Oliver's parents and colleagues. I don't know about Jack's friends. I don't know that he has many; he's a very solitary boy. If you need to speak to him Inspector, do please be very gentle.' Treloar and Sam both nodded.

'Did you know of anyone with a grudge against Mr Osborne?' asked Treloar.

Helen threw back her head and laughed loudly. Then, realising that this was perhaps not appropriate behaviour, shook her head quickly and spoke quietly. 'I'm sorry. I know this is no laughing matter, but you have to understand that Oliver Osborne was almost universally despised. He was a bully and a boor; a cruel, sadistic man who abused his wife and ignored his child. You'll be hard pressed to find anyone other than my husband with a good word for him.'

'If you disliked him so, why holiday with him?' asked Sam.

'For David. David and Oliver are, were, the very best of friends since childhood. David adored him, and Julia and Jack aren't so bad. Julia can be extraordinarily dim but she has a good heart and a hell of a lot to put up with. I feel sorry for her, I always have. She's Oliver's second wife. Becca, Rebecca, Jack's mother, drowned; oh it must be five years ago. We were all on holiday in the south of France. We often went there; I knew the region from childhood holidays. Becca was at Oxford with us. She read History. She was very sweet, quiet and gentle. I do believe Oliver loved her at first, in as much as Oliver could love anyone, but she became sad. Over time she just became sad. After Jack was born she suffered terribly from depression. It was as if she could see no purpose in life, not even Jack. I sometimes think Jack's gloom was born within him. Anyway as I told you she drowned. It was ruled death by misadventure. There was no note, no tidied affairs. She just swam out one morning and kept swimming. She did so love to swim. I like to think she was peaceful at the end, out to sea away from everything.' Helen fell silent, gazing back into the past.

'Excuse me,' Treloar stood abruptly and strode from the room. *Christ*, thought Sam, *he's thinking of his father*.

'Julia married Oliver three years ago. She's very young, too young. She has more in common with Jack than Oliver and the boy dotes on her. They share a bond as fellow victims of Oliver. It probably has a name like Stockholm syndrome for the kidnapped. Her one skill is that she can ride like the wind. Last year we were in the Camargue. I used to holiday there as a chid and so did Julia coincidentally. Anyway, Julia was bareback riding at incredible speed, as if glued to the horse. Jack was enthralled watching her, we all were, even Oliver. I've never seen the like. And as for the joint holiday, well it's only two weeks. This year, a month, was an exception, and Oliver was not staying for the whole time he was going to be travelling back and forth to London after the first week, so I thought it would be bearable.'

Treloar walked back into the room pocketing his phone.

'You say your husband liked Mr Osborne, but you seem to dislike him actively,' said Treloar.'

'You may as well know Inspector, I'm sure you can find out; Oliver Osborne raped my housemate when we were at Oxford. I made a statement to the police, so it's on the record somewhere, but there was insufficient evidence to proceed.'

'We were all friends, we'd all been drinking, and of course Kate was the daughter of a country GP and Oliver was the scion of a banking dynasty, generous benefactors to his college, but perhaps that's just the cynic in me.'

'Anyway, it was through Oliver I met David and thus had Robin, so every cloud?'

'Does your husband know about the rape allegation?' asked Treloar.

'No and I don't want him to. What purpose would it serve now? At first it was too soon, and then... well time passed and soon it was too late. I truly believe Oliver thought it was consensual, if rather violent, but I get the impression that Oliver prefers, preferred, his sex on the rough side. Anyway, it was a very long time ago, before I met David, before any of us met Julia. It didn't kill Kate so I guess it made her stronger.'

'Nietzsche, Sir,' said Sam to a quizzical Treloar.

'You have to understand Inspector, David and Oliver have deep-rooted ties, bonds that endure from childhood. I don't know the details, David refuses to talk about his schooldays, but Oliver protected David, took his part against bullies at Eton. I know how vicious children can be from teaching. These boys, removed from their parents so very young, they grow tough hides, they have to. Oliver never shed his, not in my presence, but with David he was different. I don't think it has hit David yet that he's gone.'

'Could you give us some idea of what you've all been doing since you arrived?' asked Sam.

'Well if you want to know what we did on each day I'll fetch my diary. I am keeping a detailed account of our holiday for a school project I am running with the children in my class.'

'Well just a summary...,' but it was too late. Helen had leapt to her feet and rushed from the room before Sam could finish her sentence.

'Christ we'll be here all day,' Treloar rolled his eyes, 'I hope you're paying attention Sergeant there may well be written questions.'

'Now let me see...,' Helen had returned with a spotted A4 ring binder, 'Where are we? Ah yes... Right. We arrived on Saturday 10th at Newquay Airport on flight number SZ105...'

'Mrs Cavendish thank you,' Sam interrupted, 'just a broad outline will suffice.'

'As you wish,' Helen snapped frostily, 'Well, the next day, the Sunday, Julia, David and I went to Padstow leaving Oliver in charge of the boys. I understand they spent most of the day on the beach and then went up to that big house where the students are staying. Monday the weather was poor so we stayed around the house. Tuesday we all went to the Eden Project...'

'Including Mr Osborne?' Treloar asked.

'Yes indeed. I too was surprised but of course when we got there he spent the entire time in the various eateries drinking. Wednesday Julia and I went to Truro. I wanted to see the cathedral and the museum, Julia just had to shop, though when we met up she had bought nothing. Apparently there was nothing she liked. Actually I thought it rather odd at the time. Gone for hours and not a single bag, and Julia who could find something to buy at a funeral,' Helen blushed, 'sorry, poor taste.'

'Not at all,' Sam smiled.

'Anyway where were we? Thursday was a glorious day and David and I went to the Lost Gardens at Heligan. Julia went riding and Oliver and the boys stayed around the house and beach. Friday Julia, and I and the boys went to Trengissey where amazingly Julia found plenty to buy. Though I must say she did buy some colourful, metallic confetti shaped like cows which she thought Jack might like to use in his drawings, so you see she can be quite thoughtful where the boy is concerned. Then I took the boys to look round the Pentreath estate house, Polgwynn. The men stayed here. Saturday we all went to Fowey and Sunday, well we were all here. Today we were supposed to be off to the Tate at St Ives and St Michael's Mount but obviously that's out of the question now,' she added ruefully.

'If it's any consolation St Ives is unbearably crowded at this time of year,' Sam said smiling.

'Can you tell us more about the day before yesterday Mrs Cavendish?' said Treloar.

'Helen, please.' Helen took a deep breath and a sip of wine. She closed the ring binder and placed it on the coffee table. 'Right. Saturday evening we'd all been drinking, but Oliver more than the rest of us, not that that was unusual. As I said we'd been to Fowey for the day. We'd hired a sailboat. I've sailed since childhood and David and Robin crew. Of course the Osbornes are horse people and totally useless on a boat but they only had to sit still and move when told. Oliver spent the entire time with a beer bottle in his hand, but Jack was really interested and asking quite sensible questions.'

'What about Julia?' asked Sam.

'Oh she was faffing about as usual, opening all the stows for a cloth to mop the wet deck so she could sit down, and rummaging about in a ridiculously large totally inappropriate tote bag she'd brought along looking for her iPod. As it turned out she'd left it behind here and anyway I had told her quite clearly before we set sail that she couldn't use it because she needed to be able to hear my calls. She really can be extraordinarily blonde at times. Well we were out for about four hours and then we went for a late lunch in town.'

'I was driving so I didn't drink at all, but the other three had two bottles of wine between them and Oliver had several large Armagnacs, plus the beers on the boat of course. He had been unusually quiet for Oliver all week but, whether it was the booze or just the old Oliver rising to the surface, he was loud and obnoxious on the way back, especially to Julia. I remember David teasing her about that ridiculous bag and Oliver turned around, he was sitting in the front passenger seat of course, and said. 'Now then 'Davy, how can you be so mean to someone so meaningless?'

'Was he always like that with her, putting her down in front of others?' asked Sam.

'Oh, yes he could be so cruel. He could be sharp with anyone but when it came to Julia he seemed to delight in humiliating her, but I'm not sure she noticed. Perhaps she was inured or just too dumb. Christ, you'll think I'm as much a bastard as he was.'

'So what happened when you got back here?' asked Treloar.

'Well, I started preparing some crabs we'd bought for supper, so I was in the kitchen with a large glass of white wine which I felt I'd earned to be honest. The boys couldn't wait to be out down to the beach, and the others took yet another bottle of wine into the garden.'

'So to recap, when you got back from Fowey, the boys went to the beach, you to the kitchen and the others into the garden, and this would be what time?' asked Treloar.

'About six thirty?'

'OK, carry on.'

'Well I was doing the crabs and some salad. I remember David came in for another bottle of wine and I commented on the amount they were getting through.'

'Did that annoy him?' asked Treloar.

'Oh, no. David doesn't do angry. He just smiled, pinched my bum and said something like 'don't worry, we're just chilling and Oliver's in the best mood I've seen all week.'

'So, nobody went out other than the boys, nobody called or came to the house.'

'No, it was just the four of us 'til the boys got back for supper about 8:00. We had two more bottles of wine with supper and the boys went up to play computer games about 9:30 leaving us at the table. By now Oliver was definitely getting drunk and frankly I was glad the boys were out of the way. About 10:30 Oliver went out, I assumed to the pub or to the students' place at the other end of the village, he couldn't keep away from there. Anyway I didn't ask and he didn't say, he just grabbed his coat from the floor where he'd thrown it earlier and slammed out the front door.'

'I went up to bed about 12:30 leaving the others.'

'So the last time you saw Oliver Osborne was when he left the house at 10:30?'

'Correct.'

'And you went off to bed at 12:30 and slept 'til the morning.'

'No. I couldn't sleep. I often can't especially when away from home. I looked for my sleeping tablets but couldn't find them anywhere so, about 01:30, I decided to go for a walk; I often do that if I can't sleep.'

'Was anyone else still up?' asked Sam.

'Yes, David and Julia were in the kitchen, I could hear them talking. It sounded serious and I really didn't want to get involved so I ran back up to leave a note on David's pillow and slipped out the front door.'

'Would he not have been alarmed, you out alone in the middle of the night in a strange place?' asked Sam.

'No, as I said I often walk at night and it's hardly downtown Chicago around here. No I just slipped out and headed up the hill. I walked for miles it was actually lovely, very still and fresh with just the sheep for company.'

'So no one saw you,' said Treloar.

'Well I saw no one Inspector, they may have seen me, I cannot say. I walked as far as the entrance to that large country hotel and spa then turned back. I got back here around 4:45 and went to bed. David was asleep and I assumed the others were too.'

'So what happened yesterday morning after you got up?' asked Treloar.

'Well, the boys were already downstairs eating cereal. I remember thinking how it's impossible to get Robin up at home, but they're so keen to be up and out down here. I made coffee and toast and read the paper which had been delivered by then. David was in the garden reading a book.'

'What time does the newspaper come?' asked Sam.

'I think about 8:00 but it varies. Today it was nearer half past I heard it come through the door when I was in the bathroom.'

'What about Oliver and Julia?' asked Treloar.

'I just assumed they were still in bed, especially with Oliver being so drunk every night. I don't know, he's always been a drinker but this summer he seems totally reckless.'

'Carry on,' said Treloar.

Helen sighed and rubbed her eyes tiredly. 'The boys went out straight after breakfast about 9:30 to walk round to Long Beach and I went down to the stores to get some fresh bread. It's a very good shop, surprising for such a small place, excellent deli, very reminiscent of Tresco Stores on the Isles of Scilly. Anyway, all the talk was about the body of a man on the beach.' In fact Porthaven Stores had been abuzz. Rumour and theories were rife giving vent to long-held grudges, wild speculation and some delicious black humour. 'I didn't wait around, I wanted to get back and call Robin and Jack. I got back and found David in the garden drinking coffee, reading the paper. I told him about the body and he told me not to worry it could be anything, and certainly nothing to do with the boys. I rang Robin anyway and got his voicemail but as you know the signal around here is very flaky.'

'Did you leave a message?' asked Sam.

'Of course, I can't abide people hanging up on voicemail answerphones. I just told them to call us when they got a signal and gave the time of my call as I always do. I tidied up the kitchen, by then it was about 10:30 then I joined David in the garden with a coffee. Then at 11:00 I was surprised when Julia walked into the garden through the gate at the back. I'd assumed she was still upstairs in bed. She said she'd been out walking up the valley to the vegetable and flower stall at the top of the lane to fetch some flowers, and she was indeed carrying a huge bunch of cornflowers. She took them through to the kitchen and came back with a coffee. I asked if she was going to take one up for Oliver and she said something like 'Do you think he deserves one?' and just sat down.'

'How did she seem?' asked Treloar.

'Absolutely normal: a bit vague, and a bit flushed and breathless, but then she had just hiked up the hill and back'.

'How was she dressed?' asked Sam.

'Normally: a sundress and sandals, sunglasses and a large straw hat.'

'What about a bag?' asked Sam.

'No, no bag.'

'So how did she pay for the flowers?' asked Treloar.

'Oh she probably took a £10 note and paid with that knowing Julia. She would have left it in the money box up there, there's a tin box with a coin slot attached to a pole. Julia does not concern herself with small change Inspector.'

'Well we were all still sitting there when DS Flowers arrived at 12:45 to break the news. The rest of the day was very quiet as I'm sure you can imagine. Julia retired to her room as soon as DS Flowers went and she hasn't left it since. When the boys got back they watched DVDs and we all went to bed quite soon after supper.'

'And where are the others now?' asked Sam.

'David is in the garden, Julia is lying down upstairs and the boys are in the Family Room watching a DVD.'

Treloar stood handing Helen a business card and Sam did likewise.

'Thank you Mrs Cavendish. You've been very helpful and told us a lot which we would have had to ask Mrs Osborne. May we speak to your husband now?' asked Treloar.

'Certainly. Follow me.' And with that Helen led the way along the hallway through the kitchen into the garden. 'David,' she called 'Inspector Treloar and Sergeant Scott to speak with you,' she added, then, turning on one bare heel she went back into the house.

Treloar and Scott took a seat in the garden where David Cavendish sat at the table, glass of whisky to hand. He was a tall slender man with greying hair dressed in faded jeans and a baggy washed out Weird Fish T shirt.

'Tell me something about Oliver Osborne Mr Cavendish. You must know him better than anyone, certainly longer than most. What was it, Eton and Oxford?'

'He was a complex man Inspector. Oh he was very intelligent, very ambitious and he could be totally ruthless and utterly cruel, but I'm not sure he realised that he was being cruel. Imagine finding yourself destitute having been well off, it's the shock, the change that knocks you off kilter. If you've always been poor you don't know any different so what's to miss? Well for Oliver it was like that with love and kindness. He'd never known them, so how could he show them? It was an unknown land to Oliver, a foreign language. Oliver was not a 'nice' man.'

'So why did you holiday with them so often?' asked Sam.

'As I said Sergeant, Oliver was a complex man. On the one hand there was his insensitivity and boorishness but on the other his fierce intellect and total, unquestioning loyalty. I often thought he played up the brutishness as a shield, you know, attack being the best form of defence as Napoleon said,' he smiled wistfully, 'actually Oliver had a lot in common with Napoleon physically and intellectually. Let me give you an example of his complexity. When my business failed it was literally just weeks before we were all due to go to Italy. I was shattered, physically and emotionally void. I dreaded Oliver finding out, the very thought was unbearable. Then on that holiday after a few too many bottles of red wine I told him. He was silent for ages. Then he said, I remember verbatim; "Let it go Davy, it's gone." He went on to say something along the lines of: 'What you need right now is cash. I can help you there'. He wrote me a cheque for £250,000 there and then. 'I don't need it back. Let's not speak of it again.' And we never did. Most people who knew of him, knew his reputation, would have expected him to rub my nose in it at every occasion. Let's face it most people would have been tempted to mention it now and again to glow in their own generosity of spirit. But not Oliver. Never a word. Never a hint. And he didn't tell Julia, I know that for sure. And he didn't mention it to Helen. So not a total shit eh? I owed Oliver Osborne more than money, I owed him my life. He was a true friend to me Sergeant. Always.'

'We have heard from your wife most of what happened yesterday. I understand she left you and Mrs

Osborne downstairs when she went up to bed after Mr Osborne had gone out,' said Treloar.

'Yes that's right sometime after midnight.'

'And you stayed up with Mrs Osborne?' asked Sam.

'Yes. Julia was rather tipsy and a little maudlin. She had heard recently about the death of an old friend and she was rather dwelling on it. I took her through to the kitchen for some tea and we sat talking until about 3:00 am. Then I put her to bed and went off myself. Helen was not there, out walking I assumed, rightly as it turned out. She was there when I woke this morning about 7:30.'

'And you saw nothing further of Mr Osborne after 10:30 Saturday night?' asked Treloar.

'No. I imagined he'd headed up to Point End House again, and then in the morning, I, we, Helen and I, assumed he and Julia were still in bed. Then Julia came strolling in with the flowers and the next thing we knew your Superintendent arrived with the dreadful news.'

'Did Julia mention Oliver when she came back with the flowers?' asked Sam. Treloar turned to her with the slightest smile.

A few seconds was all it took for her to understand exactly what had happened. Perfectly natural.

She knew she was clever, very clever, and her notes proved it.

She had known even before Grinn had retested her IQ and found that it was 146 that she was cleverer than the others and most of the adults she had ever met; exceptional. She had christened him Grinn after his leering smile had somehow reminded her of the Brothers Grimm stories. Her favourite was the one about the boy who wanted to shudder. He eventually did and was happy. It had taken her no time at all to figure out what the upturned wine cases in the corners of his room were all about the first time she'd met him. He'd asked her to stand on the one in the white corner and recite the alphabet backwards, then the 14 times table as far as 16 x 14, then what the capital cities were of Australia, Argentina and Alaska. She had got them all completely right. Totally gobsmacked, and disappointed, he told her to go to the Champagne corner and stand on the case. He had not even asked how she had known about Juneau and Alaska. She recognised the shields and went over to what she knew were two sixes of Dom Perignon joined together, sat down, and waited for him to come back from his kitchen counter. He had opened the bottle and turned briefly to look at her, and frowned hard, probably thinking she hadn't seen.

He had carried two champagne glasses, bubbles fizzing, over to her and before he bent to hand her one she saw that his cock hung to his right and was rolling against his tight beige trousers with each step, and that a damp patch darkened the material at its end. Then it got close enough to grab or thump, and he bent and handed a glass to her and chinked his own against it, and congratulated her. Then Grinn went to his swivel chair and sat and looked at her, smiling his inane smile which froze into position as he gazed and went somewhere else for a few seconds before the corners of his mouth twitched back to life and he put his glass down and took a square grey box from his desk drawer. It clicked and turned into a weird looking camera.

He took a photograph of her and after a few seconds he pulled the photo out of the camera and looked at it and beamed. He rolled forward and showed it to her so she could see herself; shiny hair in high bunches, eyebrows raised and eyes wide, with lips carefully puckered and open slightly while sipping demurely. Then he had pushed the chair back, swivelled and put the photo and camera in the desk drawer. She had seen the red corner, where she recognised the black eagle logo on the case from the vineyard up in the mountains even though it was upside down, and now she knew that her guess about that corner had been right.

She had seen her notes from the filing cabinet and knew what was in them, all of them. One day, just after the start of a session, Grinn had rushed out after saying he would be back after dealing with an emergency in the pool and she took them from the cabinet, putting them back when she had finished reading. By leading one of their 'getting to know you' discussions to the species of the charcoal owl she had drawn on the patio he had needed to make an addition to her computer file as well as making a handwritten note for the cabinet. She was leaning close, breathing softly and looking over his shoulder at the time.

He was stupid. She knew staff were difficult to recruit because the locals wanted the chateau back, for a hotel. They had thought they would get it. Staff had left because they weren't sure what was happening and Grinn had come in because they couldn't get anyone else; the butcher had told her. Now they were lumbered. The locals had ended up with the staff cottage nearest the village as the tourist office, and the hospital would still be there until the next time some big local wanted to try it on.

She knew that the creepy Grinn bastard knew that Ma and Pa hadn't come back that next day, and that all they had done was visit the hospital and drop off two suitcases with lots of clothes that stopped the Tin Tin books, her sketchpads, pencils, charcoal, and paints rattling around. She knew he knew that they suspected she had killed the twins, but that the police couldn't prove it and that the court had sent her to the psychiatric hospital for supervision and evaluation before releasing her to foster parents.

Foster parents because her parents had gone. Ma and Pa had left the country the court discovered eventually. She knew she was suspected of killing the fosterers' idiot boy and leaving their girl with nettle sting scars that made the backs of her hands look like rough pink sandpaper, and that that was why she had been sent back to the hospital but only under light supervision – they couldn't prove she had done any of it. She had read that this time she was in long-term evaluation, waiting for when puberty had finished and her hormones had settled before the next move. Grinn would write the quarterly reports that would say just what she wanted them to say, and the stupid creep would be carrying on writing the annual reports for the court, just like the bastard's much nicer predecessor.

She knew the Lanner was from North Africa, probably Algeria, that the scorpion was a Buthos Occitanus and it had been caught by the falcon at the last minute before leaving for Sicily. It was to eat on arrival in Sicily before resting and flying on towards Greece and Eastern Europe. She knew it was angry because the wind that had left Algeria as a Sirocco and arrived in France as a Marin, had caught up with it, soaked it, and blown it West and way off course. It had been looking for somewhere to land and snack and rest when it spotted her rabbit and decided on the bigger and tastier meal, dumping the scorpion at the last minute. She had seen Buthos Occitani in the mountains and knew they stung, like wasps, but she had read in the library that the ones from Algeria could kill.

Getting to her knees she knelt, then slowly crawled forwards, big rain drops hitting her face, until she could place her left hand, open with palm upward, just behind the scorpion. She scooped it up, two fingers either side of its body so its legs rested on them and her thumb pressed the sting at the end of its tail down and forward, towards its head. It was cold and its skin felt hard and rough. Its leg tips were sharp and she felt the legs wriggle. She could see its small claws moving slowly. She gripped it tightly, twisted her wrist and bought it up to her face to look closely before dropping it into the binocular case which she had flipped open, then quickly closed it. She returned the Lanner's sidelong stare with a smile as she walked past it, quietly going chckk chckk chckk from the back of her throat, and into the roof room.

Upstairs Julia Osborne lay on the bed in the ensuite master bedroom. The windows were open billowing the cream voile curtains into the room and she could hear the conversation in the garden. *So that's where that money went* she said to herself.

Julia was quiet and thoughtful. She was not sobbing or whimpering. She had been brought up in a world where one doesn't show one's emotions, but that wasn't it. She wasn't sad, not in the slightest. She was starting to list in her head the tremendous ongoing benefits which would stem from Oliver's death, the first of which was a deep personal sense of satisfaction.

The room was cool, the light dim. Above the bed a large wooden ceiling fan circled languorously taking Julia back to her honeymoon in The Maldives. Oliver had been a bastard from the first day. She recalled him saying in umbrage 'You realise I'm missing the First Test for this don't you?' as if it had been her idea to honeymoon in The Maldives in May. In fact he had chosen the location to upstage a colleague, Emilia Irskine QC who had honeymooned in The Seychelles at Christmas. 'Maldives for the masses' Oliver had sneered. As the voices in the garden were clearly the police she decided to go down to face them.

Julia came into the garden wrapped in a cashmere travelling rug in vivid primary coloured stripes.

'I heard voices' she said dreamily pushing her long blond tresses back from her face.

Treloar and Scott turned at the sound of a voice to see what could have been a child wrapped in a rug standing at the kitchen door. David leapt to his feet and rushed across the lawn without answering Sam's last question.

'Julia, what are you doing up?' he cried.

'It's OK Davy, really, I don't want to be on my own anymore and I can't sleep despite those pills.'

He smiled and putting his arm around her shoulders led the small stumbling figure dragging her blanket over to the table.

'Julia, he said gently, these people are from the police. They've come to talk about Ollie. But they don't need to bother you just now do you Inspector?' he spoke pointedly, fixing Treloar with a cold stare.

'Indeed not. We are very sorry for your loss Mrs Osborne and we will come back tomorrow to speak with you,' Treloar said gently taking the tiny proffered hand.

'You're very kind, everyone's so very kind...' and with that Julia Osborne started to cry softly and turned her face into David Cavendish's chest.

Treloar and Sam placed two business cards on the table and with a nodded acknowledgement walked back to the kitchen door where Helen Cavendish stood scowling at the scene in the garden.

'Bloody pathetic, she'll be milking this,' she muttered as they walked into earshot.

'We'll be off now Mrs Cavendish. Thank you again for your help. We'll be back again to speak with Mrs Osborne tomorrow but if anything comes to mind you have our contact details. We'll try to keep the press at bay but call if you have any problems,' said Treloar.

'Of course, of course. We'll be out first thing. Julia has to identify the body formally, she is insisting on going herself but we'll go with her to the hospital. Perhaps you should call first to make sure we're back. Let me give you my card,' she said handing over a white business card. She led them to the front door. 'Goodbye and thank you.' With that she opened the door, ushered them through, and closed it firmly behind them.

She hadn't planned it but that day became one of the busiest ever. After putting the binocular case with the scorpion into one of her clothes drawers in the dorm she was just happy. She had heard it scrabbling around and would go out after the storm to the old barn to find it some bugs; it would be fine. She hadn't seen a Lanner before, knew they were called vagrants in France because they didn't live there normally, and thought the Shorties would probably move it on. That was OK though, she thought it looked even better close up than it did in the books, and was especially pleased that the chckk chckk from the back of her throat had worked. She enjoyed thinking back to the minutes looking at Natalie with Grinn and smiled when she remembered how she had felt, then again as an idea came to mind.

She had booked time in the art room for that morning and didn't want to waste it; she could have up to three hours on a Saturday. She had known that Eric would be there too, and after showering she had put on her black bra and matching knickers, then one of her paint marked light blue smocks. It was above her knees, quite a long way, but she was pretty sure she would get away with it because the old bag doing the rounds that weekend probably wouldn't come in. Then she had taken her knickers off. She was going to miss breakfast so none of the other staff would see her, and she was going straight there.

Eric probably wouldn't be there for a while so she had fetched her sketchpad, started a watercolour of the mountain from the back of the room and put it on her easel. Perched on a stool looking thoughtfully at it with one leg crossed over the other she decided she could start again in oils, after revising the sketch to include the Lanner. Then she went to the store to get her pallet, clean brushes, pencils, and some paints. In one hand she had the pallet, with paints balanced on it like a tray, and in the other she had the brushes and pencils and she was forced to turn sideways when she was nearly through the storeroom door because the arsehole Gilbert was coming the other way. He was 14. He laughed down at her, pushed her hard against the door frame using his right hand, which she would later realise had been coated with yellow paint, on her left tit, squeezing it, and used his left to pull up her smock and shove the other hand between her legs. Then the bastard had breathed in sharply and smiled widely.

Then he had fallen suddenly into the storeroom holding his head and landed on the floor next to the paints that had fallen off the pallet. Eric had looked at her, with her hands full, yellow finger marks and palm print on one tit, legs apart, shocked. He had taken the pallet, pencils and brushes from her and with a nod of his head and a wink he motioned her into a chair in the main room. He was 15, had sideburns, had a deep, broken voice, and she was really grateful.

'Well Sam what do you make of our happy holidaymakers?'

'Strange relationships all round if you ask me. Osborne was a right monster. To know the man is to know the killer my old DI used to say. That and the three motives are lust, love and lucre, but I think he nicked that from someone else.'

Treloar laughed and picked up his pint of Betty Stoggs. 'I know what you mean. What a crew, excuse the pun. More motives than money, and that's saying something, and weird vibes especially between the women.'

They were sitting at a corner table in The Harbour Lights. Most of the customers were sitting outside under the Stella Artois umbrellas, leaving Treloar and Scott in relative privacy tucked away at the back of the lounge bar.

Sam picked up a menu. 'I think I'll try the fish and chips, you?'

'I'm Cornish Sam, I don't eat fish.'

'I thought that was just the fishermen?'

'At heart, all true Cornishmen are fishermen. Actually I'm more or less vegetarian.'

'A Cornish vegetarian farmer?'

'Actually I'm half Spanish hence the name Félipe. My mother is from an area of Northern Spain where they ate little meat, mainly vegetables, pulses and grains. Anyway the farm is arable and flowers. The only beasts are Mum's chickens and goats and we'd never eat those. They have their own graveyard in the corner cliff top field, headstones with photographs, proper job.'

'Well you don't look too bad on it, Sir,' Sam blushed realising what she had just said.

Treloar smiled. 'Well thank you for that Sam and do please call me Phil.'

'So how do you come to be half Spanish?' she said quickly.

'A drunken young Cornish farmers' weekend in the big city. Plymouth. My father and a friend mistakenly thought a boat painted Brittany Ferries would be going to Brittany, not an unreasonable assumption I've always thought, and they stowed away for a laugh. They ended up in Santander in Northern Spain and to cut a long story short he met my mother. I've always been thankful actually. Let's face it I could have been half French.'

'I'd watch what you say in here I think that pretty little barmaid's French,' said Sam in a hushed tone.

Treloar laughed and crossed to the bar to order fish and chips and a ploughman's.

'So. No alibi for the redoubtable Helen, but the other two cover for each other,' said Treloar when he returned with the cutlery.

'Well, a friend's rape festering over the years is quite a motive. But she was very upfront about it.'

'Mmm, did you believe that 'I tolerate him for my beloved husband' line? Coming from such a strong character I'm very doubtful. And don't you think it was odd that they weren't sitting together, him in the garden, her in the sitting room? Perhaps she couldn't disguise some pleasure and he was obviously upset, or perhaps it was something stronger, satisfaction with a job well done, long overdue?'

'Well, she is fit enough. Mind you, if he was such a bastard to Julia, perhaps she and David did it when Helen was off strolling the lanes?'

'No she's too slight and from what we've heard too ditzy to carry out or even be involved in that brutal organised attack and I did believe David Cavendish. I think he really did love Oliver Osborne as his closest, oldest friend. No my money's not on him for sure.'

'What about the Helen-Julia-David relationship. That was a bit strained I thought, from Helen's side at least.'

'Yes I can see her being fiercely protective of David, jealous even, but wouldn't she kill Julia rather than Oliver?'

'Unless Oliver and David were... you know. Public school, Oxford colleges and the belaying pin up the bum,' Sam grinned.

'Really Sergeant, too much *Brideshead Revisited* methinks.'

'Is it someone close to him? It's so very personal but so very brutal, almost crazed.'

'Well, if I was going to murder my wife that's how I'd do it. It does look like the work of a madman rather than a civilized aristocratic English lady.'

'Yes but it can't be her. She has David as an alibi and I can't see him lying for her not in the killing of his best friend, however chivalrous he may be. Perhaps she got someone to do it for her. But would a third party show such hatred, why not something clean and clinical?'

'It's possible. She has the money.'

'Well Dr Tremayne did say he was universally disliked. Could it be someone he fell foul of in court or in business?'

'No I don't think so. I still think it's personal and I can see a woman's hand in it. Maybe not Julia... Helen perhaps, she has no alibi and there was certainly no love lost there?' Treloar sipped his pint.

'But she's so.......... well so very normal.'

'Yes I agree but she is intelligent, above average. She might see the savagery as a good disguise.'

'Even so. No. Why would she then be so open about her dislike?'

'Further disguise and deception?'

'No I just don't see it. Not Helen. Why wait all these years? No I don't think it's her. But I do think you may be right about there being a woman's hand in it. It is spiteful. Hell hath no fury and all that and the pin is so contrived to make us think of homosexuality.'

Sam's phone rang just as the food arrived and she went outside to take the call. Treloar looked around the pub. Behind the bar the aforementioned barmaid was serving a group of young people. She was indeed very pretty with her short black hair and pea green eyes. Treloar was looking for Sam when the doorway was blocked by an enormous figure. A huge young black man strolled up to the bar grinning ear to ear at the barmaid who clapped her hands together and cried out a greeting. One of the others at the bar, a pale red-headed girl turned away from her companion and took the young black man's arm pulling him back towards the door and shouting 'Tobes get Ben a beer I just want a word.' The barmaid frowned and stomped off to the pumps to pour a pint of bitter which she banged down in front of a tanned blond boy with hair flopping in his eyes. He smiled at her like a puppy dog and handed over a ten pound note. *Tangled webs there* thought Treloar as Sam walked back in and joined him picking up a chip from her plate.

'Well, that was Col Andrews. He's heard from the crime scene investigators. Bad news; nothing useful from the immediate scene. Good news; good set of prints on a second matching skittle thing trapped in the culvert at the side of the slipway,' Sam mumbled through a mouthful of steaming chip.

'Well, there'd hardly be great shoeprints on a recently high tided beach. Probably more pawprints and bare footmarks than anything, or those surfer sock things to stop the Weever fish stings....' Treloar trailed off, clearly thinking.

'So what would you wear? What would you wear?' Sam repeated.

Treloar turned to her grinning. 'Something dark obviously, and something that wouldn't leave traces, torn shreds of cloth and fibres oh and smooth-soled shoes to avoid footprints. How about something black, smooth, warm and close-fitting that's also waterproof and comes with matching hood and bootees?'

'Perfect. Of course, a wetsuit.'

'Indeed and there's a shopful of them just up the hill and dozens of them draped over every wall and fence in the village.'

'There's more,' said Sam looking over her shoulder towards the bar, is it OK to talk in here?'

Treloar looked up from his plate and scanned the bar. They were in a corner table with no other occupied tables anywhere near them. The toilets were on the other side of the bar so there should be no one passing near them. 'Fine for now,' he said 'go ahead.'

Sam consulted her notebook. 'The tape over his mouth was reinforced adhesive aluminium foil tape used by plumbers because it's low temperature fast stick, moisture resistant and permanently adhesive. Widely available. But now it gets more interesting. 'That skittle thing was a belaying pin probably from a vintage yacht because they're not found on modern ones. The rope was yacht racing cord; braided dyneema core 16 plait polyester cover, in purple, 2mm diameter and the knots were rolling hitches, apparently normally used to secure a rope to a parallel rope.   The sack over his head was a cotton drawstring bag screenprinted with The Porthaven Stores logo in navy blue and it was covered in Refined Coal Tar. That is as a heavy duty traditional tar coating that you brush on.'

'Yes,' interrupted Treloar 'it's used on wooden barns. But it was classified in 2003 for restricted supply, professionals only. I've used it on the farm, nasty stuff.'

'And,' said Sam 'it's a traditional coating for wooden boats.'

'Well we're being pointed at a nautical suspect. Having said that we are on the Cornish coast. Presumably no match for the fingerprints?'

'No'.

'Right. So we have our man leaving the beach in his wetsuit. Where does he go?'

'Well, there's only one way out of the village, up the slipway and straight up the hill.'

'I wouldn't go that way, said Treloar shaking his head, 'OK the time is on your side: it's the middle of the night, but the street is narrow, overlooked by houses, and they're all full of holidaymakers. Anyone up late, chancing to look out or happening to be out, would see you.'

'Yes, but Porthaven's hardly Newquay. Would there be anyone about at that time of night?'

'Helen Cavendish was.' Treloar paused. 'You'd be safe on the beach. No houses overlook it, not directly, just Crabbers and this pub. Mermaids is empty and the houses along the cliff top are set too far back. You'd need to be standing halfway down the cliff to see the beach from their grounds.'

'How about getting away by boat?'

'No. Out to sea you would be visible from all those houses, especially with the moon that night. No. I'd go west along the coastal path and then cut inland. The only house that way is Penmol. The owner lives alone, virtually a recluse. The path is quiet, dark, empty, but with the moonlight reflecting off the water it would be bright enough. That's the way I'd go.'

Treloar stood and went to the bar with their empty glasses. A cheer went up as two more young men joined the group already standing there.

'Hey dudes,' said the bronzed blond man called Tobes at the bar, 'usual?'

The newcomers looked excited. 'You'll never guess what's happened,' said the smaller one. 'You know all the police activity, well it's only a dead body found on the beach this morning. Some bloke. Suspicious apparently.'

The pretty barmaid placed two bottles of Sol beer with lime wedges in the necks on the beer towel. 'You didn't lose this on the path did you?' she said turning back to reach for something under the optics behind her, 'someone handed it in this morning.'

She held out a strange looking knife. The knife had a wooden handle and curved steel blade with a blunt tip bent at a 45 degree angle. It was much worn and obviously well used.

Treloar leaned across and took the knife by its tip with a paper napkin, showing Amélie his warrant card. 'Detective Inspector Treloar,' he said. 'Where did you say this was found?'

'On the path to Long Beach. It was at the stile at the top where the path goes two ways. A man gave it in this morning. He gave it me when I was putting up umbrellas outside at nine. He said this is the first building he come to and anyone dropping it on the path might come here to ask.'

'I need to take it for now,' said Treloar beckoning Sam who had seen the encounter and was approaching with a plastic evidence bag.

'It is cassé, broken,' the barmaid said.

'It's not broken. It's extremely sharp. You're lucky you've still got all your fingers,' said Treloar. 'It's a hoof knife. An old one but very well maintained. Someone loved this. Someone cared for this. It's a favourite tool, worn and well used, almost an extension of the hand. Someone will be missing this.'

He placed the knife in the plastic bag and using the plastic to cover his fingers pulled a strand of purple plastic away from a small nick in the handle where the shaft emerged. Sam handed him a second bag and he teased the thread into it.

'Did he leave a name, the man who gave you this?' asked Sam.

'No. I think he was Dutch or German. He was with a woman. He was not English.'

Sam was examining the knife through the plastic. 'There are some numbers or initials on the handle. Looks like 77 or T T. Does that mean anything to you?' she asked Amélie.

She furrowed her brow in thought and after a few moments stated firmly 'No'.

'Thank you,' said Treloar. 'We'll settle up now. Tell me, are any of you staying locally?'

'Yeah, we all are,' said the blond one called Tobes'. 'I'm Toby Brett-Morgan and we're all staying at my place along the cliff, Point End House.'

'Well in that case I'm going to ask you all to go back there now. We need to ask you some questions about Saturday night. The body on the beach was that of Oliver

Osborne and his last known destination was Point End
House.'

The storm had passed over, the sun was out and it was warm outside again, she had sketched in the Lanner, but hurriedly, Gilbert had gone outside to play football on the field, Eric had watched as she had sketched then gone outside to play tennis in the courtyard. She still wore the smock, was relaxed but thoughtful, standing and looking out towards the sea that was glinting again in the distance over the field. She was looking through the old sash window that was propped open with a sawn off piece of broom handle to keep the lounge cool. Nodding she felt in her smock pocket to check that the oil tube was still there then took it out and put it on the floor.

Knowing exactly what she wanted – but still not sure if she was strong enough - she had gone to the window, knelt on the floor, leaned through the gap and called out Gilbert's name, loudly. She wondered about Eric, and knew he wasn't far away, just in the courtyard.

Straight away Gilbert had looked up and seen the brightly hand printed tit through the open window, then he saw the shiny hair above it but couldn't see the face because of the reflection in the window. He knew who it was and that she was still wearing the smock. His mates had all cheered and she had seen him walk towards the building as she had beckoned, kneeling, looking out of the window, with her hand. She had seen the Shorties gliding up in circles as she had looked and stretched out to get a better view as her hand had beckoned and she had smiled and wondered about the Lanner.

He had been found early on Sunday morning. There had been a big fuss, there were staff called in from home. Police and ambulances. She would read in the paper later that no one could work out why Gilbert had been kneeling and looking out of the opened window with both arms still outside, although his mates had said they thought he was bragging when they had seen him on the Saturday.

How the window had fallen so harshly on the back of his neck with so much sustained pressure for so long that he couldn't breathe was also a mystery she would later read about in computer files. His mates didn't know that he couldn't have been bragging because his voice box had been crushed. How his shorts had come to be near the door, how the broom handle had got itself covered in yellow paint before being shoved roughly into Gilbert's arsehole had been another thing the police had not been able to work out. She knew that they had worked out that it had been held in place by his body as it had slumped back after the window had crashed onto the back of his neck and kept his head, not bragging, out of the window. She also knew that as soon as the police had seen the rubber gloves, covered in yellow paint, by the body they had thought they would have problems.

Well there's money here all right,' said Sam as Treloar drove down the bricked drive to park outside Point E'nd House. They walked up to the door and rang the brass bell.

The door was opened by the pale flame-haired girl. 'Hello again. Come through. We're all in the sunroom.'

They followed her along a hallway to a large airy room with stunning views across the bay to Penmassick Point. The group from the Harbour Lights plus several others were seated and sprawling around a large old pine table strewn with glasses, ashtrays and bottles of wine. The blond bronzed young man from the pub pushed himself up to greet them.

'Right then gang, introductions. Well I'm Toby Brett-Morgan and this is my place, well my parents' actually, and these are some of my pals from college,' he threw out an arm to encompass the group and, stumbling, sat back down sharply. *He's had a few* Treloar thought.

'I am Detective Inspector Treloar and this is Sergeant Scott and as I mentioned to some of you in the pub we are investigating the death of Oliver Osborne,' he pulled out a chair, 'may we?'

'Of course, of course please sit down,' stammered Ellie blushing 'Forgive Toby's manners he can be a total prick,' she glared at the grinning Toby who now had his head propped in his hands, elbows on the table. Sam and Treloar sat. Sam pulled out her notepad.

'Perhaps you could each give your name for the record?' Treloar nodded to Sam who pulled out her pencil.

They spoke in turn; Eleanor Constant, brothers Tom and Nick Haldane, Asif Iqbal, Jane Masterson, Harriet Jordan and Benjamin Dexter III. Sam noted the names down. Treloar spoke again.

'As some or all of you may be aware, the body of Oliver Osborne was found early yesterday morning on Porthaven beach. He had not committed suicide and it was not accidental. It has come to our attention that he was seen leaving the Harbour Lights at closing time in the company of several of you, apparently heading here. Can anyone confirm that?'

'Yes he came back after the pub,' it was Nick Haldane who spoke. 'He had done on several occasions; it's more or less open house here. He was a bit of a prick really, but he did buy a lot of booze.'

'He was plain mad dog mean,' mumbled Ben, 'you should have seen the way he was with those boys when they all came here that first afternoon. Drinking then too.'

'Yeah he was always bloody here knocking back the Cognac. He was a loud obnoxious prat to be honest, but what can you do?' said his brother Tom. 'As for your killer, my money would be on The Dwork.'

'Who would that be?' asked Treloar.

'Oh we don't know his name,' Tom continued. 'We all call him The Dwork. You must have seen him lurking. He seems insignificant at first glance, but there is something insidious about him; the way he's always hanging around, always on the periphery, it's well creepy.'

'I expect he's a paedophile,' added Harriet Jordan, 'he's always watching kids on the beach. I would talk to him if I were you. He may not be your murderer but I bet he saw something, he's so ...omnipresent.'

'Do you know his name or anything about him? Is he a visitor or a local?' asked Treloar.

'Well I'd guess he's a visitor,' said Nick Haldane, 'he's always around so he doesn't appear to be working. And he carries a shitload of kit: camera, binoculars, iPad.'

'I think he's camping,' said Jane Masterson excitedly, 'I've seen him buying gas cylinders in Porthaven Stores. Damn, I didn't think to look if he put them in a vehicle. I could have got his registration number.'

'OK thanks,' said Treloar, 'we'll ask around. Could you describe him physically?'

'I'm pretty sure we can do better than that,' said Tom Haldane, 'Asif, where's your iPad? You downloaded those pictures from the gig races. He's bound to be on there somewhere. Go fetch mate.'

Asif rose from the table and slouched out of the room followed by Toby Brett-Morgan and Benjamin Dexter.

'I'm so sorry, I should have asked,' said Ellie also standing, 'would you like some tea, coffee, perhaps a cold drink?'

'Coffee would be most welcome.' replied Sam, smiling.

With Ellie's departure and the general lull Sam took the opportunity to study the room. Everything was very 'chic shabby', and more Harrods than IKEA. Four slouchy three seater settees in seaside colours of blue and yellow were grouped around the most enormous low square wooden table. On one wall was a huge flatscreen TV and on what was once an original outside wall before the construction of the sunroom were a series of striking nude paintings in the style of Degas. Sam wondered if they were of Toby's mother; that would be in keeping with the affluent, louche, self indulgent aura the entire place exuded. But perhaps she was being a little puritanical as she judged these people she did not know.

Asif returned clutching his iPad and a cafétière followed by Ellie carrying a tray laden with mugs, fashionably unmatching, a large jug, a bowl of misshapen brown sugar lumps and coloured spoons.

'Doesn't Ben have some video footage?' asked Tom Haldane, 'Where has he wandered off to?'

'Probably off dreaming of la belle Amélie,' sniggered Nick.

'Don't be absurd,' snapped Ellie, 'he's just gone to the loo.'

Treloar and Sam exchanged raised eyebrows.

'Switch on the TV someone,' said Asif. The screen clicked into life and he proceeded to scroll through the photographs of the gig races.

'There! See! Standing at the edge of Crabbers' terrace, wearing the baseball cap. That's him!' cried Harriet. She was pointing at a slight dark haired young man standing, arms folded, scanning the beach as if looking for someone.

'Well I'm surprised you noticed him,' said Sam, 'he's so nondescript, anonymous even, he hardly stands out from the crowd.'

'Yes, but he's ubiquitous,' said Ellie, 'wherever you happen to be he's always there on the periphery, always alone, always watching. It's extremely disconcerting, creepy, and that's why you notice him. Christ you even find yourself looking for him.'

At that moment the door flew open with a bang and Toby and Ben walked back in. Without a word they took their places at the table and whilst they did not exchange a glance there was a distinctly tense atmosphere between them. Ellie as ever rushed to fill the vacuum and ease the tension.

'Guys, we were just talking about The Dwork, explaining how he's always around lurking in the background,' she said.

'Well whoever the hell he is I bet he's got a rich Mommy,' said Ben.

'What makes you say that?' asked Sam.

'His kit. He's got some seriously hot gear; top of the range, state of the art, very expensive. Phone, iPad, cameras. Makes Asif's kit look steam-driven,' he smiled at Asif, 'no offence pal.'

Asif shrugged his shoulders amicably. 'Ben's right. The guy has some serious stuff. Rich boy, must be.'

'Whatever,' Ellie interjected, 'Rich or not, that's irrelevant. He is dead creepy and he makes me feel very uncomfortable.'

'Yeah I guess, but I don't see him as your doer. I don't like him for it. No way', stated Ben.

Ellie's face coloured from her neck to her hair roots. 'Well no, of course not, not the murderer, no way,' she blurted.

Treloar and Sam exchanged another glance. 'When did Mr Osborne leave here on Saturday night, can anyone recall?' Treloar asked.

'It was about 3.00 am,' said Ellie, 'I know that because he woke me up on his way out and I looked at the clock.'

'You're sure it was him?' asked Sam.

'Absolutely. His voice was unmistakeable. He was loud even at that time of night. He was declaring his love for Amélie on his way up the drive.'

'Who is Amélie?' asked Treloar. This was the second time her name had been mentioned and she was obviously no friend of Ellie from her tone and expression.

'The French barmaid from the Harbour Lights. And a cause of many a manly beating heart,' said Jane Masterson smiling.

'And she left with Osborne?' Sam asked.

'No, no she stayed all night,' said Benjamin Dexter softly.

With that Ellie stood and rushed from the room leaving the others exchanging glances which ranged from surprise to fury.

Treloar and Sam were sitting outside Crabbers.

'I don't think it was any of them. Well, unless it was some sort of teen horror flick thing. You know, a group of kids on an island or in a wood or up a mountain go nuts and start killing each other one by one. Some sort of haze gone too far,' Sam said.

'Hazy? Seemed brutally clear to me.'

'No... a dare, an initiation. It's called a haze. Anyway I was joking.'

'No it's not them. Seem a sober, industrious bunch apart from Toby of course and he'd be too pissed to accomplish something that physically demanding and a total liability as an accomplice. This is personal and hateful and that lot scarcely knew him.'

'Still a lot of angst up there over the barmaid. The love of men is the root of evil in the relationships of girls. It's obvious that Ellie fancies the black guy, he's screwing the barmaid, Ellie hates her for it and his pal Toby is jealous as hell. Oh to be that age again.'

'Yeah very tangled webs, but does any of that have anything to do with our murder? I don't think so. Still we did find out about The Dwork. We need to track him down. From what they were all saying he might well have seen something. Let's try the campsite. And we need to get that hoof knife checked out. It looks to me as if it could have been used to cut the cord that bound Osborne; that thread is the same colour, bit of a coincidence otherwise.'

As they stood to leave Sam's phone rang. 'Hi Col. You are joking. No we've been switched off; we've been talking to the students at Point End House. What already?' Sam closed her phone. 'That was Col, obviously. You won't believe this. Winters has brought in Helen Cavendish, well had her brought in. She wants me to talk to her. Her prints were on that belaying pin they found in the culvert on the beach.'

At first she had been surprised that no one had found Gilbert earlier, but then she realised that everyone had been at the barbeque after the tennis in the courtyard, then they had gone to bed so no-one had been into the lounge.

Before getting on with the plan that had been born on the roof in the rain and going to the barbeque, she had gone down the back stairs to the incinerator, pulled off the smock, opened the door, thrown it in, then quickly closed it again. Looking at the closed door she smiled for a second, then laughed when she remembered she was only wearing her bra and trainers. She had seen the old brown work coat hanging on the back of the basement door, and thought about it for only a second before running back up the stairs and along the corridor right back to the dorm, feeling even more liberated.

She knew that Eric would be back in the courtyard when she got to the barbeque and had pulled on the pink smock with no paint on it yet, and thought for a few seconds before putting on her blue shorts that you could just see were underneath the smock, and retying her trainers. She used rubber bands to put her hair into high bunches. Then she took the binocular case from the drawer, held it to her ear and smiled as she heard the scrabble, and with the case hanging from her shoulder had walked round the corridors and up the stairs then along to Grinn's office where she used one of Eric's picks to open the door.

She took another pick, the smallest on the ring, and opened the desk drawer and saw the pile of photos before opening the binocular case, looking in to check that the scorpion was still OK. Remembering it was fat she didn't feel too badly about not going to the barn to fetch it bugs, then she tipped the case   downwards, gently shook it until the scorpion had not quite walked and not quite fallen into the drawer before she pushed the drawer closed and relocked it.

When she left the office she had made sure it was relocked, taken the case back and gone down to the barbeque, and as she walked into the courtyard with its music and barbeque smells she sneaked a look up to the office window and smiled.   Then she saw that Grinn was trying to impress, grilling duck legs, and she knew he wasn't turning them properly because they were black and he was coughing on the smoke.   Not wanting to draw attention to herself she had wandered over to a group of kids, where Eric was talking to Natalie, who was wearing a red sequined tank top and jeans, and joined in.   Later they'd eaten burgers. Natalie hadn't looked at Grinn as she had held out her plate. Then she saw him glance up at his office window and she had smiled, and she saw that Natalie was looking at her and was blushing.

Helen Cavendish had been taken to Truro police station to assist with enquiries. Treloar had not been asked to attend by DS Winters. In fact she had specifically excluded him and requested Sam Scott who felt uncomfortable about the matter and believed the action was premature. Treloar had laughed out loud when she told him what was happening. But Winters was their senior officer and she had made the call.

'Could you look at this knot please?' Sam showed Helen Cavendish a photograph of the knotted cord which had been cut from Osborne's wrist intact. 'Can you identify it?'

'If you mean do I know which knot this is the answer is yes. It's a rolling hitch typically used to secure one rope to another.'

'And this one?' Sam put down a close-up photograph of the knot from around Osborne's neck'.

'That is a bowline. What is this ...... basic seamanship? It's like that scene from *Jaws* with Robert Shaw testing Richard Dreyfuss.'

'And what is this?' Sam asked pushing a further photograph across the table.

'That is a belaying pin, an old-fashioned wooden one. What is this all about?'

'Indeed it is Mrs Cavendish, and one just like it was found rammed up Oliver Osborne's rectum. This one was found by the slipway in Porthaven the day after the murder and it has your fingerprints on it.'

'How can that be? How do you know it has my fingerprints on it? I don't understand.'

'Well, to answer one of your questions, your fingerprints are on file. They were taken after a break-in at your school last term and though scheduled for removal from the files they are still there,' said Sam.

'Yes, I recall. Well I don't know how it ended up on the beach, but I could have touched it in a number of places; they are a standard decorative feature around Porthaven. I have seen them in the pub, on the wall in Crabbers, for sale in Porthaven Stores, shall I go on? I think someone at the Estate Office must have bought a job lot. I can only assume that someone took one I had touched and dropped it or threw it way. I expect they make fine souvenirs. Some people will steal anything if it's not bolted down. As for my knowing seafaring knots, well I can't be alone in having that knowledge locally, we're scarcely in the Alps here are we?' Helen smiled sweetly and the PC standing at the door struggled with a grin.

'But why would you have touched a decorative belaying pin and wouldn't you remember doing so?'

Yes, well … you have a point. But I could easily have picked one up idly in the stores.'

'And we know that you did indeed touch belaying pins on the sailing day in Fowey. Is it not more likely that you took them from that boat?'

'Any one of us could have taken them from the boat quite possibly accidentally, gathering them up with our belongings. There was a box of them on deck and I certainly saw Jack holding one.'

'So you believe that Jack Osborne was involved in the murder of his father?'

'Well, I could certainly understand if he were; Oliver was a total bastard to the boy, but no, no I can't believe Jack was involved and anyway he was at the house that night, he couldn't have gone out without Julia or David noticing.'

'So we're back to you Mrs Cavendish.'

'This is absurd. Were my prints on the pin found on, or should I see in, Oliver's body?'

'No they were not because it had been covered by the incoming and outgoing tides.'

'And are these particular belaying pins unique or special in any way, monogrammed perhaps or inlaid with gold?'

'Of course not.'

'Well in that case I am leaving. I have answered your questions. I have no idea how one of a number of belaying pins I might have touched ended up on that beach. So unless there is anything else Sergeant?'

Before Sam could respond there was a knock and Col Andrews poked his head around the door. 'A word Sam?'

There was another fuss on Monday, not as big as Sunday's. He had been found when the Chief got so pissed off that he told the caretaker to break down his office door if he needed and see if he was asleep on his sofa. He wasn't in his cottage, he hadn't been at the regular Monday morning staff meeting and she knew that he hadn't answered his brick of a cell phone. The caretaker had found him dead, sitting on old champagne boxes in the corner. There were two photos on the floor nearby. She was in one and later everyone said they were disgusted when she had told them about the quiz and the prize. Natalie told her later that she was in the other, sticking her tongue out at the camera, hoping she wouldn't get punished for being insolent. She knew that in the photo Natalie had been wearing a blue shirt that wasn't quite buttoned as far up as it should have been, that her hair looked freshly brushed into bunches, and she was holding up a card with a capital D printed in red on it.

The Chief had called the police again who had come and looked and then called their doctor again. They had looked at the photos, which the caretaker had put back where he first saw them, and thought he was a sick bastard who had had a heart attack while he was wanking and looking at his "conquests". His trousers had been unzipped and they could see his cock. Everyone had been surprised they couldn't find any more photos, and especially surprised they couldn't find any videos once they had discovered the button behind the picture and camera hidden in the wall near the ceiling. She knew that Natalie was surprised that no-one was asking about any more photos.

She was the only one who knew that Grinn had gone up to his office after the barbeque, to sit down for a relaxing time looking through his photos, and that when he had put his hand into the drawer the scorpion had been surprised by the noise, movement and light and, in protective mode, had stung him.

When she had found him after creeping out of the dorm a few hours later it was dark in the corridors, light in his office, and he had been slumped in his swivel chair. She had picked her way into the room easily but walked a little nervously towards the desk, looking around her at the floor as she moved slowly forward. Once she looked into the drawer though she knew she need no longer be nervous. The scorpion was right at the back, it was a lot thinner, and she realised that what looked like a pale rippling movement on its back were actually scorplings, she couldn't count them all because they were so small. She heard a slight rustling sound and saw two more scorplings run across a photo then climb up onto their mother.

No need to change the plan, not really. The new swivel chair had been easy enough to push across to the champagne corner, and she had angled it so when she pushed him off it he ended up looking as if he'd been sitting on the boxes and just slumped forward. Then she flipped open the binocular case before moving to the desk and gently pulled out the drawer and placed it on top, then she put the case down so its top was open against the bottom of the drawer, and knowing she didn't know what sound to make she just shook the case slightly hoping the scorpion would see the four dead flies she had picked up from the dorm's window sill. It did. In no time at all the scorpion complete with scorplings were in the case, lid closed, photos taken from the drawer, and as she looked through them she was quite surprised by some, and the chosen two were left at the feet of the still warm Grinn.

The walk to the old barn had been straightforward because the sky was clear after the storm and the moon was bright, so she had just walked to the pile of rubble in the corner, flipped open the binocular case lid, tilted it so it sloped down onto the rubble, waited until the scorpion had walked out, and then gone back up to the dorm, hung up her jacket and binocular case, lain on the bed and gone to sleep.

'Well so much for that theory,' said Treloar picking up his pint.

Having released Helen Cavendish the previous evening Sam had stewed overnight about the news Colin Andrews had brought to the interview room. Helen Cavendish had an alibi. Now she had joined Treloar in Porthaven where he had been checking progress on the door to door enquiries around the village. He had also spoken again to Julia Osborne who had identified her husband's body, supported by David Cavendish. She had been anxious to take Jack and go to her father's at Nertherholt. With no reason to prevent her Treloar had agreed with the proviso that she remain accessible by telephone. When he had left Porth House she had been arranging for someone to drive down to collect them.

At five o'clock the two police officers were sitting in a deserted Harbour Lights.

'We had evidence though,' said Sam. 'We had the second belaying pin with her fingerprints, we had the motive of the deep-seated resentment, hatred even after that rape business; we had the knots. I know you said it was all too obvious and that she wouldn't be so stupid, but D S Winters wanted her brought in and after all she had no alibi!'

'Yeah. Well she has now. Watertight. And it isn't Winters who ends up looking like a fool is it?' said Treloar.

'No. That would be me,' replied Sam glumly. 'You weren't there, you were right. Fucking Winters.'

That afternoon a farmer in Porthtown had come forward. He had been away in Jersey looking at Guernsey cattle since the morning of the murder. He had been awake into the early morning to finish some paperwork before his trip and had taken some urgent letters down to the post at 03:30. He had seen a woman walking past the church and when asked had described Helen Cavendish to a tee. He had paid attention because it was such an unusual hour and she was a stranger to him. Shown her photograph he confirmed it. Porthtown church is three miles from the beach where the body of Oliver Osborne was found.

'Okay Phil, then someone went out of their way to try to frame Helen Cavendish. Someone who hated her and Osborne, and had the opportunity,' Sam continued.

'Well, serious candidates, if we leave out the boys, can only be David Cavendish and Julia, they alibi each other and Robin Cavendish confirms he heard them talking and saw them at the kitchen table when he went down for a drink from the fridge at 2 am. Anyway David appears to adore his wife and why would Julia hate her so? Okay, Oliver did seem to throw her in Julia's face, but I don't see it. So unless they're all in it together. No it's not on is it.'

'What about Jamie Deverell?' said Sam. Whilst she had been in Truro the previous day Treloar had tracked down The Dwork who was indeed staying at the campsite. His name was Jamie Deverell and he was a former pupil of Helen Cavendish before her marriage. Her kindness to him then had developed in his mind into an obsession. He believed himself to be her champion and having found out about the business in Oxford with the rape allegation through means about which he had been rather vague, but which seemed to involve illegal computer access, he had followed the families to Cornwall like a benevolent stalker with an ill-defined plan on gaining retribution on her behalf.

'No it can't be him. Anyway he wouldn't want to frame Helen Cavendish he worships her. We know that Mr

Deverell and his pal have been up to naughties with their computers but I'll doubt we'll prove it,' Treloar replied.

'So, we're back to square one,' said Sam.

'He did mention something odd. The morning the body was found, a dark-haired, blue-eyed Irish bloke called Trueblood or Trueman who had been pitched next to him and who had been quite friendly had packed up and left without a word. It surprised him. But I don't think he's a regular camper so he's probably not hot on the etiquette. No we need to focus on motive. Remember what John Forbes said at the beginning, 'somebody *really* hated this man, so who's prime candidate?'

'Julia. Has to be. He treated her like dirt. But as you said, alibi.'

Treloar put down his pint and grinned. 'People of the class of the Honourable Julia Osborne née Honor don't get their own hands dirty Sam. They have faithful retainers, devoted servants; they get others to do the dirty work.'

'But she's so ditzy, so blonde everybody says so and you've met her, think of the plotting, the planning.' Sam started as the French barmaid had approached their table without a sound putting out menus. Treloar waited until she had moved away before speaking again.

'She's stiff-upper lip Sam, what's that if not pretence? That vague and vacuous act is just that, an act. No, it's Julia alright I know it. Julia with help. She must have been in contact with her accomplice by phone I'd say.' Christ it's Julia and I let her go.'

'She'll be running then Sir, she can't just be sitting around thinking she's got away with it, not now Helen Cavendish is out. It'll take a while to get the traces on her phones and cards. Shall I start now?'

'Okay Sam, you get on to that. But you're right; it will take time to go through the channels. Meanwhile I know someone who can find out now. Let's get hold of Jamie Deverell and update him on the progress of the enquiry - just out of courtesy of course - and let's go apologise to Mrs Cavendish tomorrow. Didn't you say they'd moved to St Mawes? '

Outside the weather had turned again and squally showers were blowing in on an easterly wind. As they emerged from The Harbour Lights Treloar turned to Sam, 'Oh by the way my land Rover is in for service tomorrow. Any chance you could collect me from home first thing?'

She'd really liked him. Big, sexy, quite clever, knowing how to do things most people didn't; he even liking watching her paint, she had been close to Eric until he had been taken away four years ago. She was fifteen now. It hadn't taken long, using the hacking tools he'd taught her to use, on one of the PCs in the IT room, to find out they thought he'd killed Gilbert. She'd told him to make sure he didn't leave any prints, and he didn't then. But she hadn't known about the time the previous week, when it had been hot, that he had opened the window and propped it with the broom handle. Eric had been gone for three days when she had found out, by logging in to the court's computer system and reading the interview records, that that had been the day after one of the older kids had been given a cleaning detention. So, Eric's prints were the only ones found on the window frame.

She knew that Eric had not told them what had actually happened that day. He had just told them that he hadn't done anything wrong. The window had always been loose in its frame, and he didn't know what had happened, how Gilbert had died, or how the broom handle had found itself up his backside. She knew that they couldn't prove he had done it, but thought that he had, and that it was best to move him to a more secure unit for closer observation for two years before deciding what to do with him.

She knew she was what Grinn and his profession would have called a 'classic manipulator', but she also knew that whenever they had looked, for three years now, no-one had been able to find any of her old files anywhere; on paper or on the computer. She knew that there had been an investigation; that three IT people had been sacked, and that networks had been reconfigured with new firewalls.

Since he had gone she had stayed well up on firewall developments, encryption technology and databases; Eric had shown her how. Her first test, using the newer tools she had collected and written herself, had been to get into the court system and delete her own records. The hospital system had been simple, but the court and then the police had needed a lot more time. The hospital's new files, which she had allowed to build up, were innocuous, bland, containing test results and reports that she had engineered during her meetings with the new doctors, who were idiots.

Eric had shown her how to start mopeds and motorbikes, which she loved, and she laughed when she remembered taking the librarian's Velosolex moped and riding it across the estate. The librarian had told her she had been surprised when she had seen her from the library window and had wondered what was happening. The librarian had said to her later that she hadn't really minded, but that how it could be started without the key was a mystery. The librarian had asked her to let her know the next time she wanted a ride and they both smiled. She spent a lot of time in the library, and the librarian also ran the IT room, and they knew each other very well, very well indeed.

She knew that Eric had cracked the system and persuaded the court that he could earn a living on a permanent basis, and be responsible for himself. She had seen that there had been a lot of legal to-ing and fro-ing, quite a lot of it involving the different authorities not being able to find Eric's records. After a few months, when he was eighteen, the court had said it couldn't keep Eric under any kind of detention or supervision. She knew he had gone to America not long after being let out, and that he was probably still there.

Now though, she was really pleased and proud that she had finally tracked Natalie down, and amazed when she realised she could actually see her the day after tomorrow. They had become close friends once she had shown Natalie the photos and later they had watched the videos together. She smiled as she remembered Natalie's shriek when, at their first 'dorm-over' she had tugged hard on Natalie's pubic hair. She had known she had pulled quite a few out, she had wanted to; she had counted seventeen under her pillow the next day. She had said sorry and that she just wanted to see what would happen. Then Natalie had said she didn't really mind.

She had found out, from the hospital records, that Natalie had not been registered in her real name, and that that day when she was taken away suddenly, she had been taken back home to the UK. By using Eric's software and the packages she had collected and written herself, she had looked up phone numbers, including mobiles, and listened to voice mails and read emails. She knew lots of things about 'Natalie'.

She knew that 'Natalie' had been on holiday in the mountains not far from the hospital with her parents when she was 14 when her mother had died suddenly. Natalie had become severely disturbed.

She knew that her father had sent 'Natalie' to the hospital to be treated in a residential therapeutic programme. She knew that he had been assured that their family name would not be used in any records after making a donation of £30,000 to the mayor's fund, and she knew that 'Natalie' had promised to tell people she was called 'Natalie' during her two year stay. She knew that

'Natalie's' father had told people that his daughter had been abroad at boarding school.

She knew that 'Natalie's' parents had loved the Camargue, that they had a big house with stables near Casheral village. It was close to the beach where she remembered seeing the white horses when she was three years old, and that 'Natalie' and some family friends would be staying there on holiday for a week; starting late tomorrow.

People were stupid. No one had ever understood why she called fosterers fosters, but she carried on doing it anyway because 'fosterers' was a stupid word. The new ones were a breeze; no other kids, and reasonably tolerant; loads of space on the farm, close to the water. She saw flamingos all the time. She had been there for six months. They thought they were kind. School wasn't too bad even though it was boring most of the time; she was cleverer than all the kids and most of the teachers, and knew that she knew more than most of them ever would. There was a kid who would have his balls twisted the next time he tried to grab her tits, an older girl who was jealous and had been a bully for ages she had soon discovered. She had stopped bullying after her hair had caught fire one morning in the chemistry lab and the top of her left ear had been melted by a small strip of burning magnesium that had somehow lodged and got stuck.

The girl still did not know how lucky she had been. The cow's head had been held to the bench by Ben, who had not been difficult to persuade to hold her still. The magnesium was supposed to go inside, pierce the drum and go through it, but the tongs were too big so she had dropped it onto the top of the ear then flapped the hair over the bright white flame.

The girl had screamed, a lot, and when staff eventually ran into the room she knew that the girl had been holding her hand to her ear, some of her hair had still been flaring, some was smouldering, quite a lot was very short and curled at the ends with blobs that looked like full stops, and that she was still screaming.

She knew the smell the teachers had smelled; of singed hair as hands and arms went too close to candle flames and cigarette lighters, and imagined the teachers sniffing as they ran in and smelling it, wondering what had happened.

The Bunsen burner had still been going; there was a beaker of water, a tripod, and a tied coil of magnesium on the bench. She knew that the staff had thought the girl had been working on an experiment, creeping. No-one told them anything different.

There were computers at home and at school. Both had the Internet. She got some of the educational books she wanted through the school but she still saw the librarian, who would get her the really important ones; and other things. The books would arrive not long after their meetings, which were usually in one of the barns and lasted for two or three hours. After them she would see the librarian leave looking flushed, knowing that the Velosolex's seat and the rubbing of the hand-made Jute jacket would be uncomfortable against the bare skin, especially when the bike bounced over the ruts in the lane; but looking content through the grimaces.

No-one could understand why such a nice girl had been in the hospital in the first place. There were rumours, but so what, no-one actually knew anything for sure. On a clear day, with the binoculars, she could see it, up in the mountains. She knew that the fosters wouldn't have a problem with her borrowing the quad bike the day after tomorrow. It was the beginning of the summer holidays and they would be pleased to see her going to see an old friend.

21 July 06:30

Cross the Tamar at Plymouth heading west into Cornwall and you enter a different world. A land of steep wooded valleys, their depths shrouded in mist, the road sweeping and swooping through the countryside. Places at the edge; islands and peninsulas or coastal mountain terrains have a distinct and different atmosphere; light reflecting off the open sea, the seemingly boundless expanse of water, the anticipation and exhilaration of ports and harbours. The A3311 runs from St Ives on the north Cornish coast up over a barren moorland of granite outcrops and scattered sheep through Cripplesease and Nancledra and down into Penzance and Mounts Bay in the south. This far west the land feels more ancient, less cultivated; the peninsula is narrow, almost an island and the weather can be unpredictable changing quickly. At the highest point a narrow track leads off the road to the west. Following this for half a mile brought Sam to a group of derelict farm buildings in a sheltered hollow. The largest, a long barn, was partially surrounded by scaffolding and clothed in plastic sheeting.

She had come to collect Treloar. As she stepped from the car Treloar emerged from around the far end of the barn sporting dusty faded blue overalls.

'Hi Sam,' he called, 'thanks for this'.

'No problem,' she replied.

'Come in for a minute. I'll just get these off.'

'Right'.

She followed him through a stone archway connecting the long barn to a second smaller barn.

'Wow!' she gasped.

The rear of the structure was a wall of glass facing out over a narrow wooded valley down to a distant sparkling sea.

'Location, location, location,' she murmured.

'Come through!' Treloar called.

Sam walked through a sliding patio door into a large room open to the rafters. At the far end to her right was an arched doorway through which she could see a further wall covered entirely in bright jewel coloured ceramic tiles. In the wall opposite her was an enormous hearth she could have stood inside. The only furniture in the flagstoned room was three director's chairs, several travelling rugs, a folding picnic table and four large tatty bean bags.

'Take a seat. Coffee?' he called.

'Please,' she answered sitting carefully on the cleanest of the chairs. A large ginger cat with amber eyes emerged, stretching, from behind a bean bag, strolled across and rubbed against her legs purring. Sam stretched down to stroke it.

'That's Messi,' said Treloar walking in with a tray and placing it on the picnic table.

'Oh,' she said snatching back her hand and looking at her palm.

Treloar chuckled. 'No, not messy, Messi after the footballer. There's also Cruyff over there in the hearth and Pep the baby's around somewhere. My mother collects strays. They seem to seek her out. These boys came to me ready-named. She's a Barça fan.'

'Does she not like cats?'

'Oh yes she loves them... cats, dogs, donkeys, chickens, ducks, you name it. She must have half a dozen cats. She loves all animals. When they die they are buried in the farm cemetery at the cliff edge I told you about along with the chickens, goats, dogs, the odd badger, fox and owl and of course a marker for my father. It's next to the noman's land.' He handed her a rich smelling coffee in a large green glazed terracotta cup with a red rim.

'No man's land? Like in the First World War?' she asked frowning.

'Well actually it's a Cornish tradition. In these moorland areas and on the north coast where the farm is, live the Buccas or sprites. To appease them farmers would, and some will still, leave a parcel of land uncultivated. Miners would leave part of their lunch uneaten for them. They called them knackers or knockers, like the beer Cornish Knocker or that Stephen King book Tommyknockers. They thought they were souls in purgatory. My mother believes in the old ways. Even though she is Spanish she honours the superstitions of Cornwall.'

'Well you certainly both live in a beautiful part of the county so I can't blame the sprites for liking it too,' Sam smiled. 'And this is wonderful coffee. And as for this place - it's just amazing.'

'Well it will be OK when it's finished. I'm doing as much as I can myself; I find it relaxing actually. Next time you come I'll give you the guided tour. From the hill behind these barns you can see the sea on both coasts. There's a small ring of menhirs, standing stones. It's said they were young girls turned to stone for dancing on a Sabbath. I love it up there. It makes me feel free.'

Treloar was gazing out of the window, speaking very softly and slowly. Very different from the smiling, gung ho man Sam was used to. She felt the hair on the back of her neck stand on end and shivered.

He turned back to her smiling and said in his normal voice 'So let's start from the beginning; let's look at the who and the why.'

'Well we're ruling out random – whoever it was knew where he was going to be and when. I don't see some crazed lunatic wandering around that area in the early hours picking him up by chance and killing him in that way. They knew who he was, that he'd be there and the brutality of it tells me they hated him. Now normally that would narrow it down substantially, but Osborne did seem to be universally loathed. Also he did have a definite routine at nights; down the pub, back to the students' place, it would have been easy enough for anyone watching him to establish the pattern.'

'So anyone who hated him, who had watched him here, could have done it? Sounds awfully like Jamie Deverell, but I just don't see it. Jamie's too cerebral and he certainly wouldn't have wanted to frame Helen Cavendish.'

'Or they could have contracted it,' said Sam putting down her mug, 'specifying the method. I'm with you. My money's on the bimbo wife. I know she couldn't have done it but she could have financed it.'

'Yeah, but can you see her organizing it?' Treloar shook his head.

'No that's more like the hyper-efficient Mrs Cavendish. She would have made a project out of it with a dedicated ring binder.'

'I don't see those two working together. They're hardly buddies, but I agree with you, I do like Julia for it, but she would have needed help.'

'OK, who?'

'Good question. You've requested her phone records? She'd need to be in touch with whoever, to let them know where to find him and when.'

'But how would someone like the Honourable Julia know how to hire a killer? She doesn't move in the right circles even if she could afford the fee.'

'Good point.'

'Perhaps she came across someone through Osborne himself? He certainly would have known how to set it up. No. Can you picture it? "Darling, who would I go to if I wanted someone brutally murdered?" No way,' Sam laughed.

'Still she does have the best motive as far as we know. He did treat her like shit and presumably she inherits. Better check that. He's the sort to go for a pre-nup. When you check her mobile, check the boy's too, Jack. He dotes on her apparently; she could easily have borrowed his phone.'

'What about Jamie Deverell? Did you mean it about asking him to access the phone records because Winters would go spare if she found out?'

'Mmm. I haven't decided yet. We wouldn't be able to use anything we found out but it would speed things up. I don't want to involve him but of course what he does of his own accord? Well we can't control what he does when he finds out that someone has tried to implicate his beloved Helen, and if he does find something he chooses to share with us?'

'Winters already has it in for you, don't give her any ammunition.'

'Yeah, you're right about that. OK. I'll just change and we'll be off to bounce some suspicions about Julia off the redoubtable Mrs Cavendish, see who she thinks might want to frame her and perhaps just reassure Jamie that she's been questioned but is no longer under suspicion,' and with that, grinning, he walked out of the room leaving Sam alone with her thoughts.

She had left the quad bike in the field where the track from the fosters' land crossed the lane to 'Natalie's' place. She had wanted to surprise 'Natalie' so she planned to arrive quietly, stealthily. She had wanted to know the layout of the place and where everyone was to give her the best chance to catch 'Natalie' on her own. The binoculars were no use because the lane was on top of a raised canal bank which blocked the view. She had left them with the bike before walking up the slope to the lane; her dark green stiletto sandals were in the small rucksack hanging from her shoulder.

She smiled as she remembered. The white crocs would make people wonder if they had been right at first glance. She knew that most men would see her big nipples first, made big and hard by friction as they had jogged against the light green dress as she had ridden across the fields. A split second later she knew that they would take in her big tits which she knew gave her a great profile, and that her cleavage had looked really good in that dress. Then they would see her shiny hair in high bunches, and last the crocs; then they would wonder……… some of them for ages, and she enjoyed knowing that some would wonder again and again. If they had been standing behind her and watched her buttocks jiggle as she walked, and noticed that as the breeze gently pushed the thin fabric of the dress against her skin there were no strap lines to be seen, they would have known for sure. No knickers.

As she had walked up the slope to the lane she saw the three beavers look at her then quickly scamper away and a second later heard them splash, not very loudly, into the canal. She had looked at them, on the other side of the canal, looking at her, before they turned and ran into the reeds. As they disappeared she noticed two raptors circling in the blue cloudless sky and she had laughed as she was reminded of Veliz's 'Eagle confronts Beaver at Eldorado'. She had seen all of Veliz's paintings; She had been looking for Eagle paintings when she had first come across them using the PC in the library and she had been surprised how they were all so different, yet all of scenes around Juneau, that small town that was somehow the capital of Alaska that she hadn't heard of before. She remembered being surprised when she found out that Eldorado was the name of a very small creek that, mile for mile had produced the most gold in the Klondike gold rush.

Before she got to the gate she had smelled the barbeque smoke smell, could hear what she now knew was a David Bowie album, and thought that 'Natalie' would be bored and looking forward to Julian, the son of one of the friends, arriving in two days' time. She knew that 'Natalie' had plans to stay on when the family friends went back, and that Julian was staying for three weeks to buy two stallions and prepare them and get them back to the UK.

She hadn't put the rucksack down to swap shoes in front of the gate as she had planned, because as she had been thinking about it she had noticed a fyke net. It was weird to see one in a canal. She had vividly remembered being taken round the lake in a fishing punt by one of the eel fishermen when she was three, when she was on the first holiday she could remember. As he had gone from net to net collecting the eels she remembered that he had told her they were called fyke nets, and shown her that they were wide and open at one end and narrow and closed at the other. He had shown her, he had let her try to hold an eel and she couldn't because her hands weren't big enough.

He had told her that there were fewer eels than there used to be, how the fishermen couldn't put nets in the canals because that would stop the eels reaching the lake, then they wouldn't be able to get out to sea to breed, and how the numbers of fishermen was kept low by law.

She had recognised the forked salt scraper handles that were staking it from the salt-works; she had remembered seeing men using the scrapers to move the salt around when she was five. She remembered that she had thought that the pink salt looked pretty.

She could see that all these bastards had done was to steal the scrapers and take the boards off. She could see that it would have been easy, with a hand on each side of the fork, to push the other end of the handle into the silt. All they had to do then was tie the net to the handles. She knew that it was illegal and why; and that the fishermen would go ape-shit if they found out.

Not wanting to be seen, she had quietly walked through the gate towards the music, which was coming from behind a high red brick wall, and had peered through a gap where two bricks had been left out to leave space for a plant that had died. She had seen two men and a woman, in their thirties or forties. The woman had been wearing a bright orange thong, tied at the sides, and nothing else. Her breasts didn't sag and they weren't too bad for an oldie. There was a man wearing white overalls smeared with black marks and he was taking photographs as the woman posed provocatively. The other man was lying on a sun lounger masturbating.

She had been so engrossed that she had forgotten why she was there, then she had wondered where the other two *women were that she knew were staying there, and where 'Natalie' was. The whinnying had made her turn, towards a new looking stable building fifty metres away and she wondered if 'Natalie' was there. She had wondered what would happen next on the patio and wanted to stay and watch. She remembered wishing that she had put a sketchpad in the rucksack.*

She had looked around, couldn't see anyone in the windows and no one was on the path to the stable so she had walked over to it, and carefully peered through the half open door. Three horses were tethered in stalls at the far end, 'Natalie' was leading a fourth to the last stall, and she was hot; sweaty hot. Her yellow T shirt was stained dark under the arms and down the back, her blond hair was tangled, and 'Natalie's' shorts were sticking to her legs.

In the middle of the stable was a big round table; on it were brushes, clippers, bottles and soggy looking cloths. Two buckets and a sack she could see was full of horse hair were on the floor nearby. She didn't know much about horses but when she looked again she could see that the white one being led by Natalie looked newly trimmed and very smart. There was a hay bale not far from the table, and a thick wooden post holding up the roof had ropes hanging from metal loops. On the far side were saddles resting on floor-standing racks and above them hung stirrups, harnesses, crops and whips.

The glass door to a wet-room on the right was open, and there was a very old tractor just inside the door. Nearby was a long bench with what she knew were pieces of the engine scattered on it. She had still been looking round, taking it in when 'Natalie' came back from the stalls, walked towards the wet room and took off her T shirt as she went. 'Her breasts looked as good as ever, pert and possibly even bigger than she remembered.

'Natalie' dropped the shirt onto the table as she passed it. Then she had stopped to take off her shorts and walked towards the saddles and hung them over one in the middle, stretched with her arms held high and back arched and then ran her hands through her hair and looked towards the wet room. Then 'Natalie' turned round and walked back towards the table. 'Natalie' picked up one of the clippers, looked at it and nodded, turned it on and it buzzed loudly. If she had been horsey she would have known that it was top of the range; a Heniger Saphir clipper, powerful, with no cord and rechargeable batteries.

Then 'Natalie' had sat on the hay, wincing as the stalks stuck into her backside, then she laid back and winced again, more strongly, and turned the clipper so its teeth pointed upwards before putting it between her legs, onto her pussy. Then 'Natalie' had closed her eyes and started moving the clipper slowly backwards and forwards. After a couple of minutes 'Natalie's' hips had been pushing upwards then down and writhing slowly from side to side. She knew from experience that when 'Natalie' had finished, there would be red marks down her back, across her bum and down the backs of her legs. She also knew from experience that the sweat would make the grazes really sting. She had smiled as she had remembered her own first time on a bale.

She remembered the idea she had had. The stiletto sandals would have to wait. She had turned to look at the table and smiled, then pouted. She picked up the long thin dipstick lying next to the engine block, weighed it and swished it from side to side experimentally. Then she had walked round the tractor holding it above her head and then whipped it down onto Natalie's breasts, aiming for the nipples.

'Natalie' had shrieked and opened her eyes very wide, then smiled, and then nodded and kept her eyes open, and after a few seconds put the clipper back onto her pussy. She had delivered only four more welts across 'Natalie's' breasts, each covered with a thin black stripe; two had smacked and hardened and puckered the left nipple so much, she remembered proudly thinking it could probably have been used to sharpen her sketching pencils; before 'Natalie' had orgasmed...... noisily.

She smiled again as she remembered the wet room, and how she had looked forward to seeing how the welts would look in a couple of days' time. She laughed as she remembered how romantically clichéd the dust motes had looked, floating in the sunlight as it bounced off the wet room door, as they had walked towards it.

After Helen Cavendish had been released she had joined David and Robin in a small hotel in the nearby seaside village of St Mawes, some twenty miles from Porthaven. This was home to some of the most expensive properties in Cornwall; large houses set overlooking the wooded valleys which sloped down to the River Fal.

'Wow,' said Sam as she and Treloar drove down towards the harbour at ten o'clock that morning.

'Yes,' said Treloar, 'serious money here.'

The hotel chosen by the Cavendishes was modest for the area, a terraced four storey former shop which had recently been converted into a 'bar/restaurant with rooms'. The bar was on the ground floor with the restaurant one storey above. At that time of day the restaurant was deserted and the police officers took a seat at the open French windows and waited with some trepidation for Helen Cavendish. She was a formidable woman, not impressed with having been taken in for questioning even though she had not been charged.

'Good morning Mrs Cavendish. I want to apologise for recent events but I trust that as an intelligent woman you understand why we acted as we did.'

'Yes Inspector, I do actually and I accept your apology. Though had it not been for that farmer I presume I would be in one of your cells, but that's behind us now. How can I help you?'

'I want to ask you about that nocturnal walk you took. You said you went for a walk because you couldn't sleep, you couldn't find your sleeping tablets and it was your habit to do so in those circumstances.'

'Correct.'

'Who would have known that? That it was your habit I mean?'

'Well, David obviously and Robin, my mother, some friends but other than that…. Oh, Julia and Jack,' Helen was frowning, concentrating. 'I told Julia and Jack was in the room. It was earlier that week, the morning of the sea fret. It was just the three of us in the Family Room at the house, Julia was sad and for once we had a meaningful conversation. I told Julia.' Helen stared at Treloar.

'The belaying pin,' he continued, 'the second one with your fingerprints that we found lodged in the culvert beside the slipway'.

Helen interrupted him. 'I've been thinking about that and it must have been from Fowey, from the bloody boat in Fowey. I touched everything on that boat. I was sailing it. Julia had this silly great bag with her. I thought she was just being bimbo Julia, bringing make-up and hair straighteners and God knows what. She must have taken the belaying pins from the boat. She has every reason to want rid of Oliver and she's always resented me and coveted David. She must have had something to do with it.' Helen paled. 'My God, oh my God she told me that day. It's the poem, the crabs everything.'

Helen stared at Treloar. 'Tell me Inspector, over his head there was a bag I understand and it had been coated in black tar boat varnish and tied around his neck with cord in a bowline knot. Yes? That was another pointer to a boating individual, i.e. me.'

'Yes, that's right. The knot looked like a noose, another dramatic flourish. It wasn't released but the press got hold of it anyway.'

'And there were small crabs in the bag when it was opened?'

'Yes'

169

'Oh no, no,' the colour had drained from Helen's face. 'It's her, Inspector; it's her, alibi or no alibi. Rudyard Kipling's *Smuggler's Song*. You'll know it:

'Them that ask no questions isn't told a lie.
Watch the wall, my darling, while the Gentlemen go by!'

'Yes' said Sam 'I remember it: *'Laces for a lady, letters for a spy'*

Helen continued quietly. 'Later in the poem, it goes on:

'Little barrels, roped and tarred, all full of brandy-wine,

'And Oliver was small and broad-chested and he was full of Armagnac, or so I read in the paper. That same morning before I mentioned my sleeping pills she told me how Becca, Jack's mother, used to read that poem to him when he was a toddler, it was his favourite, and he had taught it to Julia. 'And the crabs, Inspector, the crabs. She stood up and stamped on a spider, crushed it, I was horrified, and she said 'Oliver hates spiders.' Crabs: seagoing spiders.'

'Yes I do follow your train of thought but this may all just be coincidence. Why would Mrs Osborne want to kill her husband, why not just divorce him?' Treloar thought this rather dramatic but it did fit their theory. 'Did Julia have any money or access to any money?'

'No, Oliver kept total control of the finances. She had pin money and accounts which he would pay. But no, she had no access to major funds.'

'So she couldn't have hired someone to kill Oliver?'

'I don't believe she had access either to the cash or to the contacts to arrange that. No Inspector, if someone did this for Julia, it was for love not for money. You've both witnessed her little girl lost act. It is very effective on men I can assure you. I've seen her pull it off many a time.'

'Have you a candidate in mind?'

'No. But remember, I'd hardly call myself a close acquaintance. Jack might have some ideas, but I doubt he'd tell you. Fellow victims as I've said. He worships Julia and he loathed his father. She doesn't confide in me. I have seen her talking with that pretty barmaid now I come to think about it. Actually I thought it was rather odd at the time they seemed very... I don't know ... friendly perhaps? And I've seen Jack talking to her too and that is definitely odd. Jack never talks to strangers, barely to people he knows. But I can't picture her killing Oliver; she's a mere slip of a thing.'

'No Julia and I are not close; we have nothing whatsoever in common, but she's always had a soft spot for David, ever since we first met and they talk a lot. I supposed it was a crush at first, but it's always there on the periphery. She always agrees with him, always asks his opinion on absolutely everything, stares vacantly at him if she thinks no one's looking. We laugh about it David and I, but never in front of her of course. That would be cruel. We were only laughing about it the other day. David was saying how she reminded him of a devoted old dog he had as a child. She'd have been devastated had she heard him. But surely she can't have. She'd gone out... I'm sure.'

'Where is your husband now Mrs Cavendish?' asked Treloar.

At that moment Robin Cavendish came bounding up the stairs into the restaurant calling,

'Mum!'

'Here Robin,' Helen waved. Robin walked across to their table and glared at Sam and Treloar.

'It's alright Robin, really it is,' Helen said, 'the officers have already apologised and they were only following the evidence.'

Robin looked at her and smiled. 'OK, Mum.'

'Robin, where is your father?' asked Treloar.

'He's downstairs. We just got back. We rowed across to the other side of the river, it was really cool Mum, there's a great boathouse and a place like a chateau.'

'Robin,' barked Helen 'where is he now?'

'I just said, downstairs on the quay. He's talking to some guy. Dad sent me up to find you.'

'Robin,' said Sam gently as the boy was starting to look scared. 'What did this man look like?'

'Quite tall, dark curly hair, really blue eyes and he talked like the The Edge.'

'Who?' asked Sam.

'The Edge, guitarist for U2.'

'Irish,' said Sam.

'Trueman,' said Treloar standing and dashing down the stairs.

'Who on earth is Trueman?' asked Helen.

Sam hurried after Treloar. Outside on the quay the only sign of David Cavendish was a Panama hat bobbing in the water by the harbour office.

She was smiling as she had walked back from the stable, after the wet room. She had stopped to look through the hole in the wall again and no-one was on the patio. There was no music, there was no-one in the swimming pool that she now took in on the other side of the patio, and the two women she hadn't seen before were playing tennis on a court that was the other side of the pool.

She was surprised that they were both wearing white, and wondered. She watched for a few seconds and laughed when she knew what her next pastiche would be. The tennis girl photograph that she knew hung on hundreds of thousands of all kinds of walls, all around the world in the seventies.

The girl would still be walking towards the net; her hair would still be blond. The girl would be looking to the right instead of straight ahead, head down and it would profile 'Natalie's' face side-on with a shy smile, and a glint in her eye. The short white skirt would still be held up by the left hand stroking the left buttock, and it would still reveal a great bum with no knickers. Then there would be the additions – it would glow pink, with two, maybe three, bright red stripes across it, and 'Natalie' would be holding a cane in her right hand rather than the tennis racket.

It was still early afternoon and she would make good progress on it before 'Natalie' visited tomorrow.

Sam and Treloar returned to the hotel where Helen and Robin were sitting talking quietly. There had been no trace of David Cavendish.

'That bloke,' said Robin 'maybe it's just coincidence. People do look and sound like people. Like that painting in the hall at the castle.'

'What are you on about Robin?' asked Helen tetchily.

'You know. We went to the castle and there was that painting in the hall of a bloke on a horse under a tree and a woman and kids sitting on the ground. The castle was in the background. You must remember! Jack pointed out how one of the kids, a girl, looked just like that barmaid at the pub, you know the French one.'

Helen blushed. 'I'm sorry Inspector; I wasn't really paying much attention to the boys that day. I was in a bad mood. I'm sorry Robin, really.'

Robin shrugged. 'Hey, whatever. It's true though, you can go see for yourselves.'

Sam gasped and put her hand to her mouth. 'I think he's right. God I do think he's right. I've seen that painting, it's huge, but I wouldn't have made the connection because I hadn't seen her. She's French not Cornish after all, and the girl in the painting is younger and has ringlets, but the face and those eyes, it's her spitting image.'

'Jesus,' said Treloar 'the castle was in the Pentreath family for centuries. Then in the twenties the lord and master, a right rogue apparently, ran off leaving huge debts and the bank foreclosed.'

'So?' asked Sam.

'He ran off to France.'

'But so what? If the barmaid is some long lost descendent of the Pentreath family, I don't see the relevance.'

'Helen. You mentioned that when your housemate was raped by Oliver, how your word, her word, was discounted because Oliver was from a rich banking family. Do you know which bank?'

'Of course. Baring Penrose and Isaacs. Isaacs was Oliver's mother's maiden name.

'That's the bank that ended centuries of tradition for the Pentreaths. They took the estate.'

Sam laughed. 'Oh come on. An avenging angel from the distant past, come to exact revenge on the evil banker. That girl is five foot nothing and anyway she was at Point End House when Osborne died.'

'Even so, even so. I don't like coincidences. We need to speak to her.'

Helen interrupted. 'But what about this Irish man? How does he fit in and where is David for Christ's sake?'

Treloar turned to her. 'I don't know' he said solemnly 'Did Julia know you'd been released without charge?'

'I don't know. I didn't tell her. Robin, did Dad speak to Julia after she left for Netherholt?'

'Yeah. She rang a couple of times. I know she phoned when we were driving over here. Dad told her you were getting out and that we were going to stay on here for a few days.'

'Robin, this is important. Did your father actually say where you were staying?' asked Sam.

'Yeah he told her the name of the hotel and where it is.'

Treloar motioned to Sam and they both walked out onto the balcony where he pulled out his mobile, consulted his notebook and dialled.

'Netherholt House.'

'Julia Osborne please, Inspector Treloar of Devon and Cornwall Police calling.'

'Miss Julia is not in residence presently Sir. She left to visit friends yesterday with Master Jack. I took them to the railway station myself to catch the London train.'

'Where were they going?'

'To London, Sir.'

'Do you know a tall man with black curly hair, blue eyes and a soft Irish accent?'

'Why that sounds like Mr Truelove Sir, his Lordship's Stable Manager.'

'Don't tell me. He's away and his first name begins with the letter T.'

'Indeed Sir, he's gone to Ireland to look at horses and his Christian name is Thomas.'

'Thank you, goodbye.'

'Sam. The fingerprints on the hoof knife, get them to the Garda in Dublin, and get hold of a photograph of Thomas Truelove ...... driving licence, passport, anything.'

They rejoined Helen and Robin. As they all sat around the table, their discussion focused on the inexplicable appearance of Thomas Truelove here in St Mawes, they failed to notice the tall man approaching them.

'Hello there, what brings you two here?'

David Cavendish stood smiling at them. In his left hand he clutched a dripping Panama hat.

'For Christ's sake David where the hell have you been, the Inspector was about to put a nationwide alert out!' Helen roared, leaping to her feet.

'Me?' he asked innocently, 'I was just off getting some help to rescue my hat. It's a dear old thing and I would be very sorry to lose it.'

Helen exhaled loudly and sat down heavily, placing her elbows on the table and her head in her hands.

'Mr Cavendish,' said Treloar calmly, 'I understand from Robin that you were talking to an Irish gentleman. Could you tell me what that was about?'

'Oh you mean Thomas, Thomas Truelove, he works for Julia's father.'

'Yes,' Treloar continued as if speaking to a child, 'yes but what was he doing here?'

'Oh that's simple. He brought this,' he held up a battered brown leather wallet.

'What was he doing with your wallet?' asked Helen brusquely.

'Well it seems that when they packed to leave they must have swept it up with other stuff. Obviously when they unpacked at Netherholt they found it in Jack's backpack and darling Julia thought I would miss it, so she despatched Truelove hotfoot on his trusty Harley. Bloody kind of her if you ask me. Seems like a really nice chap actually and surprisingly knowledgeable about cricket for an Irishman. Still a bit tetchy about Owain Morgan, but I can't say I blame...'

'David!' Helen barked.

'Right,' he said softly looking at the floor.

Treloar and Sam exchanged a look which expressed sympathy for this perfectly pleasant man suffering yet another onslaught from his overbearing wife.

'It's perfectly fine Mrs Cavendish, no harm done,' said Treloar, 'so Mr Truelove was just here to return your wallet. I'm surprised Mrs Osborne didn't call you when they found it to say she was sending it down with Truelove and I'm surprised that you hadn't missed it.'

'Oh Mum pays for everything doesn't she Dad?' said a smiling Robin.

'Yes, yes Inspector, I'm sure my wife will tell you I'm hopeless with money,' he shot a brief sharp look at Helen. *The worm turns* thought Sam. 'And she may well have phoned; I'm afraid I've also mislaid my mobile, but it must be around somewhere because I had it yesterday, so don't go blaming Jack for that Helen.'

Helen Cavendish was not a stupid woman and she picked up on the changed atmosphere and remained silent.

'Anyway, he was bringing it to the hotel when we bumped into each other by the quay. We had met when he came to collect Julia and Jack – Robin, you were out walking so you didn't meet him – and we were just chatting, when my hat blew off. So I thanked him again and went to fetch help to recover it. He said goodbye, wished us all the best for the rest of the holiday and left. Ordinary, civilised behaviour; nothing remotely suspicious; no cause for alarm. '

'How wonderfully kind of Julia,' Helen laughed falsely, 'we must telephone to thank her,' and with that she started to gather her belongings together.

Treloar and Sam took their leave and headed back to Sam's car. Treloar was deep in thought as they drove up past Henry VIII's castle heading out back to Porthaven.

'Right,' he said, 'we've got Julia linked to Truelove, possibly Truelove owning the knife which cut the cord on Osborne's body, and now this French girl seen talking with both Julia and Jack and possibly linked to the Pentreath family. Let's go see this picture.'

'Sexually promiscuous'. That was what the notes had said. She had been five, when she had first gone to the hospital and the first dirty old man that had called himself a doctor had asked her about playing with herself, and about playing with other kids. The notes had been updated every year. Every year some dirty-minded person, sometimes a man and sometimes a woman, would ask the same questions and she'd read what they'd written in their notes before she had deleted them. She had read that she used seduction tactics, understood vulnerabilities, and that her manipulation skills were growing. "Right", and she had laughed as she had remembered thinking to herself, "when I was ten they grew as quickly as my tits".

They had asked her to be honest so over the years the notes had been updated. All the stuff about the bouncing clowns between her legs when she was three, beads up her bum, beads up other kids' bums and pussies, hairbrush handles, candles, bottles, fingers up bums, playing with cocks, and peeing on the kids who had wanted to know what it was like. It was all there. She had known that it was normal, and that most kids didn't talk about it to adults and most kids weren't asked about it by dirty bastards that called themselves doctors. She laughed as she remembered how she knew she could do all of it legally now, and remembered thinking how she would have been legal two years earlier if she had lived just a little way south, and how she had known from experience that the local gypsies didn't give a fuck and had sex according to their own law from thirteen anyway, like their cousins did legally over the border.

They had thought they had known it all, but because she hadn't talked about it they hadn't written about her having sex, how she had learned young to put on a condom using her lips and mouth to slide a cock into it, how she was proud that she was the only girl she knew that had practised and overcome what they would have called the 'gag reflex' to be able to get the condom rolled right down, how semen tasted salty, how she had enjoyed fucking some of the older kids who were getting condoms smuggled in by the butcher; or that she had found out that if you're naked and bent over a hay bale while screwing Eric you will get seriously scratched, and your nipples will stay sore and mega-sensitive for days.

She had remembered all this as she finished sketching the Tennis Girl. She was pleased, it was looking good. She had finger rubbed a few lines out and re-drawn the skirt being lifted a bit higher and more to the right so she could see more of 'Natalie's' bum.

To the west of Porthaven a further wooded valley ran down to the sea. At the head of this valley, set in acres of woodland and ornamental gardens stands Polgwynn, ancestral home of the Pentreath family, now the residence of the Hardcastles, but open to the public between 10am and 4pm Tuesday to Friday from Easter to the end of September.

The house is a mixture of architectural styles, extended through several centuries and building fashions, but the original medieval tower still stands, housing the main entrance to the baronial hall, albeit that no baron had ever lived here. Treloar and Sam crunched their way across the gravel courtyard and passed from bright sunlight through massive oak doors into cool gloom.

Having shown their warrant cards at the ticket office, thus avoiding the £12 entrance fee, they were directed onwards to the main hall where, they were told, Ms Lander would be expecting them. Once their eyes had adjusted they realised they were in a small vestibule with a further oak door ahead of them. Treloar led the way, pushing the heavy door open and ushering Sam through.

They found themselves in a huge galleried hall its walls lined with paintings. Lighting came from a suspended wire net with hundreds of lamps angled towards the walls.

'How wonderful,' said Sam.

A thirty something woman in casual expensive linen shirt and trousers approached them smiling, her hand extended.

'Millie Lander,' she said taking their hands in turn. 'How may we help you? I must say I was intrigued by your call. Is this to do with that dreadful murder?'

'Not directly,' Treloar answered smiling. 'We wanted to take a look at some of your paintings.'

'But of course. Which paintings interest you?'

Sam had moved across to look at a large gilt-framed landscape. 'This one interests me,' she said pointing.

'Oh yes, that's a favourite,' Millie Lander said with a huge smile. She walked across to join Sam, the clip-clip of her kitten heels echoing in the vast space. Treloar followed.

It was the painting Robin had described. In the background stood an earlier version of Polgwynn, the tower they were now standing in to the right of the canvass with the adjoining Tudor extension. In the centre was the White Lake smaller than its current size. In the foreground were a family group posing under a massive cedar tree, the pater familias mounted on a white horse. But the eye was drawn to the teenage girl seated on the ground at the base of the tree's enormous trunk. She was indeed the spitting image of the French barmaid. Beneath the painting a small brass plaque was engraved '**Polgwynn 1776**'.

'The sixteenth century Pentreath family with a daughter who looks exactly like the barmaid at the Harbour Lights,' said Sam quietly.

'Hah!' cried Millie Lander, clapping her hands in delight. 'That's exactly what you're supposed to think. A Gainsborough. But look more closely look at the birds on the lake, look at the tower roof.'

Sam leaned in focusing on the lake. The birds she had originally taken for swans and heron were in fact a rosy peach colour and standing on one leg. 'Flamingos,' she murmured.

'And the flag on the tower,' said Treloar 'It's the Jolly Roger; the skull and crossbones.'

'Indeed! Indeed!' cried Millie 'now look at the boy seated far right.'

Sam peered at the tousle-haired boy in blue. 'Well, well. It's Toby Brett-Morgan and he's sitting on a surfboard.'

'Isn't it marvellous?' asked Millie with pride.

'It's certainly very clever,' replied Treloar. 'Who painted it?'

'I've absolutely no idea. They're anonymous. We came across this and several other pastiches in an outbuilding one day, just left there. We all agreed that they are so good and such fun we'd hang them. Would you like to see some of the others?'

'Bizarre,' said Treloar as they walked back to the car. They had been shown two 'Audubons', a 19th century French-American artist famed for his 'Bird of America'. These pictured a Pels Fishing Owl and a Kynsna Lourie, both birds native to South Africa. They had seen another 'Gainsborough' featuring the landlady of the Harbour Lights posed as Georgiana Duchess of Devonshire and a 'Turner' seascape complete with pedalo and windsurfer.

'Extraordinary,' said Sam. 'An amazing talent; brilliant imitations of very different artists. And did you notice how your eye was drawn to the barmaid figure in the picture of the house? The divine proportion; a painting perspective used by da Vinci, for one, in 'The Last Supper' to draw your focus to the Christ figure. And did you see in her lap the same owl as in the Audubon? Spooky.'

'How the hell do you know all this obscure stuff: artists' techniques, philosophical quotations? Benefit of a university education I presume?'

'Well that and four years in a very successful pub quiz team.'

'Well ratio or no ratio if I was a fifteen year old boy my eye would be drawn to the French girl rather than

Toby. I'm not surprised Robin remembered her. So, the barmaid Amélie is not a long lost Pentreath, just a pretty girl who caught the artist's eye, though I agree the owl thing is rather sinister. I am curious to know who the artist is but I don't see any relevance to the murder.'

'We could ask around the village,' suggested Sam.

'No. Let's ask the models first.'

The Tennis Girl had been finished, 'Natalie' had seen it and cringed and then smiled. She had rung the librarian, who she knew would blush and be jealous when she saw it. She had known that the librarian's jealousy would be gone by the time she left the barn. When the librarian had left on the Velosolex, bouncing painfully over the ruts, smiling, the painting was slung over her shoulders in the carry case on its way to the Reno Gallery in town. She knew this one would bring in good money again even if it wasn't as much as she could have negotiated personally if she had been older. She had reckoned that getting reasonable payments made, electronically, into the bank account she had opened on line in her false name was the main thing, and missing out on a few thousand francs wasn't the end of the world. The librarian knew about art, and she knew the gallery owner, so she made quite a good agent and the prices she got weren't that bad. She was on her way to see 'Natalie' and saw the big black SUV noisily and dustily going down the lane away from the farm just after she had parked the quad bike in the same place as last time. She knew the man driving was going to pick up Julian at Montpellier Méditerranée after dropping off the three women in town to go shopping. She didn't know what the guy who had been wearing the dirtied overalls from working on the tractor would be doing. She soon found out.

He had been in the canal struggling with the fyke net and shouting. She had seen that he was wearing waders, still in his dirty white overalls, and was wrestling with the end of the net that would normally be closed. One of the stakes had come out and was half submerged and half lying on the bank. He had reached into the net and pulled out something dark and thrown it into the reeds on the other side of the canal. He did it again, and then again, and at the third throw she realised she was seeing him throwing dead beavers. She knew they must have swum into the net, become entangled, and drowned because they couldn't get out and couldn't breathe. Unconsciously she had been walking towards him as he had been throwing and was on the lane just above him as his arms reached, struggling, into the net, bent over with water pouring into the top of his waders, looking for more. Between his curses she could hear that he was panting hard. It was a very hot day.

She had put down her rucksack with the stiletto sandals still packed, taken off the white crocs and walked down to the water's edge. She smiled as she remembered picking up the scraper handle and hefting it up and down to test it, to see if her idea would work before deciding it would. Then she had walked into the water quietly, and calmly but firmly put the forked end over the man's neck and pushed down suddenly and hard so he was quickly lying flat; his body was thrashing and his head was under water, his arms getting more and more tangled inside the loose net. She had leaned hard on the handle and he hadn't thrashed for long.

She had wiped her hands quickly up and down the handle before putting it in the water next to the man; then she had looked over to the beavers, waded across the canal and through the reeds to them. She could see the mum and dad were dead, their bodies were twisted and they were completely still. She could see that the kit looked as if it was just sleeping, but with no movement. It wasn't breathing. She picked it up and cradled it in the crook of her right arm and pressed the heel of her left thumb against its chest to the beat of a song she remembered. After around thirty seconds it puked water into her face and opened its eyes.

She smiled as she remembered the beaver kit's face, only a foot or so away from her own, and could remember its whimper. She had put it down and she remembered that it had been still as she had waded back across the canal and walked up the bank to the lane. She had looked back and heard it as it had begun to make a haunting cry. It was like nothing she had heard before, like a cross between the cry of a scared calf and the call of a raptor, repeating again and again and she had imagined it running from mother to father and back again. She knew it would be upset for a few days but that the crying would stop soon; and she could see that it was strong enough to get its own food and survive. "Shit", she remembered thinking, "I was left behind when I was only five and on my own and I managed to make it."

Back on the lane she had wiped her feet on the grass, put on the white crocs, picked up her rucksack, and walked quickly but quietly to the barn, where 'Natalie' was waiting. She had peered through one of the windows and had seen that 'Natalie' was wearing a short, flared, red dress and strappy red pumps and was bending over one of the saddles. A red riding crop was leaning by 'Natalie's' side, against the saddle rack.

She had gone straight to the wet room, quietly, and tossed her now wet and smelly dress into the shower cubicle before changing quietly into the stiletto sandals and leaving the crocs by the dress. She had run a finger between her legs and remembered how surprised she had been that she was already damp. Then she had strutted noisily, heels clicking on the concrete floor, over to 'Natalie' who had waited even though she was five minutes late. The others wouldn't be back with Julian for two or three hours, so they had plenty of time, and she knew they wouldn't be disturbed by the overall man even though 'Natalie' didn't.

Afterwards she made sure she was first into the shower and that the water ran straight onto her dress and crocs to clean them up. She would ring out the dress and they would laugh as she set out back to the bike with the dress moulding itself to her body. She knew that on such a hot day it would be dry by the time she got home.

'Natalie' had changed into shorts and T shirt and had waved goodbye before turning back to the stable to go and do something with the horses. She was looking forward to meeting Julian in a couple of days' time, and as she walked past the overall man she wondered if the police would be finished with the canal by then.

They drove into Porthaven and walked into the Harbour Lights looking for the barmaid Amélie, Toby or the landlady. They were unlucky. They hadn't found Toby Brett-Morgan either.

'Oh well let's have a drink and collect our thoughts,' said Treloar pointing at a corner table. Sam went over and sat down. She took the postcards and the guidebook she had bought at Polgwynn out of her bag and spread them across the table, picking up the portrait to study it again. Treloar came over with the drinks.

'Did you know that the name Polgwynn comes from the Cornish meaning white pool in wooded valley?'

'No,' said Treloar putting down a pint of bitter and a cider, 'sounds native American.'

'And look at that,' she said pointing at the postcard, 'by the lake with the flamingos there's a dead tree that looks like a gibbet. Another creepy image. I wonder if there's anything about the painting in here?' She picked up the guidebook and found the right page. 'Well apparently it was a gibbet or scaffold used for hangings and for duckings and it burned down in suspicious circumstances in the early 1800s. Back in 1776 hanging was punishment for anything from theft to murder for men, women and children alike.'

'And ducking was for witches. If you drowned you were innocent and if not you were guilty and hanged,' said Treloar.

'Pub quiz?' asked Sam.

'Superstitious mother, as I told you,' Treloar answered downing a third of his pint. 'And witchcraft covered a multitude of sins including childbirth out of wedlock and healing the sick. And women convicted of petty treason were burned at the stake.'

'Petty treason?'

'Yes, a wife murdering her husband or a female servant her master, was tried for petty treason. Let's call it a day for now, tomorrow I want to call in on the reclusive Dr Brookes at Penmol. Nobody's spoken to him yet.

It had all taken longer than she thought for the police to sort out. They had come round to interview her because they thought he had died round about the time everyone knew she was with 'Natalie'. So she had sat down with them and the fosters and explained that she had seen him doing something with a net as she was leaving and had said hi. The fosters were worried that she might have been upset; she said she wasn't because she hadn't known him, but that it was a shame that someone had accidentally drowned in that way.

When she had logged into the police system she had laughed when she read in the case's official summary that the man was described as being on holiday and as being a novice fisherman. It had said that he had drowned after becoming tangled in his net and falling over. It also made the point that although his net was illegal and unknown to the authorities, because there were no suspicious circumstances the approved fishermen would not be interviewed. 'Natalie' had not liked the man so didn't care that he was dead. 'Natalie' had been over once and they had talked and walked and enjoyed each other's company in the barn for three or four hours. She had spent a lot of time thinking, then sketching, and putting together her new pastiche – 'Eagle and Beaver Confront Bastard in Eldorado'.

Stand facing the sea at the slipway in Porthaven. Turning left and walking eastwards will take you up onto the cliff road and past the large detached houses and on to Point End House. Turning right walking westwards will take you on a very different path. Once past Porth House and the Harbour Lights pub, the road peters out into a rough track which itself dwindles into a path which heads up steeply onto the cliff-top and on to Long Beach and beyond to Deadman's Point. The cliffs are overgrown with ferns and gorse and, on a July day, honeysuckle clambering seawards. Wild foxgloves grow scattered amongst the lush green which extends onwards to the horizon, stretching out into the sea at Deadman's like the paw of a giant velveteen cat. Up here there is but one residence, the large ramshackle house which stands alone at the cliff edge, home to Dr Hugo Brookes: Penmol.

Brookes had been a senior housemaster at an exclusive boys' private school in Surrey until lurid accusations of sexual abuse, albeit unsubstantiated, drove him from office in the nineties. Since then he had lived in isolation at the rambling property on the cliff.

Once part of the Pentreath estate, surrounded by a high wall now poorly maintained and crumbling in parts, Penmol is approached by vehicle via a gated road veering seawards from the main drive to Polgwynn. Treloar had noticed it when he and Sam had visited Polgwynn and had asked Charlie Hendra about the place. They were getting nothing from the door to door in the village and as Penmol stood overlooking the route leading from the beach that he, Treloar, would have taken from the beach that night had he committed the murder. It was worth a try. As Treloar and Sam turned off the main drive and passed through the gate the sky suddenly darkened with storm clouds moving in from the north east. Sam shivered.

'Brrr. There should be a sign: "Beware the Ghosts".'

They drove on through an avenue of overhanging trees emerging into an open space in front of a second high wall with a gatehouse, the gate ajar.

'Christ, were they trying to keep something in or something out?' Treloar laughed.

'It's creepy,' Sam whispered getting out of the car. She walked up to the gate and pushed it open with difficulty for Treloar to drive through. Leaving it open she climbed back into the car. The pot-holed drive continued through overgrown parkland scattered with a variety of mature trees. They drove on curving round until a large chimneyed house came into view with the sea beyond. Treloar pulled up on the weed-strewn, gravelled cobbles opposite a large wooden front door. Sam looked up at the huge dilapidated house with its mullioned windows and crenelated towers.

'*Hammer Horror* or what?' she said.

'Mmm,' Treloar replied, 'he's a very private man according to Charlie Hendra, but he has no record, causes no problems, and is generally respected, if warily. Cornwall is home to many running away from their lives.'

As they were talking, two huge grey wolfhounds rushed up, paws scattering the gravel as they ran from the side of the house.

'Whoah!' cried Sam in alarm but Treloar slowly opened his door and got out of the car holding up his hand in a 'stop' gesture. The dogs skidded to a halt and sat watching him quietly, their tongues lolling from their mouths. A tall man with flowing blond locks who looked to be in his forties appeared in the doorway calling out,

'Donal! Colm!'

'Christ, a bloody Viking,' Treloar said beneath his breath.

The man advanced, hand extended, and as Sam stepped gingerly from the car he broke into a glorious smile which lit his face. Treloar took the man's hand.

'Good afternoon. I am Detective Inspector Treloar and this is my colleague Sergeant Scott. Mr Brookes?'

'Why yes. Good afternoon. How may I help you?' His voice was deep and sonorous with a hint of humour, Sam thought.

'We're investigating the recent death in the village.'

'Ah yes, I've heard something of this. But please, come in, come in.' He turned clicking his fingers to summon the dogs, and led the way inside the house.

She was 19, it had been a Friday in mid-August and she remembered being on the patio at the pub. A good swell was rolling in and it was hot in the sun even with the strong breeze. Most people were watching the surfers and body boarders, and the big fuck you Cougar catamaran that was rolling on the swell the other side of the quay. It was sleek, at least 20 metres, and all white with black windows and portholes. Still wearing the short yellow dress she had been wearing earlier, she had been watching the banker, the wanker from Hong Kong, bragging to his pal, another wanker, who had been at the wheel when he and his wife, who looked about sixteen, had arrived on the catamaran earlier. There had been much braying and back-slapping.

The wife was olive skinned and attractive with shoulder length black hair tied back in a pony tail with a red band; small breasts though, and she remembered thinking the girl was probably Thai. She was wearing a very short red dress that was flared from the thigh, and red plimsols. They were big guys, not unattractive, in their mid to late thirties and in good shape. They were both tanned and they both wore black jeans and white T shirts. They were loud.

She had known that the wanker from Hong Kong was here to make sure his house was finished before his wife and two girls arrived for their summer holiday before the girls went back to boarding school. She knew from the locals that the house had been a not very popular guest house before it was sold, and that the previous owners hadn't been able to maintain it properly. It was big, with three floors and an attic. The house should have been finished by Easter, but there was more work needed than had been planned. She knew that now, the main thing was to finish the 'sea-room' on the top floor. It would look out over the beach to the small rocky islands in the distance. There had been scaffolding all over it and lots of noise for months; the locals were furious, the builders didn't care, and the owner would never understand why people didn't like him.

She knew from speaking to one of the younger builders that a big problem had been that the sea-room floor needed very expensive reconstruction to take the marble tiles that the wife had insisted on. She remembered being told that if it wasn't done the grout would crack. Then he had explained what grout was.

She had been told they had tried it, but it hadn't worked properly because the walls were too thin and not strong enough to take the new supports so they had decided on faux marble panels instead. She remembered that he had looked sceptical when she told him that he didn't need to explain what faux meant. Then he had been impressed when she had said that it meant that they weren't the real thing but looked just like it. He told her they were Italian and hand-made to the interior designer's exact specification and she had seen that about three quarters of them were now fixed in place. She had seen that there were some exposed joists, and some bare floorboards with tools scattered on them along the side that needed finishing. There were a few tools lying underneath the window on the other side, and the polish spray being used to shine the floor panels.

He had been there setting everything up, he said, for the gang when they arrived. When she had seen that he was there she hadn't cared why, she had seen the wanker around and heard him and thought that some knowledge about the house might be useful at some time.

She remembered that if you looked up you could see tarpaulin covering the roof at the end of the house where the sea room was being created. She remembered that there was one piece of plasterboard that had still needed nailing to the ceiling and a few floorboards and the rest of the marble panels needed fixing to the floor. She smiled as she remembered walking up the stairs not far ahead of the builder, who had been really pleased when she had asked if he would show her around. She remembered that she had been wearing the same short, flared, yellow skirt she had been wearing when the new wanker had arrived.

The wanker with the Thai bride had arrived in the fuck you catamaran anchored just outside the small harbour that morning. She had been looking, with binoculars, at gannets diving for fish, way out near the point, when a boat sped round it very quickly with the longest and highest rooster tail she had ever seen, and the birds had scattered. She remembered looking in amazement because although she had seen power boats racing on TV a few times she had never see a boat travelling that fast in real life. The sea had been calm at the time and it had looked as if it had been going faster than a car on a distant motorway. When it had passed in front of the rocks of the small island a mile out in the bay the rooster tail had completely obscured them.

The wanker from Hong Kong had bragged about how much money he had spent on the house, talking about how stupid his wife had been about the marble. He had talked about how easy it had been to con the local council into approving his planning application, and about how fucking stupid the locals must have been not to complain.

He had bragged about how his wife's maid would do anything for him because he had been fucking brilliant and made sure she got a work permit for Hong Kong after he had agreed to his wife's request to get her a passport even though she had no papers. It hadn't cost him that much he had said, and that it had been money well spent to get the regular use of her backside and mouth which his wife still wouldn't let him near. The Cougar prat had nodded knowingly, looked at his wife, who lowered her eyes, then back at him and said that what you could get these Thais to do was fucking amazing.

The Hong Kong wanker had laughed as he had said that he hoped it would rain so his wife and girls would go shopping in Truro, leaving him to catch up with work while the maid "cooked and cleaned".

They entered a dim, dusty hallway which, whilst in fact wide, was cluttered with huge stacks of newspapers and books which covered the floor restricting the width for passage to about three feet. The chandeliers overhead sported mostly empty sockets with an occasional dusty low wattage light bulb accentuating the gloom. As they proceeded down a corridor a dull distant booming echoed around them.

'Alas not a bittern, rather a naval exercise in the bay,' Brookes said.

The uneasy feeling Sam had felt since they had turned off the main drive returned. The voice seemed to come from behind her although Brookes and Treloar were ahead of her surely? She turned instinctively to see that indeed Brookes was following her and spooked, she reached out to grab the hem of Treloar's jacket as they passed through an archway into an enormous shadowy sitting room.

As her eyes adjusted to the gloom she could make out large ugly pieces of old furniture and a grand piano. A filthy Persian carpet covered most of the wooden floor and the walls were half-panelled and largely lined with bookcases. It was a dismal place. Brookes was standing in front of a huge open hearth where a large log was smouldering even in July, perhaps in an attempt to dispel the gloom. The two dogs were flanking him. As she turned to look at Treloar, a second version of Brookes emerged from behind her to join its mirror image at the fire. However, on closer scrutiny this second Brookes was greyer, faded and somehow more insubstantial, but when he spoke his voice was equally powerful and captivating.

'Another Mr Brookes,' said Treloar, 'and which would be Dr Hugo?'

'I am Hugo,' said the more ghostly Brookes, 'and this is my brother Nathaniel, younger by eight minutes.' Hugo Brookes stepped forward to take Treloar's hand and then her own and Sam sensed a quiet sadness emanate from the man. Albeit strikingly handsome like his brother Hugo Brookes seemed somehow defeated. The second Brookes also shook their hands.

'Now how may we help you? I live very quietly here having little contact with the village or the estate. Nate is visiting for a few weeks but he only arrived yesterday. Shall we sit?' They moved to a pair of shabby leather Chesterfields.

'There has been a violent death in the last week and we are speaking to everyone. I appreciate that we are at the height of the season and there are many strangers around but we wondered if you had seen anything or anyone suspicious particularly along the coastal path here, anything that struck you as out of place? It is possible to leave Porthaven via the path, passing close to your house.'

'Well from the upper floors one can see the coastal path running down to Long Beach and then further on to Deadman's Point. There are occasional campers on Long, and walkers of course, but I cannot say that I have seen anything untoward.'

'Hugo, would our guests not like some tea?' asked Nathaniel.

'No, no thank you,' replied Treloar to Sam's annoyance, 'Are you aware of the identity of the victim?'

'No,' said Hugo, 'I understand a summer visitor, but I know no more.'

'Well he was Oliver Osborne a London QC staying with friends and family at Porth House above the beach. Does that name mean anything to either of you?'

The two brothers shook their heads.

'How is it that you come to be living here?' asked Treloar.

'Do you know the history of Penmol?' Hugo said.

'Only that it once formed part of the estate,' Sam replied, eager to contribute something to the conversation.

'Ah well,' said Hugo with a deep sigh, 'it is as sad and tragic a tale as you will encounter. The house was built at the end of the 18th century as a dower house by the incumbent lord of the manor. He particularly disliked his wife and consoled himself in life with the thought that after his death she would be despatched to the cliff edge encircled by high walls far removed from the main house. He named the house Penmol meaning 'bare end' with some irony I like to think. At the turn of the last century the house was not in use as there was no dowager, David Pentreath's grandmother having predeceased her husband. So when it was decided that David's elder brother Howel be 'put away', he raised his fingers to indicate quotation marks, 'Penmol was the ideal place.'

'Put away?' queried Sam.

'Yes,' Hugo continued, 'Howel suffered from a neurological weakness, what we would probably now determine as a form of autism, but then a secret and shameful thing. Lady Pentreath, the boys' mother, decided that Howel should be banished to Penmol at the age of eight with a loyal nanny and suitable servants. She forbade anyone to visit or speak of him again. It was as if the boy had never been.

'How terrible,' said Sam.

'But not uncommon alas, yet there is a brief light in the darkness. David Pentreath defied his mother, visiting Howel in secret. The poor boy adored his younger brother. But then our story turns to tragedy. One day ten years after his incarceration David and Howel had been walking in the garden and on his departure David forgot to lock the gate on the seaward side of the wall. Howel got out and with his first true taste of freedom ran laughing along the cliff path. David realised his dreadful mistake and chased after him calling out his name. But Howel kept running, for the first time in years he knew no boundaries, and he went straight over the edge falling onto the rocks below, dying where he fell.'

'Brother's Leap,' murmured Treloar, 'I saw the name on the map.'

'Yes Inspector,' that point on the cliffs has since been known by that name. On that day, having turned her face against Howel, Lady Pentreath now turned her face against David. She never spoke his name again. Sadly David was devastated and it is said that ultimately the tragedy drove him to drink, debauchery and ruin. And ironically that is also how I come to occupy this house. It was not sold with the rest of the estate when the bank foreclosed and remained the property of the family. Our grandfather won Penmol in a card game with David Pentreath in Paris in the thirties.'

'So, every cloud ...?' Nathaniel smiled but he was alone in doing so.

'And you arrived yesterday Sir?' Treloar asked coldly. He had taken an instant dislike to the charming, debonair Nathaniel Brookes with his insouciant, bemused air.

'Indeed Inspector. Just staying with bro' for a couple of weeks between trips.'

'Trips?'

'Yes Nathaniel travels the world 'facilitating',' said Hugo again stressing the word with raised index fingers.

'Yes, I find solutions; bring people and projects together, troubleshoot situations. It sounds exciting, globetrotting, but it's really quite mundane and international travel can be extraordinarily tedious I assure you.'

'So you have nothing to tell us that can help with our investigations,' Treloar stated.

'Well no, I suppose not,' he seemed put out at being dismissed as immaterial.

'And I fear I cannot help either Inspector. As I have said, I have seen nothing unusual in the last week and I have not visited the village in over a month. If there is nothing else please allow me to show you out.' With that he stood and motioned them from the room.

Treloar rose and Sam walked to the front door. 'If we have further questions for you Dr Brookes we will be back, but thank you for your time today.'

She had been sketching and writing on a plain white card as she listened to the wankers' table making the occasional contribution to the general blur of conversations that drifted in and out between the tables. She had disappeared for a while after smiling as an idea had dawned, but when she sat down in the same seat on her return no-one seemed to have noticed she had been away. She had carried on sketching. She hadn't been back for long when the Cougar prat had said cheerio to the Hong Kong wanker, after first using his mobile to try and book a hotel room. No deal, it had been high season and everywhere was full. He had rung the Trengissey harbour master and booked a berth, saying he would be there within the hour. Then he told Hong Kong wanker that he needed to get through the surf while the RIB could still make it. A summer storm was brewing.

She had been surprised how effortlessly he had lifted his wife into it, and not at all surprised when she saw several people on the beach telling him to get in too, clearly offering to push the RIB out. He had started the engine then expertly guided the RIB through the surf and although the front had seemed to be out of the water and pointing straight at the sky a few times it always landed the right way up and carried on. As it moved out of the surf and round the end of the quay and began moving over the swell people on the beach had applauded. Not long afterwards the same people had shaken their heads in disbelief and some had applauded again as a few seconds after the catamaran engine had started the rooster tail had appeared and was huge in just two or three seconds. The boat seemed to move like a rocket with a noise to suit. Less than two minutes later it had disappeared round the point.

While everyone had been admiring the boat's departure she had walked over to the Hong Kong wanker and given him the card she had she had worked on. Then she had walked to the seat next to the one she had been at, now without the table between them. She smiled as she remembered his surprise when he saw a sketched pussy, close up, as seen from between the legs of a prone woman. They were spread widely with the knees raised. A tattoo of a diamond patterned snake ran down to her pussy from just above the left thigh. Its head couldn't be seen.

Underneath the sketch she had written PTO, so he did; then he had read the instructions. Just as he had finished reading he looked up at her and watched as she had slowly and flamboyantly uncrossed and re-crossed her legs. She had seen the surprise on his face as he had realised that she had revealed, for a short and tantalising time, that she had sketched herself. She had smiled as she was now certain how good the liquid latex snake had really looked.

What she knew he had seen as an erotic but painful tattoo was really the quickly, but carefully, painted latex snake she had created when she had left unnoticed earlier. With ten minutes for each of the black, then yellow, then red coats to dry it had taken three quarters of an hour, and she had been keen to get back before she was missed. She hadn't had a chance to see the finished article properly in the mirror.

She had slightly tipped her head to one side and raised her eyebrows in question, and after about two seconds thought he had nodded. She had nodded back and smiled. Then she stood up and walked over and retrieved the card; then she had put a finger to her lips and, looking at him, and gone sshh.

Well what did you make of those two?' asked Treloar as they drove back to the main Polgwynn road.

'Hugo seemed rather sad I thought but Nathaniel, well he was really very charming,' Sam replied with a grin.

'Huh,' Treloar grunted, 'certainly fancied himself with his posy dogs.'

'Well I rather liked him. But seriously, I don't think they can shine any light on the murder. If the Irish police records match those prints on the knife to Truelove I think that's it. It'll be back to drunken holidaying teenagers disturbing the Newquay peace for us.'

'You sound almost wistful Sam,' said Treloar answering his mobile.

Within hours Sam would rue her statement and never again doubt the folly of tempting fate.

She had known that he had heard her red stiletto pumps clacking on the still to be carpeted stairs on her way up to the third floor because he was looking towards the door as she had walked through it; he shouldn't have been. He was standing exactly where she had instructed, naked, feet one metre apart, hands by his side, facing the window and one metre from it. There was no light on.

His eyes had widened as she had stepped, high heels clicking on what he would have called the marble flooring, towards him. She saw that he recognised the snake curling down from her thigh as he had looked, nervously. Then she saw him relax and look forward, as he should have been. Her jeans, sweatshirt, and sandals were downstairs next to the door she had locked after walking in from the wind and the sound of the waves breaking noisily against the slipway and sea wall. It had been light outside but gloomy because of the storm, and the only people about were either riding the waves or on the viewing area above the beach watching them because the tide was right in and the beach had disappeared.

All she had been wearing apart from the red stiletto pumps was a black, latex, full face mask that extended down to the top of her neck and round the back of her head where it was tightly laced to keep her hair completely hidden; and elbow length black latex gloves.

The hand that he had seen as she stepped through the door had been holding the ball gag he had been expecting; the other which had been behind her back was holding silver grey duct tape. By the time she was standing just in front of him he was completely erect and she had smiled, bent down, and gently blown. Then she had walked round

208

behind him, told him to put his hands behind his back and then she had put the duct tape on the floor well behind him. She had reached up after telling him to open his mouth wide, then reached round with her left hand and put the gag into it then she had drawn the straps together before fastening them tightly at the back of his head. She had made sure that he felt her hardened nipples grazing upwards on his back as she carefully leaned in and reached up in order to fasten the gag securely.

She had told him to lay on the floor, leaving his feet exactly where they were, then to stretch his arms 'above' his head with the palms of his hands facing upwards. When he was in place she had squatted over him while looking into his eyes, which were beginning to look desperate. She stood and moved until she was standing between his legs, looking away from him and out of the window, then reached down and grasped her ankles. As she looked back through her legs she had seen that his head was raised so that he could see her; it shouldn't have been. She stood up, turned round and by the time she was wagging her finger at him and shaking her head she had seen that he was looking at her but his head was back on the floor.

She had smiled at him and pouted as she walked to the duct tape, peeled a length off the reel and wrapped it round his left wrist, making sure the tape was running underneath the back of his hand before peeling another metre off as she moved towards one of the bare joists. Then she had wrapped the reel round the joist three times, reached for the knife and cut the tape. She then taped his right wrist to the joist in the same way, walked until she stood with her legs apart either side of his shoulders squatted again. She had looked down and stood up quickly as he lifted his head again. By the time she was looking at him and wagging her finger and shaking her head at him again his head was back on the ground.

She had then walked back to pick up the duct tape and knife, then one metre from the right side of his head she had reeled off a short length of tape and stuck it to the smooth 'marble' and reeled it out pressing it to the floor as she went, then lifted it over his forehead pressing it down and sticking it as she went, then back down to the floor and out to a metre on the left side of his head before cutting it and putting the reel down. Then she had made sure it was stuck to the floor by rubbing it with her finger tips right along its length.

Then she had walked until she was standing between his legs and put the finger tips of each hand, which she had known would be warm from the friction of rubbing the tape, around his erection. She stood up, walked round so her feet were either side of his shoulders and he would have been able to see the latex snake's body glistening, as she worked her pelvic floor muscles, before standing up, looking into his pleading eyes.

She walked back until she was standing between his legs, knelt on the floor and bent slowly towards him, then reached behind to pick up the nail gun which she knew was lying on the floor against the wall under the window, and shot a round head nail through his left foot. Then she had moved quickly to fire another through his right foot before he had the chance to register the pain and wonder what was happening.

Then, she had walked past him and knew that he was trying to scream but couldn't because of the ball gag and carried on walking until she was standing over his right arm close to the shoulder so he was able to see her, snake and all, then bent down and fired again, through his right wrist just above the duct tape, before moving to stand above the left arm, bend down and do it again. She had heard the young builder talking about the Bostitch nail gun in the pub, how it was the latest - very light, no need for a cable and could fire nails up to 90mm long to any depth needed. He had said that it was loaded with round head nails at the moment so they could finish off the last bit of roof. She had looked it up on the Internet and checked out the instructions in the user manual.

After standing and moving to the side of his head, she could see that he was straining in pain to try and lift himself from the floor. She had smiled as he was failing completely. His eyes were open, bulging and he could still see the snake. He had looked shocked and was still trying to make a noise; "noooooooooo" she had thought he was probably trying to shout. She had altered the depth gauge, then put the nail gun close to his left eye, it had still been open, and fired; it quickly filled with mushy blood. A few slimy red tears slid to the floor. She remembered that the muffled screaming had stopped immediately and that his right eye had bulged and stared straight up, unmoving. For good measure and completeness though, she had put the nail gun close to it and fired again.

She smiled as she remembered how calmly she had stood for a few seconds listening to the wind battering the tarpaulin and the waves crashing, before putting the nail gun back at the base of the wall, then using the knife to cut the tape from the wrists and joists. Then she had pulled the tape from the floor and his forehead before putting the knife where she had found it and balled the tape together.

She had sprayed the wrists, right round, with the floor polish, which she knew contained a solvent that 'would dissolve anything' to dissolve any adhesive that may have been left from the tape, then did the same with his forehead and the floor where the tape had been. Then she had taken a clean cloth from a packet that had been next to the polish and polished the floor where the tape had been. The rest would evaporate.

Then she had dropped the cloth on the floor near the window, picked up the roll of tape, walked back to the ground floor and removed the mask, taken off her stiletto pumps and put her jeans, sweatshirt and sandals back on. Then she had opened the rucksack and dropped in the roll of tape and mask, unlocked the door and walked out into the wind, closing the door behind her. Then she had taken off her gloves and put them in the rucksack before fastening it, and dropped the balled up duct tape into the first litter bin she came to, which she knew would be emptied first thing the next morning, just like every day at that time of the year.

'I don't believe this,' said Treloar closing his mobile phone as they drove into the village.

'What?' asked Sam.

'There's another body in Porthaven. Trader of some sort called Christopher Bond. Naked, tied spread-eagled, eyes put out, nail-gunned to the floor, top storey of his newly refurbished holiday home. Happened last night.'

'Christ.'

'Yeah. You spoke too soon.'

'Someone's really got it in for the grockles this year,' Sam said.

Treloar, Sam and Dr Tremayne were standing in the kitchen of Mermaids, Christopher Bond's newly refurbished holiday home on Chapel Hill. Formerly the property had been the Mermaid Tavern but it had closed as a pub in the fifties since when it had been a rather shabby guesthouse up until Bond's recent purchase. He had hired a local design firm famed for their work with celebrity chefs acquiring Cornish venues, and had given them a free hand and apparently limitless budget with the vague briefing 'modern seaside'. Consequently there was a lot of driftwood and washed out shades of blue and yellow.

'Emmetts, Sam. Grockles in Devon, emmetts in Cornwall,' said Dr Tremayne, 'could be an extreme faction of Merbyon Kernow, but they'd probably just poison the pasties.'

'This is personal again,' said Treloar 'but these are not stupid men. How is he doing this and what is the connection? We're missing something. It has to be the same killer; the scenes are too alike, too staged. If it is Thomas Truelove how the hell does he know this bloke?

213

The victims must be linked somehow. How does Julia Osborne fit in?'

Sam ticked the points off on her fingers. 'Well they're both men, both rich, both from London, albeit one via Hong Kong, and from what I can gather both utter shits. We know Truelove was here again. He could have done this.'

'Maybe that's it,' said Treloar. 'Perhaps they were both shitty to the same person and that person took offense big time, perhaps Truelove came to do Osborne and came across Bond. What are the chances of two unrelated individuals both visiting, both pissing off the same person in the brief time they were here to such an extent that he slaughtered them? Unless we have a visiting psychopath. Bloody tourism.'

'Well, psychopaths need holidays too,' said Tremayne with a smile.

Sergeant Colin Andrews walked down the open staircase to join them peeling off his latex gloves.

'Nasty way to go.'

'Very,' said Tremayne, 'first nail to the head probably killed him. He wouldn't have felt it but of course he would have seen it coming. That's probably when he lost control of his bladder.'

'So what do we think?' asked Treloar.

'Well, according to Charlie Hendra,' said Andrews, 'he was a total letch, always ogling and pawing any female he could get near.'

'Sounds remarkably like Osborne,' Sam commented.

'Yeah, and definitely no hint of anything homosexual,' Andrews continued, 'so either he was forced to lie down, say at gunpoint, or he volunteered. If he was willing, there must have been a woman involved. Perhaps she lured him, got him into position then called in her accomplice who did the deed. A woman working with Truelove?'

'Or a woman acting alone,' said Sam.

'Or an acrobatic troupe from the local circus? Christ knows, we certainly don't,' muttered Treloar. 'It has to be connected to Osborne, has to be. Things like this don't happen here, and now we have two similar killings within days. Has to be the same guy.'

'Or gal,' added Sam.

'You seem fixed on a female suspect Sergeant,' said Tremayne, 'surely such grizzly acts are unlikely to be the work of the fairer sex?'

'Why not? Once he was down he would be at her mercy. If she had enough rage, if he'd really pissed her off or done her wrong or threatened her or cheated on her, I can think of lots of reasons a woman might want a man like him dead. I admit the nail business would take some balls if you'll excuse the expression, but maybe it just came to hand and it was bloody effective,' Sam said.

'Indeed it was,' the doctor agreed, smiling.

'Yes, OK, but if we all agree we're looking at the same killer, and we rule out Truelove because he's not a woman, how could one woman be so enraged by two separate men?' asked Treloar.

'Well, equally, how could one man be? Unless he was paid of course but if it's a contract it's extraordinarily overcomplicated and contrived. Why not just shoot them or slit their throats?' Sam was on a roll. 'No. A woman is involved somehow, trust me.'

'I see what Sam means,' said Andrews nodding his head, 'it does feel very vindictive, woman scorned, a bit Bobbitt. What about the wives?'

'Which wife, Treloar was sounding irritated, 'the ditzy blonde or the Hong Kong matron or maybe they acted together, even though they've never met? Come on people get real. It's not the wives. We need to find the connection between Bond and Osborne.'

'Well good luck my sweet ones, I must love and leave you,' said Tremayne picking up his bag from the marble worktop.

'Cheers, Doc,' said Andrews whilst Sam waved and Treloar raised a hand.

'Thanks Doc. Right let's get out of here and back up the road you two. I want to go over everything and everyone. Like the advice Dave Robicheaux's father gave him in a James Lee Burke novel: when you searched the whole marsh for the bull 'gator that ate your hog and you haven't found him, go back and start again because you've walked right over him.'

She remembered it had been almost quiet outside when she woke at around 6.00am, satisfied. When she had put her head out of the window she had seen and heard that the storm had blown over but its tail end was there as a strong onshore breeze. It had been a bright morning which she knew would warm quickly and she had decided to go out later to look at the Peregrine falcons she knew would be hovering in the wind, as it flowed up and over the cliff, while they waited for prey. It was birds and rabbits up there mostly. They were nearly as beautiful as the Lanner she remembered from the hospital roof years ago. Sometimes there would be buzzards, but they were bigger and less agile and preferred the cliff top on calmer days.

She remembered that that morning she had dressed in dark blue denim jeans, the Meindl Lady Lite boots which she still wore, and a yellow sweat shirt. Her hair had been tied in a pony tail and her binoculars had hung from the strap over her left shoulder. She was walking up the road and about to turn left up the very steep, narrow hill that led to the gated cliff road when she had noticed a seagull intently pecking at something on the road.

She had heard the throaty rumble of a car behind her and stopped walking, standing instead close to the brambles at the side of the road. As the car slowed and rumbled past she saw that it was a grey Porsche Boxter with the roof off, and that it had a German number plate. 'Bastards', she had thought. It was being driven by a blond haired man and there was a dark haired woman passenger. After passing her the car accelerated quickly with a squeal of tyres, leaving blue smoke drifting behind, straight at the seagull before it had a chance to take off. She had heard the woman's roar of laughter through the rumble of the car as it had turned left to go up the hill.

She had seen one of its wings flapping uselessly and when she got closer she could see that the other was flattened on the road, and that the rear half of its body was squashed. She could hear the gull trying to make its distress call but it was stuck in its throat and came out through its quivering beak, from which blood was seeping, as a high pitched burble; Her eyes had watered, and tears had rolled down her cheeks. For a while she wasn't sure what to do as she had looked around. There was nobody else in sight, nor were there any sticks or handy bricks or stones. So, she had walked up to the gull and stamped hard on its head. It had become still and quiet straight away. She was seething, tearful, and for a while she still wasn't sure what to do.

Then she had remembered walking past someone digging in a garden and walked back and asked if she could borrow his spade, explaining that she wanted to move a dead bird from the road. He had looked surprised and then bemused but handed it to her without question. She had scooped the seagull from the road and tipped it over a fence into long grass by the side of the stream which ran by the side of the road. Then she had taken the spade back and thanked the man. He had surreptitiously inspected it and looked relieved that all he could see on it was soil. Then she had thought she might as well go back to plan A and cheer herself up by going up to the cliff road to look at the raptors.

In the hope of minimising the impact of the police's comings and goings - all those patrol cars driving up and down the hill, cluttering the lanes and unsettling the visitors - the estate's PR people had suggested the loan of one of the larger properties as a base for the investigation. Consequently the team were occupying Hillside, a large house set in a large garden half way up the hill, currently undergoing redecoration and major roof works and thus vacant. It was ideal as it had an enormous knocked through kitchen and dining area the length of the ground floor, three smaller living rooms on the first floor and several bathrooms. Only the second floor was unusable as the workmen had installed their roofing materials and tools and there were tarpaulins and plastic sheeting everywhere. Needless to say the workmen had withdrawn for the duration. All in all the team were very happy with their accommodation which saved them the journey to and from their various bases. As they turned into the drive Treloar noticed a Volvo estate parked in the driveway.

'Shit - that's all we need - our esteemed leader.' The car belonged to Detective Superintendent Suzanne Winters. 'Come on follow me. We're on foot and we may just get away with it. Anyway it's a nice day and the fresh air is good for the brain,' Treloar swerved off the gravel drive behind a row of large rhododendrons onto a narrow path which led down the garden to a paved sheltered patio with a 10 metre swimming pool, an incongruous striped beach hut and a set of heavy wooden garden furniture.

'Shouldn't we check in?' asked Andrews nervously.

'No. We came in through that gate there,' Sam pointed to a tall green metal gate below them at the bottom of the garden which opened onto the road, 'we didn't see her car, we don't know she's here.' Sam shared Treloar's antipathy towards Winters albeit for a very different reason. Whilst he found her overly obsessed with procedure and regulations Sam had received an unfortunate proposition of a sexual nature from her at a Christmas party and since had avoided her at every opportunity. Only Treloar knew of this.

'OK,' said Andrews outnumbered and outranked, 'I'll put up the umbrella.'

'Shame there's not waitress service,' said Treloar sitting and stretching out his long legs, his hands clasped behind his head.

'So, where do you want to start?' asked Sam sitting next to him whilst Andrews drew up a chair opposite facing uphill towards the house.

'I'll keep an eye open,' he said sheepishly.

'Sam. You've got the fastest handwriting, you keep notes. Let's start with a timeline from The Porth House set arriving up to today with the finding of Bond's body. We'll note down what we know and that should highlight what we don't, talking of which,' he glanced at Sam's spiral notebook, 'you're gonna need a bigger book.'

On the way up the hill a few people had driven up past her, and she knew that most would be turning into the National Trust car park, about three hundred metres before the gate, to park up before their passengers walked to the coastal path. She was glad she had worn her jeans because the road was so narrow that she had had to stop and lean right into the brambles for the cars to get past. One car, a black Mini Cooper S driven by a woman with red hair, and two kids on bikes had come down the hill. It had taken around half an hour to get to the gate across the single track road and even before she had reached it she had seen the birds, hovering in the breeze in the distance, facing seawards, scanning the ground. Maybe six or seven, just inland from the cliff top, about 30 metres from the road. She had thought she would sit on the edge of the old stone horse trough that she knew was next to the wall set back from the road and watch them.

She had just closed the gate behind her, after smiling at the notice informing would-be pilots that the road was not to be used as a runway, when she caught sight of the bumper of a car behind the edge of a gateless opening into the first field, the opposite side of the road to the cliff, and she was instinctively curious. As she got closer and heard an excited female voice throatily telling someone what to do, she recognised the colour of the car and knew it was the German couple and their Boxter.

As she walked through the gate and round to the far side of the car she had seen the woman, naked, kneeling astride the man's face, rubbing herself over his mouth and nose and clearly getting a great deal of pleasure. The woman saw her, stopped and sneered, then spat, "Also, Perversling, willst du mitmachen?" She hadn't wanted to join in but she had smiled as she had had an idea so she had replied "Später, wo übernachten sie?"

The woman had been amazed that she had not been embarrassed and turned and walked off, and was completely taken aback when she had said that she would join them later and asked where they were staying. Then the woman had laughed and told her that they were staying at the only hotel in the village in room Tresco, and to arrive at 8.00 that evening.

She had nodded and smiled, then walked up to the woman, and in a flash quickly took her left nipple between the thumb and forefinger of her right hand and squeezed it hard. Her mind was racing. She was sure she could get the bastards, and already had the beginnings of a plan. After a few minutes of perching against the old horse trough she had realised she was looking through the birds and not really seeing them, not really looking at them. She needed to plan and organise herself properly, so she left.

Overnight it had rained heavily. After the deluge the vegetation looked bruised and battered. The daisies in their terracotta troughs outside Porthaven Stores huddled together like miserable refugees. Small sandbanks had formed in the road as the rain had driven the blown summer sand downhill to catch against manhole covers and ridges in the tarmac.

Sam opened the passenger door of Treloar's Land Rover and tossed the bag of sandwiches and soft drinks over onto the back seat. 'There wasn't much choice I'm afraid so it's cheese and onion again for you.'

'No problem.'

'So Dr Brookes knew Christopher Bond. He taught him. He was at the school when Brookes had his little difficulty.' They were on there way up to Penmol again. Colin Andrews had discovered the school link. As they left the main drive to Polgwynn to turn towards Penmol Sam felt the same uneasy feeling she had on their first visit.

'Yes I remember him,' said Hugo Brookes. 'But he was not known as Christopher. He was Leonard to the staff, Leo to his peers and acolytes.'

They were sitting in the back garden where they had found Brookes at a huge worn wooden table reading a battered Evelyn Waugh paperback. There was no sign of Nathaniel or the dogs.

'What kind of boy was he?' asked Sam.

'He was a leader. He had a group of boys who worshipped him. It was one of those boys, Dominic Wells, who made the allegations against me.   There was speculation that Bond had put him up to it. What did you say he became, a trader? Yes I can imagine that suiting his psychology: arrogant, vain, ruthless, greedy, driven and dominating. I can imagine him chasing the big bucks. And he was a wanton boy; cruel and lewd. I can imagine him being sexually obsessed.'

'Was he homosexual?' asked Treloar.

'Oh no, far from it. He was always chasing after girls in the village, it became quite an issue. No he wasn't homosexual, but I can see him manipulating his followers sexually. Forcing them to fellate him and each other; watching them perform for him. Oh yes he was a warped, nasty boy.'

Treloar's mobile buzzed and he glanced at the display. Rising from the table he spoke, 'Excuse me, I need to take this,' and he strode deeper into the garden.

'Your brother is not here today?' asked Sam as her eyes followed Treloar.

'No, Nate is out of the country. He left shortly after your visit yesterday. Purely coincidental I assure you; an urgent summons from an important client. He travels for his work as I believe he mentioned. I expect you'll be asking where I was at the time of Bond's demise. I assume that is the reason for your visit. Well, I was here, alone, as I am most nights. I did not know that Bond had bought the property in the village. I would not have recognised him as Christopher, as I have said, and Bond is not an uncommon name. I have not seen him since his schooldays, not to my knowledge. I have not been to the village, indeed I have not left the house and grounds for over a month, as I believe I have already stated.'

'You will appreciate that given your previous connection with the deceased and the nature of that connection we are obliged to ask.'

'Oh yes. I understand. But this is pure coincidence I assure you.'

'OK which way now?'

Treloar was driving Sam home from a meeting at the station with DS Winters at which very little had been achieved apart from the reinforcement of Treloar's very low opinion of Winters as a detective, a superior officer and a human being.

'Turn left at the end and it's the second on the left. Thanks for this, I would have walked.'

'Don't be ridiculous; it's no trouble,' Treloar snapped. 'Sorry Sam; that bloody woman brings out the worst in me. Did you hear her? "Deal with your problems Inspector before you make them mine." '

'I know what you mean. She's insecure and she feels the need to exert her authority to bolster her self esteem. A lot of woman in authority are like that. It's as if they don't believe they deserve to be there. Of course in her case she's right,' Sam laughed.

Sam Scott lived in the upper flat of a large white Georgian house situated in a road overlooking the city. It was within easy walking distance of the police station and she had left her car at home that day.

Treloar turned into the road and pulled up where Sam indicated. They were alongside a tall privet hedge and a high wall with two large stone gateposts. A gravel drive swept round in front of the house and back out to the road some fifty yards further down the road.

'Nice place. I'll see you to the door.'

They got out of the Land Rover and scrunched up the drive. To their right was a bank of flowering hydrangeas, to their left several cars were parked against a ten foot high side wall. Treloar looked up at the imposing property. The house was double fronted with huge bay windows on the ground and first floors. A row of large terracotta pots containing agapanthus flanked steps to the front. They climbed the steps to the imposing red gloss front door and he noticed two brass name plates with push bells illuminated by a carriage lamp. As Sam fished for her keys in her handbag a car door slammed behind them and they both turned instinctively. The furthest car parked against the wall was a dark TVR and stumbling from it towards them across the gravel was a tall well built man.

'Fuck,' said Sam beneath her breath.

'Well, well, well, didn't take the saintly Sam long to move on did it?' the man spoke in a deep voice with a slight slur but no noticeable accent other than that of privilege it seemed to Treloar.

'What are you doing here Adam?' Sam spoke softly and slowly as if to a child.

'Just wanted to see my darling ex, make sure she's not broken hearted,' he was swaying and clutching a bottle of whisky in his left hand whilst he gesticulated with his right as he spoke, 'and who have we here then, some handsome, lusty yokel who knows how to satisfy a maiden?'

Sam sensed Treloar bristle and placed her hand on his arm as she answered.

'This, Adam, is my boss Detective Inspector Félipe Treloar, and this, Inspector is my *former* fiancé, Adam Hanbury.'

Treloar looked at Hanbury and spoke. 'I trust you do not intend to drive that vehicle in your current state of intoxication Mr Hanbury?'

Adam staggered backwards and bellowed, 'Don't you dare speak to me like that! Do you know who my father is?'

'No I'm afraid not, and I'm very sorry to hear that you don't. Perhaps you could ask your mother?' Treloar could not resist the remark and was not ungratified when he heard Sam stifle a laugh, 'now may I suggest we call a taxi for you or would you prefer to be arrested for causing a disturbance?'

Adam sneered at them, turned on his heel and staggered off across the drive and through the stone gates. As they turned back to the door they heard a bottle smashing on the pavement.

'Should I go after him?' Treloar asked; a question he would reflect upon with bitter regret within hours.

'No. Leave him. He'll be fine. He leads a charmed life, even when he's drunk. It's as if he has a guardian angel watching over him. I've never known him come to harm and he is not my responsibility anymore, thank God. Would you like to come up for a coffee?'

'Thanks, I'd love one.'

'I can't promise it'll be as good as yours though.'

They entered the house and climbed a wide wooden staircase to the first floor where Sam unlocked a second red gloss door.

'Come in.'

Sam switched on the lights and led the way down a hallway with vibrant apple green painted walls. She opened a door on her right and showed Treloar into a large spacious room with a huge bay window. He would later look back and recall his first impressions of this room. The lights of the city stretched out below filled the room with a pale glow before the overhead light came on and illuminated the room. Treloar looked around him. In stark contrast with the hallway the walls and high ceiling were painted in an icy white. The floor was polished wood with a large rectangular seagrass rug positioned in the centre of the room. The furniture was a mix of antique and modern; an old wooden dresser with shelves of mismatched plates, a grandfather clock with a mellow tick and small rolled top desk contrasted with cream leather stressless chairs, a large square pine coffee table and a four seater sofa covered in rust coloured canvas with vivid striped and spotted cushions in primary colours. One wall was lined with fitted shelving full of books, the opposite housed a large open fireplace with a tiled surround and wooden mantelpiece. It was a comfortable, peaceful room, pleasantly cool and delicately scented by a glass vase of roses which stood on the coffee table.

'Coffee,' Sam walked in with a tray bearing two mugs and a plate of cookies. She placed the tray on the table and sat on the sofa. Treloar took one of the chairs opposite.

'Who is his father anyway?' he asked.

'You've heard of Hanbury Telecom? Well that's Adam's father: Tim Hanbury.'

Treloar whistled through his teeth. 'OK. Plenty of money then, shame about the manners.'

Sam handed him a mug. 'Oh he's not bad when he's sober, just a total prat when he's drunk. He does this from time to time: just turns up on my doorstep proclaiming undying love and seeking forgiveness. Strangely, he didn't declare his feelings tonight, but I suppose your presence put him off. He's basically harmless and can be very sweet. I was engaged to him after all, and I like to think I'm not a complete idiot when it comes to judging character. If he remembers saying that about his father he'll be really embarrassed. He shouldn't drink like that he's diabetic, but no one can tell him anything. He listens to no one, not even his father. Anyway Tim thinks that's a sign of strength, of will, but he's always spoiled Adam, always. It's been the ruin of him. And as for his mother… well, don't get me started. She worships Adam, idolizes him. It's positively unhealthy.'

'So, what happened to end it? I take it from what he said that it was your call.'

'Yes. We were living in Bristol, it was before my promotion and transfer, and I came home unexpectedly one afternoon and found Adam with one of our neighbours naked on the sitting room floor, giggling and rolling around amongst several empty wine bottles.'

'I see.'

'It wasn't that I cared that was the shock, it was that I didn't care and that's what made me realise we were finished. He was very apologetic, floods of tears and pleas for forgiveness, going on and on about how it was just one drunken mistake, but it was to no avail. I knew I didn't love him, in fact I didn't even like him anymore. So I applied for the transfer and here I am.'

'Well, Bristol's loss is our gain,' Treloar smiled at her and Sam felt the colour rising in her cheeks.

'Anyway, what do you think about Winters' ideas?' she asked, quickly moving onto safer ground. She was becoming disconcerted by her feelings around this man.

Wearing baggy, knee length, blue denim shorts, a red T shirt, and blue elasticated slip-on plimsolls, with her trusty rucksack over her shoulder, she had climbed the outside staircase to the fire door on the first floor of the hotel. She had been pleased that she had been right about it being open; she had known that the hotel air conditioning was proving unreliable that summer and that because it had been a warm day there was a good chance that the door would have been propped open to create a through draft. Just before 8.00pm most residents would have been in the bar or restaurant she had thought so she had decided to surprise the German couple to gain the upper hand quickly.

Just inside the door, almost pulled to, it had been dark at the end of the corridor. She had quickly slipped out of her shorts, T shirt and plimsolls, reached into the rucksack and retrieved, put on and tied the black latex hood, taken out and pulled on the freshly powdered and polished black latex gloves, and lastly taken out and slipped on the red stiletto pumps. She was wearing nothing else.

Then she had removed the hammer, chisel, knife and duct tape from the rucksack, folded the shorts and T shirt and laid them at the bottom and put the plimsolls, upside down, on top of the clothes. Then she had carefully replaced her tools so they would be easily accessible when they were needed. Folding the top of the rucksack over but not fastening it, then unfastening the pocket with the thin rubber blanket folded inside, she had picked it up and walked quickly down the corridor to room Tresco and knocked.

"Herein!" the woman called, so she opened and went

through the door and the woman looked at her and laughed throatily. The man, on his hands and knees on the bed with the woman underneath him with her head on a pillow, had turned and stared, while the woman had smiled.

Looking round the room and seeing the sex toys laid out neatly on the desk, she had looked again at the German couple and realised that it was going to be easier than she could possibly have imagined, and turned, put the rucksack down and locked the door.

The man was struggling to bend his head as fully as he needed to because it's movement was restricted by stainless steel nose hooks, which were holding in place small hollow nose plugs. The hooks were attached to a leather strap which stretched back over his head and was attached securely to a leather collar, at the back of his neck.

She had walked to the side of the bed, smiled at the woman, then squeezed her left nipple hard, then harder, and twisted it before letting it go. It was still swollen and coloured from that morning. The woman had gasped, looked at her, then smiled again.

She picked up a shiny metal spreader bar from the desk, there had been two, each with integral straps at each end, walked back to the bed and strapped the man's ankles to it. They had been either side of the woman's head and just behind it. She had had to pull the foot nearest to her about half a metre to secure the second strap. The man had yelped.

She went back to the desk and took the second spreader bar and attached the woman's right ankle to it then leaned on the bed and reached to squeeze the woman's right nipple, hard. The woman had sighed as she had released it; she smiled as she remembered being pleased that the plan was working and that her assumptions about desire and control had been spot on. She had then fastened the woman's left ankle to the bar. Her feet were now a metre apart. She then slipped a latex gloved finger across the woman's lips and the woman had sighed.

Then she went back to the desk and picked up two pairs of handcuffs, cuffed the man's left wrist to the woman's left ankle and then his right wrist to her right ankle. With his arms stretched out in front of him and hands wide apart he was trying hard to avoid collapsing, although his backside was now humping up and down.

She went back to the desk and picked up a length of soft rope, walked back and tied one end round the woman's left elbow before pushing the other end underneath her back. She had walked round the bed to the other side, pulled the rope and tied it round her right elbow, so that the woman's arms were held tightly into her sides. She had reached between the woman's legs again and this time pushed two gloved fingers into her and wriggled their tips. The woman had moaned again, more loudly.

She went back to the desk and admired the collection of dildos. There were latex ones, glass ones, black ones, red ones, a fine collection. She looked back to the writhing couple on the bed and listened to the groans and smiled and then picked up the tie on dildo which was red, and quite thick.

Afterwards when they were still she could remember looking at them, to take it in for a couple of minutes, pleased with herself, thinking back to how cruel they had been. She had then carefully removed her mask and pumps, putting them in the rucksack after removing and donning the shorts, T shirt, and plimsolls. She had then left the room and closed the door after wiping the base of the man's back with a face cloth she had dampened after finding it in the bathroom, then flushing it down the toilet. Once outside the fire door she had removed her gloves, put them in the rucksack and fastened it then walked down the staircase, though the car park and away from the hotel, content.

'Well this is not at all bad. If you are going to die violently I can think of far worse places; grubby cellars, underground car parks, derelict buildings, no this is definitely five star; la crème de la crime scene. Do you think they'd send up some Earl Grey?' Dr Tremayne was his usual laconic self.

'Jesus Tony, if you had to find this bastard you wouldn't be so flippant,' Treloar snarled.

'Now then Phil, I have always found a little levity in the face of atrocity helps keep one's sanity.' Treloar closed his eyes and shook his head.

At one point in the late fifties Porthaven had boasted a thriving local business and social community: two pubs, a baker, a butcher, a greengrocer, a chemist and a school. But over time the properties had been sold and converted into accommodation leaving only Porthaven Stores, the surf shop, Crabbers and The Harbour Lights as going concerns. The school was now a self-styled bijou hotel, very exclusive, very expensive: The Gig; one of the few properties in the original village to be privately owned and not part of the Pentreath Estate. The hotel was located amid terraced gardens, set back from the main hill leading down to the harbour, with a swimming pool located on the former playground site. The rooms were named after places on the Isles of Scilly and decorated in bold vibrant primary colours in sharp contrast to the muted seascape tones of the estate properties.

At 11:00 that morning the housekeeper had let herself into room *Tresco* to discover the bodies of Herr and Frau Bauer of Stuttgart. She had been deeply shocked at the sight of the two naked distorted bodies. When Treloar had arrived he had found the police doctor already in situ.

'So Tony, what the hell has happened here?'

'Well, at first glance it looks like a rather adventurous sexual encounter gone awry, but bruising indicates that there was a third player involved here. Look at her nose, see the bruising where someone or something has clamped the nostrils shut whilst she choked on his penis, and look at the man, it's faint but something or someone has applied pressure to his lower back, perhaps stood or sat on him whilst pulling back on those ties and forcing that dildo contraption deep into his throat. They could not have achieved all this alone. With the extreme erotic element again I think it's the work of the same perpetrator as the Osborne and Bond killings. It beggars belief that there are two violent sexual psychopaths frequenting one small Cornish village simultaneously.'

'So the cause of death is asphyxia?'

'Yes I would say so unless John finds something when he opens them up. But whoever this is, they know what they're doing, they understand the physics of leverage and pressure. The bruising you see, it's relatively slight but the weight was applied in exactly the right spot to achieve the result.'

'So what are you saying Tony, we're looking for an engineer?'

'Possibly, but it's more what you're not looking for. This would not have required a great deal of strength or mass. It could easily be the work of a small or very young man or indeed a woman. In fact in all likelihood a threesome would consist of a man and two women, statistically speaking; it is not just a male fantasy, unless of course it's a second couple? No, I think we have an excellent example of equal opportunities in action here; I think we are looking at the work of a lone female.'

'Christ almighty…. Why is it so stuffy in here, can we not have a window open?'

'Ah well there's a reason for that,' said Colin Andrews who'd just entered the room, 'the air conditioning is playing up. I've just been talking to the owner and she says that because they're waiting for some spare parts to come in from Europe they've been leaving doors propped open, particularly the external doors and French windows. Rather than obliging people to come in the front or garden doors the place has been wide open for days: fire exits, patio doors, kitchen doors, you name it.'

'Didn't they think of the security issues?' asked Treloar.

'Well as Mrs Henderson pointed out, this is a hotel not a private house and they have not broken any fire or health and safety regulations. Anyone could have come in yesterday without being seen by the staff at reception.'

'Any CCTV?'

'Only covering the car park.'

'Terrific.'

'Well Phil,' Tremayne said, ' I don't think there's much more I can tell you, it's over to John from here but I think you'll find he'll concur. Fascinating creature you're seeking here my friend.' The doctor picked up his bag and left the room leaving the police officers deep in thought.

'Col, have you heard from Sam?' Treloar asked.

From the outside the house looked just as it had the night when he had brought Sam home from the meeting at the station. The agapanthus pots stood sentinel either side of the front door, the hydrangeas were in full bloom in the afternoon sunshine. But today the front door stood open and two police cars were parked against the wall. As Treloar took the stairs two at a time he recalled his first impressions of the sitting room, the relaxed comfort, the peacefulness and the scent of roses.

'Col?' he called out as he walked through the front door and along the hallway.

'In here,' came the reply from the sitting room. He walked into a scene of utter devastation.

The floor was covered with broken china and open books. The dresser shelves were empty and the bookshelves showed large gaps where books had been torn out and hurled to the ground. The vase of roses lay shattered in the hearth. Cushions had been slashed and tossed around leaving trails of feathers and the cream voile curtains were hanging in shreds and streaked with yellow stains. There was an overpowering smell of urine overlaid with a sickly sweet, almost fruity note. But in all the chaos his eye was drawn to a large red mark on the seagrass rug: blood.

Police had been called to the house at 11:45 am by Abigail Warner, Sam Scott's downstairs neighbour, who had left her flat to collect the post and found the front door standing wide open. This was very unusual as both she and Sam were very security conscious, so she decided to go up to Sam's flat to check that all was well. Sam's front door was also open and when Abigail walked into the flat calling out and walked through to the sitting room, she found Sam lying unconscious on the floor. She immediately picked up the telephone and dialled 999 summoning the ambulance and the police.

Attending paramedics established that Sam was probably suffering from a blow to the head and that she showed severe bruising on her face and arms. Later in the hospital it was found that in addition to her other injuries she had severe bruising to her stomach which appeared to be the result of repeated kicking. At 2:30 that afternoon as Treloar surveyed the wreck of her sitting room Sam was still unconscious in the Intensive Care Unit of The Royal Cornwall Hospital scarcely a mile from where he was standing.

'Jesus, what the hell happened here?' Treloar asked Colin Andrews.

'Well, somebody beat the shit out of Sam, trashed this room and left.'

'Surely the neighbour heard something, there must have been a hell of a row?'

'Unfortunately not. Miss Warner is over seventy and partially deaf. Without her hearing aid and with a couple of sleeping pills inside her she was dead to the world. Luckily she acted promptly and with the hospital so close Sam was in the ICU within half an hour of the call. I've spoken to John Forbes and he's going to look in on her and give us an update. They won't let you see her yet, family only. Her mother's on her way from Winchester. She's young Phil and very fit and she got there fast. It must have happened in the early hours because Miss Warner says the front door was secure when she went to bed just after midnight, she checked. And the bastard left his DNA all over the curtains. So if we can find a match, we'll have him.'

'Mmm. I don't think you'll find a match, but I bet I can.' With that he turned and left with Andrews calling after him.

'What do you mean Phil? Don't do anything daft!'

Treloar opened the boot of his car and grabbed a pair of latex gloves and an evidence bag. Donning the gloves he walked down the gravel drive and turned left on the pavement scouring the ground as he walked down the road. He found what he was looking for thirty yards along. Lying in the gutter were the remains of a bottle bearing the Famous Grouse label. Treloar shovelled the remains into the evidence bag, managing to retrieve the bottle's neck and a substantial piece of glass where the label had held it together. *Gotcha* he thought.

It was rare for John Forbes to venture forth from Pathology so when he entered the ICU at 3:00 that afternoon consultant Patrick Burke was surprised to see him.

'What brings you to the land of the living? Not touting for business are we?'

'No, just checking on Samantha Scott, the police officer.'

'Oh of course, you must know her.'

'Yes but not well, she's new to the area. But from what I've seen so far she's keen, capable and also very likeable which isn't something I'd say of all her colleagues.'

'Well it's early days but the prognosis is good. There's no fracture, just a lot of swelling and bruising and a very nasty gash on the back of her head. She should wake up soon and then we'll know more.'

'So you reckon it was the ex?' asked Andrews when Treloar returned with the broken bottle.

'Yup, and I think this will prove it if we can get his fingerprints and DNA.'

'If you're right and Sam ID's him, he's totally stuffed.'

'Well he's got one thing going for him,' said Treloar glumly.

'What's that?'

'A very rich, very powerful father who dotes on him apparently. How long before we get a "back off" call from Winters?'

'Na. We'll have too much on him for daddy to pull any strings.'

'Mmm.'

Treloar flipped open his mobile to make a call. He wanted Adam Hanbury picked up. But before he could dial it rang.

'Treloar. What? When? Is she OK?'

Andrews saw the anxiety on his friend's face, 'What is it?' he whispered.

Treloar hung up. 'The bastard's only tried to finish Sam off.'

She told them what he'd told her. She was tired and fed up with their questioning. She'd been on duty on ICU for ten hours. He looked like a doctor, he spoke like a doctor and he'd been so charming and very good looking, rather like a young Brad Pitt. So she'd buzzed him in without a second thought.

Adam Hanbury had made a decision. He'd thought that he had killed Sam and that thought had made him feel good. That surprised him but it was true. Now it turned out she was still alive. It was all over the radio. She would identify him and he'd be fucked so she had to go. It had been stupid to piss on her curtains but that had felt good too and they didn't have his DNA or his fingerprints on any database so he was in the clear there, but Sam would identify him, he knew it. Still, he was smart and he was persuasive and he had a plan.

What Adam hadn't taken into account was that with a violent attack, and particular Sam being a police officer, there would be more than the usual number of police at the hospital. When he walked through the double doors and spotted Sam's room there was a PC sitting outside her room reading a newspaper. But Adam was nothing if not confident and decided to brazen it out. I can do this he thought and with his right hand clutching the syringe of insulin in his white coat pocket he approached. Just as he reached the door and smiled at the policeman the double doors behind him swung open again and he turned instinctively to face a tall middle aged woman with turquoise eyes.

'Adam, what the hell are you doing here and why are you wearing that doctor's coat?'

Sophie Scott was just returning to the ICU after a brief break from her daughter's bed. Simon froze, then unable to think of any excuse for his presence he turned from the door and started to stride quickly down the corridor.

'Stop that man!' shouted Sophie Scott and the PC leapt to his feet calling on his radio oblivious to the fierce looks from the nurses. Adam made it as far as the stairs where he was stopped half way down by two security guards and escorted to the bottom to be met by Charlie Hendra who had just arrived for an outpatients' clinic.

'Would it have been enough to kill her?' Treloar asked Colin Andrews.

They were en route to the station to wait for Adam Hanbury to be brought over from the hospital.

'Probably not, but he couldn't have known that and it was obviously his intention.'

'Christ, and he's claiming he loves her.'

'Yes but she rejected him and he clearly loves himself more.'

'So, what do we have?'

'We have the CCTV of him walking into the hospital dressed in that white coat and we have the syringe in the pocket with his fingerprints on it. We also have his fingerprints and DNA all over Sam's sitting room.'

'Christ it's not enough. We need Sam to wake up and remember.'

When Treloar arrived at the station that morning he was told by the desk Sergeant that Adam Hanbury's solicitor had arrived and was waiting for him in his office. Hanbury had refused to say a word since his arrest, insisting that his solicitor and parents be summoned. He had been released on police bail but told to remain in Truro. Treloar met Colin Andrews in the corridor outside his office and asked him to join the interview. As they walked in a tall slender woman rose to greet them extending a hand. She was dressed immaculately in a black business suit and ivory silk blouse. Her chestnut hair swept back in an elegant chignon.

'Emilia Irskine,' she smiled and shook their hands then gave them both a business card. 'We act for Hanbury Telecomm and the Hanbury family in all matters legal.'

Treloar glanced at the card and was struck at once by the name of the firm embossed on it.

'Didn't Oliver Osborne belong to these Chambers?' he asked.

'Indeed, Inspector. And whilst I cannot see that it has any bearing on the current situation, I will say that he was the Senior Partner on the Hanbury account for many years until shortly before his death when...' she hesitated briefly, 'there was a disagreement on a business issue.'

Before he could ask anything more there was a knock on the door.

'Mr Hanbury Senior has arrived, Sir.' said a young PC on opening the door.

'Right. Do you wish to see Mr Hanbury, Ms Irskine, or would you prefer to wait here until your client, Adam Hanbury is brought over from his hotel?' Treloar asked.

'No, I have spoken with Tim already this morning so I would prefer to wait here if I might have some coffee?'

'Of course,' Treloar replied, 'Coffee for Ms Irskine please constable. Col you go on down. I just want to ask Ms Irskine something.'

Emilia Irskine settled herself in a chair and started to pull papers from her briefcase as Treloar took his seat behind the desk.

'Something of a coincidence this business with Hanbury happening here and coming so soon after Oliver Osborne's death also here,' he said.

'Oh I don't know, the ex girlfriend lives here, and as for Oliver's being here, well Cornwall is scarcely an unusual destination for old Etonians. Half the Cabinet come to Cornwall to be seen holidaying.'

Her slight barb didn't escape Treloar and he smiled. He was definitely warming to the splendid Ms Irskine. 'So coincidence rather than connection. I know it is not relevant to your role here, and of course you don't have to answer, but may I just ask your opinion of Oliver Osborne?' he asked.

'Well. I see no harm in answering that question; I'm only offering an opinion. I didn't like Oliver Osborne. I respected him, even admired him professionally, but I didn't like the man. He was utterly ruthless; a formidable opponent and a peerless advocate. Had I been in need of a barrister I would have selected him without a moment's hesitation, but I would not have invited him to dinner. I think that's a fair summation.'

'Well thank you. It's always useful to have different perspectives. We did speak with some of your colleagues after his death, but you were away as I recall.'

'Yes, I was in the Seychelles. My husband's family has an island there.'

Treloar rose from his seat and held out his hand. She took it in her cool slim one and shook it firmly.

'Well thank you again, and we'll let you know when Adam Hanbury arrives,' and with that he left her to her papers.

Tim Hanbury was a thinner, greyer version of his son; the same easy charm, the same winning good looks. Whilst waiting for his son to arrive at the station he had asked for the opportunity to speak with the officers handling the case.

'Yes, Oliver and I disagreed fundamentally about a new subsidiary I wanted to create for Adam to head up. Oliver had a very low opinion of Adam, shared by many I know, but there is potential in the boy... he just needs focus and a purpose in life. He was amply qualified for the position, even Oliver conceded that, but he questioned Adam's temperament and application. It became unpleasant and intractable on both sides so Oliver decided to step aside from the business element of our relationship in favour of Emilia Irskine. I had yet to make a decision about my personal and family legal matters but obviously that is now forced upon me and Emilia seems eminently competent. Oh, and before you ask, at the time of Oliver's demise Adam was in rehab. And not for the first time unfortunately, it has proved ineffective.'

There was the sound of a commotion in the corridor outside the interview room; a woman's voice high pitched and gabbling. Tim Hanbury slowly closed his eyes and spoke through gritted teeth.

'My wife arrives gentlemen.'

A brief knock at the door and it was opened by a flustered PC.

'Er, Mrs Hanbury Sir.'

As he stood aside to hold open the door a short dumpy middle aged woman rushed into the room in a waft of heavy perfume and flung herself at Tim Hanbury who stood up to receive her with obvious distaste.

'Where is he, where is he, what have they done to him?'

'Hush Annabelle, he's fine and he's not here yet. He's not hurt and the police just want to talk to him.'

Well that last bit's an understatement thought Treloar but he could see that Hanbury was trying to calm his wife down.

'Tim, Tim, what has that Scott bitch done to my boy now?'

'Why do you infer that your son's detention is in any way related to an action on the part of Detective Sergeant Scott?' asked D S Winters who had just entered the room presumably alerted to the presence of persons of standing in the station.

'It's always been about that bitch, always, since the first day he set eyes on her,' she spat, 'what else would drag him down to this poxy little city?'

Tim Hanbury grabbed his wife by the arm.

'Annabelle, be quiet for once for God's sake!' he barked.

'Your son is being brought here to answer questions in connection with a vicious physical assault and subsequent attempt on the life of Samantha Scott. If charged, prosecuted and convicted he will go to prison for a very long time,' Winters continued in an icy tone.

'If he did anything, she made him do it; she made him I tell you! And you, you just watch yourself lady, my husband has powerful friends,' she hissed.

'We are all aware of who your husband is madam, but as the United Nations uphold we are all equal before the law. Your money and influence will curry no favour in my station, especially when we are concerned with one of my officers, so I suggest you follow your husband's advice and SHUT THE FUCK UP!'

As Annabelle Hanbury slumped shocked and deflated into a chair she could not have been more astonished at Winters' tone and words than the others gathered in the room. Treloar and Andrews exchanged a quizzical look and a slight smile respectively. The ringing silence was broken by a further knock at the door and the flustered PC heralding another arrival.

'Ma'am, Sir, er Sir, Adam Hanbury has arrived.'

'I'll go… unless you want to Ma'am?' said Treloar.

'Go ahead Inspector,' Winters purred, 'I'll take Mr and Mrs Hanbury to my office for coffee.'

A cowed Annabelle Hanbury smiled weakly at Winters. 'Please,' she murmured.

25 July 19:00

That evening it was busy in The Old Ale House in Truro. Because the weather had been damp and overcast all day holidaymakers had flocked to Truro to enjoy the delights of the city leaving the beaches deserted. Having filled the tills of shops they could easily frequent at home and traipsed around the Cathedral and the brewery they were now ensconced in the pub. Treloar was grumpy. But luckily Dr Tremayne was a frequent visitor to the splendid public house and with a little help from the staff he had secured a large window table for the gathering. Tremayne, Treloar, Colin Andrews and John Forbes were occupying their space, spreading themselves around the large table with Treloar glaring at anyone approaching their territory looking to share.

The Old Ale House was a large traditional public house in true style with wooden floors and furniture, no soft furnishings, beer, more beer, live music and a nod to food. Having suspended the interview with Adam Hanbury overnight for a statutory period of rest, and before he either burst into uncontrollable hysterics or launched himself at the suspect across the table, Treloar had declared himself in need of a drink. Colin Andrews had rounded up the usual gang and they now sat supping pints of Betty Stoggs and London Pride.

Treloar had been recounting the tale told by Hanbury and Ms Emilia Irskine to explain his fingerprints and DNA in Sam Scott's flat and his appearance at the hospital. As far as the flat was concerned, it was scarcely surprising that his DNA and fingerprints were found on numerous items. He had lived with Sam for several years and touched many of her possessions; indeed he had visited the flat on more than one occasion, as the Inspector himself could confirm, and had been there only earlier the evening of her dreadful assault. He had begged her to come back to him and reconsider their engagement. She had been fine when he left and he can only assume that her assailant had turned up later that evening. As for his DNA in urine on the curtains, well he had visited the lavatory and it was his occasional petty childish habit not to flush. Presumably the attacker had taken advantage of his slovenliness and thrown the contents of the lavatory bowl over the curtains to spread confusion. As the assembled party roared with laughter Andrews pointed out that the estimable Ms Irskine had had the decency to look sheepish at this point.

His presence at the hospital was not an attempt to injure Ms Scott but a desperate attempt to see his beloved. He had heard of her plight on the radio and knowing there would be restricted visitation had devised the ruse to dress in a white coat and impersonate a doctor so as to gain access to the ICU. The syringe full of insulin was not intended for Ms Scott but for himself and he had taken it with him to remind himself to take the dose as he had been forgetting recently owing to his distraught mood at the continuing estrangement and his beloved's plight.

'You couldn't bloody well make it up,' Treloar muttered.

'Well,' said Dr Tremayne, 'The urine business is far-fetched, but if he were suffering from diabetic ketoacidosis at the time due to his slapdash approach to his insulin regime, the urine would have been very noticeable giving off a sickly, fruity smell. It could have drawn an intruder's attention, but why said intruder would have opted to strew another's urine about the place rather than relieve himself if he was minded to act in such a beastly fashion, well that is more the domain of the marvellous Mrs Forbes.'

'As you mention my lovely wife Anthony, she has been giving me some insights into that business in Porthaven... from a psychological perspective.'

'Really?' Treloar perked up and turned to the pathologist whose wife had always impressed him both professionally as a psychologist and personally as a beautiful woman.

'Well, obviously these are only general points as Priscilla is not privy to the case details, but she thinks you are definitely looking for a woman and that the sexual elements indicate a need to control and humiliate which probably stems from previous abuse.'

'What about a homosexual man?' asked Andrews.

'Possible, but more likely a woman. It's to do with the lack of violence, torture, or disfigurement and the fact that the last three victims seem to have been willing participants in a sexual scenario; there are no signs of compulsion. It would be difficult to coerce somebody even with a gun or a knife and tie them up at the same time.'

'Could be a couple acting together,' said Andrews.

'Possible, but Priss thinks they were lured to the location with the expectation of sex, especially since we appear to be talking about alpha males with a low opinion of women.' Forbes commented lifting his pint.

'Well that is interesting. Assuming it is a lone woman, she's putting them down like dangerous animals?' asked Treloar.

'Exactly. The very analogy Priss used: veterinary.'

'Yeah, but what about Osborne? He was full of ketamine and even Angelina Jolie couldn't lure me to a deserted beach in the middle of the night for a spot of bondage!' said Andrews.

'No, but maybe she did do Osborne with a partner and found out that she enjoyed the experience and wanted more. Shit,' said Treloar.

There was a lull in the conversation as each man thought this over.

'I hear your esteemed leader was showing her more forceful side this afternoon. DS Winters?' Dr Tremayne smiled as he spoke.

'Yes indeed. I don't know who was more shocked, the Hanbury woman or Col and me. It was actually very impressive and certainly effective. Like pricking a balloon. You could see her deflate. One minute shouting the odds, the next quiet as a lamb. I wouldn't have believed Winters capable of it. Raised voice and foul language, and in front of the rich and famous!'

The noise levels in the pub were rising but as the door was open and they were sitting next to an open window Treloar heard his phone ring. He pulled it out of his pocket.

'Treloar,' the others watched as he leapt to his feet, smiling, 'bloody great, thanks Jim. We'll get over there straight away.' He put the phone back in his trouser pocket and dragged his jacket from the back of the chair.

'That was Jim Carstairs on the desk. Sam's come round. Come on Col.'

Sam Scott opened her eyes gingerly. Her head was pounding and her mouth felt like it was lined with dried moss. She could see that she was lying in a hospital bed in a single room with a lot of machines and not a lot of light. Either that or she had eyesight problems. She turned her head towards the main source of light which appeared to be a window. Sitting at her bedside, reading a paperback book, which Sam recognised as an old Faber and Faber copy of the Collected Works of T. S. Eliot, was her mother.

'Mum,' she whispered.

Sophie Scott dropped the book and shot to her feet.

'Sammy, Sammy are you OK? Poppet can I get you some water?' She smiled at her daughter stroking the hair across her brow with one hand whilst ringing for assistance with the other.

'Cca... can I have some water please, yes I'd love some water,' she cleared her throat.

'Here you are my sweetie. Can you reach the straw? I've called for the doctor. Oh my God Sammy, you've had a lot of people very worried, me most of all.'

'I want to sit up.'

'No Sammy, I think we should wait for the doctor.'

'Christ Mum I don't feel that bad,' she raised a cannulised finger to point at the paperback, 'T. S. Eliot... did you think I'd had it? It's not good night sweet lady yet.'

Patrick Burke walked in on a scene of the two Scott ladies giggling and wiping tears away. Alerted by the voices PC Tate stuck her head around the door and grinned.

'I'll let them know down at the station.'

'For fuck's sake you silly cow; how could you scare me like that? I need you. I don't want to be without you - not now.'

'Whaat?' Sam asked groggily raising herself on one elbow. Had she been dreaming?

'So you're back with us then. About bloody time. Winters will be after you for some dereliction of duty, you just watch.' Treloar was leaning over the bed smiling.

Ah, so what I thought he said, it was just a dream thought Sam, but she did notice that he was looking rather pink in the face. *Just the heat in here.*

'What do you remember about the attack, anything at all?'

'No. Sorry. I remember Adam coming round; the usual pleas and nonsense. I remember making camomile tea for him, trying to get him to calm down, him going to the loo, him coming back and sitting down, then nothing 'til I woke up here with my mother.'

'OK, don't worry. They say it's probably temporary and if you don't push it, it'll probably come back to you. You do need to know that we've taken Hanbury in and we are now holding him on suspicion of the attack.'

'No. He's out.'

'What do you mean he's out?' Treloar spoke very slowly and softly.

'He's out, released by Winters on bail with conditions. Mum told me.'

Before Treloar could speak again the door opened and Mrs Scott walked through laughing followed by Colin Andrews.

'Our esteemed leader has released Mr Hanbury,' said Treloar through gritted teeth.

'Yes she said you haven't enough to charge him yet, but she expects to when some test results are back, with grievous bodily harm and criminal damage I think,' Sophie Scott said, 'but he has to remain at his parents' home.'

Andrews could see that Treloar was seething and could guess why. What about the attempt on Sam's life? But he knew this was not the time or place for that discussion and he shot Treloar a glance which said exactly that: later.

'What the fuck is she playing at?' shouted Treloar as he and Andrews stormed back into the station after spending a few more minutes with Sam and her mother. Sam was clearly tiring and in need of rest so they left, promising to be back soon.

'Calm down Phil, calm down or you'll be in the shit again,' Andrews replied hurrying to keep up with Treloar as he strode along the corridor toward DS Winters' office. Without knocking he hurled the door open and walked into the room which was lit only by a desk lamp. DS Winters rose to her feet and held out her right arm hand raised as if she were directing traffic.

'Stop right there Inspector. Sit down, keep your mouth shut and listen. Colin you take a seat too. There has been a development which I can see you are not aware of, but from your demeanour I imagine you have heard about Hanbury's release.'

'Yes we have heard about that,' Treloar snapped, flopping into one of the two armchairs arranged to the side of the large desk. Andrews took the other.

'After you left for the hospital we had a telephone call from a friend of Adam Hanbury which effectively provided him with a solid alibi for the time of the attack on Sam. This friend had been staying with Hanbury at Mannings in Truro but has now returned to Bristol. I have arranged for you to speak with him tomorrow.'

'Rubbish. I don't believe a word of it,' blustered Treloar.

'I am inclined to agree with you Inspector but we have to check it out. You may not like it but the Hanburys do have influence and a very good barrister in Ms Irskine and we need to sew this up tight as a duck's arse. Then we will charge Hanbury with the assault, the damage and attempted murder. Let a jury decide if he would take an insulin loaded syringe in an open pocket on a hospital visit, just for personal use.'

'Yes you're right, you're right,' said Treloar calmly.

'Who is this friend?' asked Andrews.

'I have his details here,' Winters replied rifling through a pile of papers on her desk. 'Here we are: Tobias Anderson. Friend of Hanbury's from University; still lives in Bristol.' She handed Andrews the piece of paper.

At that moment the phone rang.

'Winters. Yes he is. You can tell me. Right. Give me that name again. Thank you,' she replaced the handset and made a note on a piece of paper.

'A message for you Inspector. Please could you call a Mr Deverell urgently? He says you'll know what it's about.'

'Hello Jamie what can I do for you?'

Treloar was back in his office checking through the messages that had piled up over the course of the day. He was tired and he wanted to go home and he really didn't need a conversation with this strange young man, but he thought it unlikely he would use the word 'urgently' lightly, so he had made the call.

'Well I was looking at Julia Osborne's credit card account again, and yes I know that's illegal but... well .... anyway I came across a payment to a motorcycle dealership in Great Missenden and I thought it a bit odd so I checked it out and I found that it was for a Harley Davidson Gull Wing and it's the same registration as that Irish bloke's who was parked up next to me when Osborne was killed. Just thought you'd be interested. I know you can't use illegally obtained stuff; fruit of the poison tree and all that, but if you looked into him? Bit of a coincidence that he'd be there just that one night.'

'Give me the details Jamie and I'll look into it on the quiet.'

'Hang on there's more. Well as I say I thought it was a bit odd at the time so I had a word with my friend Alisdair, gave him the bloke's name and got him to poke about. Then with these other murders I assumed it must be some maniac and nothing to do with Julia so I let it slide. Anyway I chased Alisdair and it turns out this bloke Thomas Truelove is the Stable Manager at Netherholt House Julia's family pile. Coincidence or connection?'

'Well that's very interesting Jamie. We've already come across that name. Thanks. And we didn't have this conversation.'

As he was closing his mobile Colin Andrews walked into his office.

'Early start tomorrow then, will you pick me up?'

'Yeah. I'll be at yours at six then we should get to this bloke's place before he starts work. Let's go see what his motive is for lying to the police. Adam Hanbury is guilty, no fucking doubt about it. And get an alert out for Thomas Truelove. I want him picked up. I want to know how he fits in.'

'Hello Samantha, how are you feeling today?'

Priscilla Forbes had called into the ward to see Sam Scott. She was out of ICU and staying in a private room on a general ward for observation.

'Hello Doctor Forbes. I'm feeling so much better, I just wish they'd let me out.'

'Do you have a release time yet?'

'Later today when I've seen the consultant. I can't wait. I want to get back to the investigation.'

'I've been thinking some more about all that.'

Sam bristled. 'Yes I understand you've been advising Inspector Treloar.'

'Scarcely that; nothing so formal. Just a few thoughts shared with a very old, very good friend,' she smiled as she spoke, emphasizing the word friend.

'Right... of course,' Sam stammered.

Priscilla laughed. 'Don't worry Sergeant Scott your secret's safe with me. I wouldn't dream of talking to Phil about how you feel.'

'What?' asked Sam, her eyes wide.

'If it's any comfort, he has been like a wounded bear since your attack. I don't think that's just concern for a colleague, but that is very much between you and me. OK?'

'Right... thanks,' Sam blushed deeply.

'Anyway, the killer. In my opinion the sex is not primarily about sex; it's about physical control. Think about it. How does a less physically powerful individual subdue a more powerful one? How does a woman, and yes I believe we are talking about a woman here, how does she overpower a strong fit man such as Christopher Bond or indeed two fit people in the case of the German couple?'

She uses the promise of sex. They relax, they obviously allow her to get close, they allow her to restrain them, they abet in their own deaths. It's classic.'

'She must have tremendous charisma and sexual appeal.'

'Oh yes, and she's manipulative and credible. Classic psychopathy. Have you come across anyone like that yet in your enquiries?'

'No. Not really. Well Julia Osborne does appeal to men but not in that way, I don't think so, she's more the damsel in distress, helpless and vulnerable and a bit dim.'

'No that's not the type at all. You're looking for a strong personality and a fierce intelligence. I don't believe she would feign weakness, certainly not consistently.'

'Well there's Helen Cavendish. She's certainly intelligent enough, but she's just not sexy; more of a wholesome, pony club type; Joan Hunter Dunn, a John Betjeman gal. There is one of the students, Eleanor Constant, she's certainly very beautiful but she seems to have a thing for the American student. She could be putting it on as a ruse, but I don't think so, she seems too self-conscious about it, almost embarrassed that she's letting other people see how she feels.'

'No that sounds like genuine emotion.'

'And then there's the French barmaid. She's very pretty but quiet and always seems to be in the background. Although there was that business with the woman from Polgwynn.'

'What business?'

'Well the woman who manages or whatever at Polgwynn, her name's Millie Lander, she voiced concerns about The French girl, but it was to do with a perceived control over children rather than adults. She was uncomfortable with her daughter being around her.'

'Mmm. That is interesting. It could show a manipulative personality trait. How is she around men?'

'I haven't seen enough of her to form an opinion. But now you mention it there was definitely an atmosphere between the American student and Toby Brett-Morgan, you could almost smell the testosterone when we first visited Point End House, and that didn't seem to be over the lovelorn Ellie. And one time in the Harbour Lights I did see Toby mooning over the French girl. I wonder?'

Treloar had got hold of an unmarked traffic car for the trip to Bristol. This had proved very useful to get them through the odd patch of slow traffic on the A30 and past Exeter and now they were steadily doing 95 mph in the outside lane of the M5.

'What I don't get is the link between Osborne and the others,' said Colin Andrews. 'I know it's one hell of a coincidence if there are two killers at loose in a tiny place like Porthaven, but we've already agreed that Osborne was personal, vindictive and probably a male killer and that the others most likely are, or involve, a woman. Then there's Hanbury knowing Osborne and Osborne blocking his nice new job in daddy's empire. How about Hanbury wants rid of Osborne but he has a clear motive so he disguises that by making the murder look personal or crazed? Then just to further muddy the waters he kills Bond and the German couple to make it look like a serial killer?'

'Christ Col you'll be on about the grassy knoll and the Paris tunnel soon. Just keep it simple or you'll do your head in. Your scenario is the plot of The ABC Murders by Agatha Christie! No. I think the Porthaven murders are connected and the Hanbury/Osborne business is pure coincidence. As the lovely Ms Irskine pointed out, her Chambers work for most of the FTSE 100, and Hanbury Telecomm is in that league. Adam Hanbury is just a nasty little bastard who was spoiled rotten by his doting parents and probably inherited a few dodgy genes from his mother. I doubt he'd even heard of Oliver Osborne. Daddy was going to ignore Osborne's advice so why would he even mention him to his son? He attacked Sam because he couldn't have his own way for once and then didn't want her to tell on him. Simple as that. No, the Porthaven business is much darker and deeper. Whoever is behind those killings is far more sophisticated and troubling than Adam Hanbury.'

They were coming up behind a dozing BMW and Treloar flashed on the blue lights twice to get the driver to move into the empty middle lane. He was tempted to stop the idiot but they were out of their jurisdiction and he didn't have time.

They followed the River Avon into Bristol past the Clifton Suspension Bridge then swung up to the Triangle and took Whiteladies Road past the BBC and on up towards the Downs. Tobias Anderson had agreed to wait for them at his home in a converted Georgian terrace just off the main road. They parked in the street and strode up to the door. It opened before they reached it and a nervous looking young man smiled and extended his hand on the doorstep. With introductions made he seemed disinclined to move, so Treloar spoke up,' Shall we go inside Mr Anderson?'

'What? Oh yes, yes of course, please excuse me, do come through.'

He led them along a corridor into a bright kitchen which was housed in an extension at the rear of the house. A small table stood next to a window with a bench seat and two matching wooden chairs. The room was filled with shiny stainless steel; appliances, microwaves, kettles, toasters, cupboards, it was like a hall of smeared mirrors.

'Please sit down. I have coffee ready if you'd like some?'

'That would be most welcome Sir, and would it be OK for me to use your loo?' Treloar asked. He wanted to get a feel for the place.

'Of course, of course, just to your left and down the stairs. It's straight ahead of you.'

Treloar followed the directions down a polished wooden staircase to a door. He opened it and went through into a tile-floored area which must once have been a cellar. Ahead of him was indeed a toilet and next to it stood a large open shower and a further wooden door into a glass walled sauna. Opposite stood a row of wooden shelves and a stainless steel heated towel rail. On the only bare rough plastered wall was an enormous painting of a naked woman. Interesting thought Treloar and very surprising given the meek and mild appearance of their host. He used the facilities and went back up to the kitchen.

'Everything OK?' Anderson asked. He and Andrews had taken seats at the small table and sat with steaming mugs in front of them. A third mug stood at an empty place and Treloar took it.

'Yes indeed. Interesting basement you have.'

'Oh it's not mine. Well... I mean it is mine in as much as I live here, but I'm only renting. The house belongs to a footballer. His taste in the décor I expect.'

'Right. Well it's good of you to wait in like this. We appreciate your taking the time out to meet us. You must have accommodating employers.'

'Well yes, of course. I am my own boss actually so there was no problem with time off,' he giggled nervously and spilled some of his coffee on the waxed cotton tablecloth.

'Really?' asked Andrews.

'Yes. I'm starting a small web company, just selling stuff online. It's early days.'

'I understand you also took some days off to accompany Adam on a trip to Cornwall. Business must be looking good if you can take time out like that at this stage.'

'Oh... well... yes it was just a few days and I did come back early,' he said as if justifying his actions.

'Right, but you were with Adam Hanbury on the evening of the 23rd I understand. Can you tell us about that night?'

'Yes of course. Well... Adam wanted to see Sam --,' he shot a hand to his mouth, 'Oh ... How is she, how is she? I should have asked, I should have asked,' he muttered as if reprimanding himself for forgetting something important.

'She has regained consciousness and is talking about that evening,' Andrews stated.

Anderson's reaction was almost tangible. The blood drained from his face and he spluttered, 'What is she saying? What has she said?'

'Oh she is having trouble remembering much detail but the mist is clearing slowly and the doctors expect it all to come back to her in time.' Andrews replied.

As they had been talking Treloar had been taking in the surroundings and he was now scrutinizing the papers and post lying on the table. He noticed the edge of a cheque poking out from beneath an opened brown envelope. Picking up his mug he took a sip of coffee and put it down again nudging the envelope in the process. He had revealed the bottom right hand corner with the name of the account holder: Mrs A T Hanbury.

Well, well he thought to himself surreptitiously pushing the envelope aside to reveal a cheque made out to Tobias Anderson in the amount of £100,000.

'....so he came back about eight and we sat in my room drinking a few beers before we went down for something to eat.'

'And what time was that?'

'Oh … about nine, half nine I think. I understand poor Sam was attacked later that evening. I wonder if they waited for Adam to leave, you know, perhaps they were stalking her or something?'

'Might I trouble you for some cold water?' Treloar asked. Anderson rose from the table and as soon as he had turned his back to move towards the sink Treloar pulled out his pen and used it to turn the cheque to face Andrews whilst kicking him under the table. Andrew flinched at the kick and frowned but looked at the cheque and his eyes widened. As Anderson returned to the table Treloar turned the cheque back to its original position and drew the envelope back across with his pen.

'Thank you,' he said, 'so to summarise the evening of July 23rd. Adam Hanbury was with you at Mannings hotel in Truro from eight o'clock until after midnight when you left the bar, and he was not out of your presence during that time except for brief trips to the bathroom. And when he came to your room at eight he was his normal self and in no way anxious or agitated.'

'Yes. That's absolutely it,' Anderson beamed as if he had just answered the prize winning question correctly.

Treloar stood and held out his hand. 'Well I don't think we need trouble you further Mr Anderson and thank you so much for your help. You'd be amazed at how many people choose to keep out of a nasty business like this, just don't want to get involved. You have been an exemplary citizen. Oh, how did you find out that we were talking to Adam?'

'Ah… well… Annabelle, Mrs Hanbury telephoned me very upset to let me know.'

'And why would she do that?' asked Andrews.

'Well… she knew that I'd been down there with Adam, and that as his friend I would …. be concerned of course. Oh… and to tell me about Sam in case I didn't know… but I did. Know that is. I had heard about it on the radio on my way back up here of course. '

'Of course,' said Treloar, 'well we'll just need you to call into your local station to sign a statement confirming these facts and then that should be all we need from you.' Anderson smiled as he saw them to the door.

'Unless, of course, the matter goes to court in which case you will be called upon to give evidence,' Andrews added and they watched Anderson's face fall.'

'Oh yes. There is that possibility… of course,' said Treloar smiling amiably.

'Well, I'd say were looking at accepting a bribe, conspiracy to pervert the course of justice, suborning perjury, blackmail, who knows what else. If we could get confirmation of when Hanbury got back to that hotel; there must be CCTV coverage of him somewhere en route from Sam's. I'll ring and see how they're getting on with that. Then we'll have all three of them,' Andrews was driving back and he was excited, 'the confidence, the arrogance of these people beggars belief. For her to give him a cheque, presumably more convenient, less effort than getting her hands on some grubby cash, and for him to leave it lying around in plain sight when he knew we were coming.'

'Yes well money doesn't buy sense, especially when you haven't actually earned that money yourself,' said Treloar quietly.

'So now what?'

'I'm going to check my messages and you are going to drive in a sober fashion.'

Amongst Treloar's messages was one from Winters herself to say that scrutiny of the Truro CCTV had shown Hanbury running down Lemon Street and past Lemon

Quay on his way from Sam's flat to Mannings hotel. The footage was timed from 20:26 to 20:38. She had ordered the arrest of Adam Hanbury and Tobias Anderson. When he told her about the cheque he felt sure she would extend that to include Annabelle Hanbury.

'What I don't understand is how Truelove fits into all this. I can understand him killing Osborne. I can understand him coming down to collect Julia and Jack Osborne after the first murder. I can believe he brought back Cavendish's wallet, but I can't see him being involved in the other murders, what possible motive could he have?'

Treloar was sitting at Sam's bedside.

'How do we know he *was* here the night of Osborne's murder?' she continued.

'Ah. Well. You remember Jamie Deverell?'

'Yeeessss,' said Sam anticipating Treloar's next words.

'He saw him at the campsite. Truelove was pitched next to him. He traced the registration number of his Harley and … well to cut it short it was definitely Thomas Truelove.'

'OK. So what do we know about him?'

Treloar started to tick the points off on his fingers.

'He's called Thomas Aidan Truelove and he's thirty eight. He's worked at Netherholt since he came over from Cork when he was sixteen. He is currently Stable Manager and he's supposed to be in Ireland looking at horses. He rides a Honda Gull Wing which was purchased on Julia Osborne's credit card a week after she booked Porth House. He was in Porthaven the night Osborne was killed and gone the next day. His initials are T T and those initials were on that hoof knife found on the coastal path. He's known Julia all her life and is probably devoted to her.

266

They share a passion for horses and riding. He's tall, dark, handsome and extremely fit; he could easily manhandle an unconscious Oliver Osborne.'

Treloar and Andrews were talking to Adam Hanbury again. He had waived his right to have Ms Irskine present saying he just wanted to tell them what had happened. He was explaining how there was a new woman in his life and he believed that in order to break with the past he had to be rid of Sam, to 'move past' that relationship as his therapist had been telling him for months.

'Her name is Marthe and she's from Bruges and she loves me. We are destined to be together.'

'How did you meet her?'

'She was watching me play cricket in Truro. She came to the pub afterwards. That's how it started.'

'When was this?'

'Last month.'

'Last month?' asked Colin Andrews incredulously, 'You met her last month and in that short time you decided that you had to attack Sam, someone you had known for years, someone you had lived with and were going to marry?'

A confused expression crossed Hanbury's face as he thought about this. 'Well, y...yes,' he stammered. 'She told me it was love at first sight, a coup de foudre. She explained to me that I needed to confront Sam and end it once and for all in order for us to be together. And she was right. Afterwards I did feel better. But then I realised that to be free I had to finish it; Sam would identify me, I would go to prison and Marthe and I *wouldn't* be together.'

'So she didn't actually say 'beat the crap out of your former fiancée'?'

'Well … no. Just that I had to move on; forget Sam.'

'What does she look like?' Treloar was thinking about Julia Osborne.

'She's luminous. She has beautiful hair like that woman who works for Rupert.'

'What woman, Rupert who?'

'You know she works for Rupert, Rupert Murdoch, my dad knows him. She has long red hair.'

'My God that sounds like one of the students at Point End House. What's her name...the Scottish one? Eleanor Constant,' said Andrews.

'No, no I told you her name is Marthe and she's Belgian not Scottish for Christ's sake. I think I can tell the difference!'

A satisfied smile crept across Hanbury's face. 'Do you want to see her?' he asked quietly looking around as if someone might be listening. 'I have a photograph. She said I mustn't because photographs steal the soul, but I had to have one so I took it when she wasn't aware I had my phone on. It's on my mobile. Your custody people took it.'

Treloar looked at Andrews who dashed from the room to fetch the phone. He switched off the tape. A worried expression on his face, Hanbury leant back in his chair trying to distance himself.

'If I had my way you'd be having a nasty fall or an accident in the cells you creepy little shit. It's not too late for an unfortunate incident you know.' He switched the tape back on as they heard Andrews open the door.

'Show us,' Andrews said holding the phone in front of Hanbury, 'and no stupid tricks. You tell me how to access the photo.'

'Just turn it on. The photo's the wallpaper.'

Andrews turned on the phone and it powered up. He showed it to Treloar.

The photo showed a small, delicate girl with cascading red tresses and huge green eyes. 'That's not Eleanor Constant.'

'No. It's the French girl.' Andrews replied.

She remembered she'd been doing mostly poppies. The daydreams had been mostly about men and she knew that anyone looking on would have been surprised to see the scowls, grimaces, grunts and occasional smile as the poppies had flown off her brushes, quickly towards the light.

She remembered laughing as she'd remembered painting Polgwynn 1776 and how much Tuscan Cypress she'd used for the greenery; the trees and grasses, and laughing again as she had remembered it was Flaubert's favourite colour. She remembered smiling again as she remembered the librarian, how good she'd been in the barn, and how she had introduced her to great authors. After finding Flaubert years ago, he was still her favourite.

Eric and Ben reminded her of Mathô in Salammbô, her absolute favourite book; strong, physical and attractive. Especially Eric, with his gifts for 'accessing' other people's data, and stealing. She didn't know Ben that well though, which was a pity as she probably now never would.

She remembered paint-dreaming of Adam and Toby, poppies still flowing. They both reminded her of Rodolphe in Madame Bovary - shallow, vain and self-centred...especially Adam. She hadn't been sure about 'Tobes' in the end, maybe he'd just been trying to forget who he was by being someone else for a while. That fucking Adam though, what a prat. All he had to do was get over the policewoman and fall for her. The he could give her access to daddy's latest technology so she could carry on hacking and syphoning cash. Christ, he could have been running a new business, what an absolute idiot, losing it like that with the policewoman and thinking he'd get away with it.

She remembered switching to daisies and thinking that it had been years ago she first thought that most men were idiots, simple and a waste of time apart from being useful for what you could get out of them; driven by food, sex and violence, and she remembered smiling when she thought about not needing much food herself. Women were much more interesting, more worthwhile, more layered. Ellie, lovely Ellie, sweet and obliging until Ben was around, then fierce as a lioness, and that policewoman Sam, desperate to be treated as an equal by the others but fawning over her boss. Mostly, with anger, she remembered Millie Lander; showing such cleverness, perception and potential with her appreciation and displaying of the paintings but such a huge disappointment with her clinging, suffocating protectiveness of her so promising daughter.

She remembered she had relaxed, seen how the poppies and daisies had spread, grown nearer to the light, thinking how much she would miss this house but knowing that none of it, none of them really mattered, because soon she would be with Natalie again. Soon they would be somewhere hot.

The Harbour Lights pub was virtually empty when Treloar and Andrews stormed through the doors. Behind the bar a stocky shaven headed man was cleaning the beer lines, pulling on a hand pump to flush water through into a plastic bucket.

'Where is your French barmaid?' demanded Treloar.

'Amélie? She's off this week, back on Monday,' he turned back to the task in hand.

'Excuse me. Do you know where she is?'

'Not a clue mate.'

'Does she have a room here?'

'Yeah.'

'Can - we - see - it?' Treloar enunciated each word making his impatience clear.

'Sure. Upstairs, turn right, last room on the left.'

'Key?'

'It ain't locked. She don't lock it. Never.'

Treloar and Andrews took the old wooden stairs two at a time and hurried along the narrow dim landing to the last door. It opened into a small neat room with a curtainless sash window overlooking the patio and beyond to the sea wall. Andrews hesitated at the door.

'Err… don't we need a warrant for this?'

'Fuck that. She might be lying in here injured,' said Treloar with a smile.

'It's like a dormitory room, institutional, so tidy and impersonal. Weird,' said Andrews.

'Yes I see what you mean but we'd better take a look around anyway.'

Other than a small double bed with a brass bedstead the room contained a whitewashed single wardrobe which contained a few T shirts, plimsolls, a couple of cotton dresses and a pair of cut-off jeans. A bedside chest of drawers contained several pairs of socks and knickers and clean towels. There was a spotless hand basin with a new pump-action bottle of lavender handwash. There were no other toiletries: no toothbrush, no toothpaste, nothing. The only personal touch was a large framed poster above the bed. It showed two dogs and a wheelbarrow in an empty street with grey shuttered houses and was obviously French.

'We'll have to ask Priss about this,' murmured Treloar. It seemed inappropriate to speak in a normal voice somehow... the room was like a tomb.

Back in the bar they collared the barman again.

'Her room seems very tidy almost unoccupied. I take it you've been in there.' Treloar fixed the man with a cold stare.

'Yeah,' he smiled sheepishly, 'well she don't stay here much.'

'What do you mean?'

'Well she only kips here once in a blue moon. She spends most of her free time up on the cliff with that bent old bloke. Still, she's safe enough wiv 'im,' he grinned at them unpleasantly.

'Do you mean Dr Brookes?' asked Andrews.

'Yeah, that's the fella. She kips up there an' all. Says she likes the space. Come to think of it, she's more 'n likely there now mate.'

Brookes was out. The house was closed and locked.

That evening Treloar called in to see Sam who had been discharged from hospital that afternoon.

'But I don't understand,' she said.

'Adam was angry with you for ending the relationship. The French girl wanted him to forget about you. Remember she is very clever, very manipulative. We know she exerts power over people, especially men, using sex or the promise of sex as a snare.'

'Oh I can believe it of Adam, being seduced, but what was in it for her, why would she want rid of me and how could he be so easily and quickly persuaded to go so far?'

'Well Priscilla Forbes thinks she was just having some fun at our expense. She had researched you, discovered Adam and targeted him. She probably just wanted access to his money.'

'And he was easy meat.'

'For her, yes.'

'But why the disguise?'

'Well if we got to Adam and he described his new love as she knew he would, he couldn't resist the opportunity to talk about her; she knew that description would point us at Eleanor Constant. Think about it. The long red hair is what anyone would notice and mention; a very distinguishing feature. We would waste time tracking down Eleanor and checking her version. She was the perfect choice to distract us. But she actually underestimated her effect on Adam. He has admitted that she only told him to forget about you not to attack you. He was drunk and got carried away and then he was scared of what you'd say. Apparently she forbade him to take a photograph, but not only could he not resist the temptation, he couldn't resist showing her off.'

'So Adam has admitted everything?'

'The attack yes, but he insists that at the hospital he couldn't go through with finishing you off.'

'So is he going to help us find her?'

275

'He can't help us. He had no contact numbers for her, no address. She always called him. He thought it was wonderful, all part of the mystery and intrigue of it all.'

'So now what?'

'Tomorrow we're back up to Penmol to see Brookes.'

'I'm coming.'

'I'm not sure Sam; you're supposed to be off for a few days.'

'I'm bloody well coming. I want that bitch.'

Treloar's phone rang. It was Andrews. They had Truelove.

Thomas Truelove had been apprehended speeding on the M4 and brought back to Cornwall. He was sitting in an interview room at Truro with Treloar and Scott. They had been through the formalities and Truelove was cooperating, almost relieved to be doing so.

'As you know, we're charging you with the murder of Oliver Osborne,' said Treloar.

'It was all the idea of that little French witch. To be sure Miss Julia didn't care for the man but she was made to marry him by that witch and his Lordship. It all goes back to that loony bin in France where Miss Julia met her. She knew about Osborne, all about him. Knew he was loaded and that Julia's father needed money and Osborne would love her title. She planned the whole thing, when his first wife was still alive. Boasted to me about it, laughing she was," 'ow lucky that she drowned eh Tommy?" Drowned my arse, the bitch killed her somehow, betcha. She knew that I loved Miss Julia and that Osborne was a bastard to her so she knew I'd help with the "leefting, moving ze body, ze rough stuff",' Truelove spoke quickly, spitting his words out.

'Oh I know Miss Julia loves her, and I mean sex not just friendship, turned me on a bit truth be told, but that bitch loves no one. I was all for just stabbing the bastard, making it look like a mugging, but oh no, that evil little cow wanted all the bells and whistles. She wanted him to suffer; she who'd never met the man except in the pub. The staking out, the bag over the head, the crabs... all of it was her idea. And all that shit with the knots and that wooden pin up his arse. All to point the finger at that other stuck up cow, God, does Miss Julia hate her, but all the fancy detail, it was all that French bitch's idea. "A geeft for Julia." Miss

Julia just giggled and clapped her hands as the witch spelled it out and made *me* write it down "zo you don't fook up Tommy". Bitch! And she was watching, I don't know where from but she was watching alright, I just know it. She scared the shit out of me man, Jeez she's a touched one, fucking scary, watch yerselves if youse come up against her. Take reinforcements, take a bloody battalion!'

'What about Christopher Bond and the couple at the hotel, do you think she could have carried out those murders?' asked Treloar.

'Oh yeah, she'd have been up for that no problem. She'd have enjoyed herself too. Poor sods probably didn't say please at the bar or give her a tip. Wicked she is underneath that pretty little face. I bet she ratted on me the little cow. She did, didn't she, some anonymous tip with something to nail me, the bitch.'

'Actually we traced you through your hoof knife.'

'My hoof knife?'

'Yes.'

'What do yers mean?'

'We have your hoof knife Mr Truelove,' said Sam patiently, 'it has your fingerprints on it. They are on file with the Garda in Dublin. We know you work for Lord Netherholt. There were threads matching the cord used to bind Osborne caught in the handle of your knife. It is not rocket science. We joined the dots.'

'The bitch, the bloody bitch. Where did you get my knife?'

'Sam and Treloar exchanged glances and Sam continued, 'well… it was handed in at the pub actually.'

'Bejesus she's got youse too! Handed in my arse. She stole it from me after I'd cut the lengths of cord. She was there 'soopervizing'. She's fitted me up well and proper,' Truelove let out a long sigh and seemed to deflate before their eyes. 'Oh I never said she wasn't clever,' he continued after a long pause. 'Clever, but pure evil.' Truelove shuddered and made the sign of the cross.

'Do you have any idea of the current whereabouts of Amélie Bonnard, Julia Osborne or Jack Osborne?' asked Sam.

'Not a clue. Why don't you ask those poncey twin brothers? She spent a lot of time up at that creepy house. A right bunch they are. Not my kind of fellows for sure.'

'Do you believe all that stuff about the first Mrs Osborne?' asked Sam.

'Who knows? If it is her, everything she's done has been clinical, exact and very calculated. No I think she was winding him up; establishing a persona that would put the fear of God into him with his beliefs; maintaining control through terror. He's clearly scared of her and he's trying to hide it behind anger. But we'd better check. You know Winters. All we have is his word. But he is a great fall guy; he could well have known where they were holidaying, he's clearly devoted to the Honourable Honors especially Julia, the knife is his and the story of it being handed in by anonymous Dutch or German tourists – well we wouldn't even try to trace them with so little information. No it's clever. He's right about that. '

'What about Julia and the French girl meeting in this French 'loony bin'?

'I don't know. We'll have to check somehow. I'll ask Priss how we go about it.'

Treloar and Sam were on their way to see the Brookes brothers at Penmol. They had agreed to arrive unannounced.

'I've been talking to Priscilla; off the record, Winters won't foot the bill to bring her on board, but we go back a long way-'

'Really?' Sam said, eyebrows raised.

'Oh yeah,' Treloar smiled wistfully, 'I introduced her to John, more fool me.'

Sam bristled.

'Anyway, what she said came with all the qualifications, you know, not having met the subject and all that, but she believes it all stems back to childhood and lack of love and intimacy. The French girl meets a lot of the criteria for a psychopath apparently: lack of empathy, narcissism, social deviancy, sexual promiscuity, lack of guilt, charisma, ruthlessness --'

'Bed-wetting, arson and cruelty to animals?' scoffed Sam determined to undermine the precious Priscilla.

'Well we don't know, apart for any obvious fires or cruelty to animals. Mind you, apparently there was a Scottish serial killer, Peter Manuel, who murdered a family of three at New Year and returned to the house over a period of days before the bodies were discovered to feed the cat.'

'So she's just a run of the mill serial killer? No, it's all about Osborne. He must have suffered dreadfully when he came round staked out on that beach in the dark. No I think the others were a little light recreational killing after the main event. The target was Osborne, the others were incidental. He deserved pain in her eyes.'

'Or in Julia's perhaps?'

They drove in silence for some miles, each deep in thought. Then Sam spoke.

'I'll tell you something else about Ms Bonnard; apparently she has a strange power over children, so perhaps by extension over weaker adults too.'

'Where's this come from?'

'Millie Lander at Polgwynn. I didn't give it much credence at the time; she does come across as rather excitable don't you think? Anyway I was having a coffee at Crabbers and she walked up from the beach and stopped to say hello.'

'When was this?'

'Oh, days ago, not long after we'd first met her. We were just chatting and she was watching the beach, keeping an eye on her daughter apparently. Then suddenly she stopped talking and froze. Then she started shouting her daughter's name and waving her arms frantically. I looked around and saw the French girl down by the water's edge with a gaggle of small children around her. She spoke to one of the little girls and a miniature version of Millie Lander started walking up the beach towards us, very reluctantly I thought. When she reached us Millie knelt down and took her hand and spoke very slowly; "Chloe, I have told you not to go near that girl have I not?" the child was very quiet and subdued. I asked her what the issue was and she said, I remember her exact words, "There is something of the Pied Piper about that French girl. She fascinates children, it's unhealthy. It troubles me deeply." I asked if it was a matter for us but she shrugged it off and laughed saying something about mother's intuition and over-reaction. I looked back and the other children were still down by the water but the French girl was nowhere to be seen. I dismissed the episode from my mind until

Truelove started with all the witch and demon talk earlier and brought it back.'

'I'll run it past Priscilla when I get a chance.'

'Great,' said Sam under her breath.

'I did speak to one of Priscilla's colleagues on the phone. She made the referral for us. Bloke knows a lot about perverse criminal behaviour. Interesting stuff.'

Priscilla Forbes had pointed Treloar at a colleague, Marcus Sinclair, who had a specialism in aberrant criminal behaviour. Whilst Superintendent Winters was still reluctant to fund the official involvement of a profiler, Priscilla had called in a favour and Sinclair had agreed to an unofficial opinion based on what Priscilla and Treloar had told him about the case. Treloar wanted to understand what drove Amélie and the dynamic of her relationship with Julia Osborne, starting with their first meeting at the psychiatric institute in the south of France which they had discovered was not just a figment of Truelove's fevered imagination. This was Sinclair's account:

'It was not quite Broadmoor sur Mer but there were a lot of disturbed children and adolescents there. It was a classic example of something that seemed like a good idea at the time; the road to hell paved with good intentions. You must understand that psychiatry is not an absolute or exact science but a matter of opinion and interpretation. There are no nuances in the treatment of a broken leg, but a damaged mind? The patients or inmates or guests, however you choose to describe them, would have been exposed to dangerous difficult and deeply unpleasant individuals and not only among their peers. There was a predilection for sexual diagnosis; every ill caused by sex and every treatment centred on sex. It appals me to say that these people, the people running the Institute, were highly qualified, highly distinguished professionals. Up until the exposé by the television company every authority, every governing body heaped praise upon the place. Looking back now it reminds one of a Mel Brooks' film or it would do had it not been so tragic. Those girls would have witnessed and been subjected to behaviour most of us are spared thankfully.

The French girl was obviously sent there after the drowning of two children. Apparently there were accusations at the time but there are no records of her history; they were lost or destroyed. But Julia Honor? I can only assume that some well meaning doctor or even a friend or family associate had heard of the place and she was sent there having apparently suffered a breakdown after her mother's death. As a private admission she would have fared better than most, better accommodation, more privacy, and the expense, which would have been considerable, might have lulled her father into the false assumption that he was doing the right thing. Once there she would have been cut off completely. There was no contact with the outside world; that was a major part of the therapy. It is no wonder to me that she turned to the French girl for succour. Julia Honor was Natalie. It was not unusual for patients to be registered under pseudonyms. Julia Honor is the acolyte. It is the French girl who is the master.

There are several classifications, definitions and checklists if you like, of psychopathy: One is the Macdonald triad. It was first proposed by American psychiatrist. Basically it purports that a history of bedwetting, arson, and cruelty to animals, are three key indicators of psychopathy. But he went on to describe factors observed in psychopaths: aggressive narcissism which would include superficial charm, manipulation, lack of remorse, lack of empathy, pathological lying, and socially deviant lifestyle which would include proneness to boredom, parasitic lifestyle, and irresponsibility; plus sexual promiscuity and criminal versatility. It strikes me that you have these traits in the French girl and to a lesser degree in Julia Honor. Yet the French girl is by far the more complex. She manifests a marked degree of loyalty and commitment to certain individuals and a contradictory devotion to animals. She is highly intelligent, highly competent, self controlled and self reliant. She would certainly be a fascinating study, but look, now I'm sounding as bad as those charlatans at the Institute. As for which of the two is the more dangerous, well the French girl appears to have purpose, a rationale, but Julia Honor in my opinion has a total moral vacuity. Her actions will be governed by her inferior intelligence if she is operating alone now, and she has crossed a Rubicon, she has achieved her desire through violence, she is by far the more unstable of the two and the more to be feared. If we know how something or someone has become broken it is possible to fix them, but some people are just born broken. I fear Julia Honor is one such. To paraphrase Dickens: beware them both, but most of all beware Julia. If Jack Osborne is with her he is in peril. Thus far she has shown fondness and kindness toward the boy, but that is only superficial. If he becomes tiresome, at best, she will abandon him. We must never forget that victims have victims too.

Find him. If he's still with her then you'll need someone with influence over her. Ideally I would enlist the aid of the French girl. She has no issue with Jack and probably sees him as a defenceless creature. We know from people at the institute who remember her, that her positive feelings for birds and animals predate her relationship with Julia. The business with Osborne was essentially for Julia, not a personal act. With Bond and the German couple there must have been a trigger, most likely they manifested some cruelty towards birds or animals or perhaps even people who the French girl valued. She would fiercely defend and avenge those significant to her. The French girl would be deeply conflicted if she believed that Julia might harm the boy if she valued him. Your best hope of keeping Jack Osborne alive is to enlist the help of the French girl.'

'So all we have to do is find the French girl and appeal to her better nature?'

'No Inspector, not her better nature, just her nature. There is no better or worse with this girl. You may have good days and bad days, so may I. This girl, she has days Inspector, just days.'

'So,' said Sam, 'if she knew about Bond's history with Dr Brookes that would explain why he was selected. But that doesn't explain the German couple. When we find her we'll just have to ask her.'

'If we find her,' Treloar added glumly.

As they drove through the gates to Penmol Treloar's phone rang. It was Col Andrews and he was excited.

'We've got her on camera at The Gig. It's a complete bloody fluke. They'd had some work done on the trees around the car park the morning of the murder and the camera had been twisted round and not put back. It was pointing at the fire escape not the car park but you wouldn't have known from looking at the housing from ground level. They only noticed when they reviewed the footage because there was a prang. No coverage of the accident, but there is the French girl climbing the staircase and coming back down again in the timeframe, carrying a rucksack.'

When they arrived at Penmol and drew up outside the house Hugo Brookes was standing at the open front door looking sombre. As they climbed from the Land Rover Treloar's phone rang again and he indicated he would catch them up. Brookes led Sam through to an enclosed sun room at the rear of the house. The original wall of the house appeared to be papered which struck Sam as odd, but looking more closely she could see that it was not in fact wallpaper but paint. Someone had hand-painted hundreds of flowers: cornflowers, daisies and poppies, climbing the walls and stretching out onto the ceiling. It was remarkable. Brookes sat heavily in a cushioned wicker chair and sighed deeply.

'I found her in the garden when I arrived home from Truro on Easter Sunday. She was sketching the house. I offered her tea and matters progressed from there; she told me her story. She is descended from David Pentreath and his irresponsible attitude to offspring was passed down through the generations; she was largely neglected and then abandoned by her parents. I offered her house space to stay and to paint. She did not strike me as a dangerous creature. You have met her I presume, did she put you on your guard? Then once she'd met Nathaniel, that very first day, I knew I would lose her, I knew he would take her from me. I could tell at once that there was chemistry between them. I am not a sexual being, Sergeant but I do recognise it in others. You and the Inspector for instance.'

Sam blushed and stuttered, 'I don't know what you mean.'

'Really?' said Brookes with a wry smile, 'my mistake perhaps?'

A jangling rang out from the front of the house. 'Ah, saved by the bell.' Brookes strolled from the room and returned with Treloar. Sam brought him up to date with the conversation.

'Did you know that Oliver Osborne's maternal family were the bankers who forced David Pentreath from Polgwynn?,' Treloar asked.

'No I did not. That would have enraged her. She was extremely bitter about the loss of the estate, her birthright.'

'Sufficiently bitter to orchestrate Osborne's death?'

'That would be speculation on my part Sergeant.'

'Then please speculate Sir.'

'Yes… I would surmise so; however I cannot accept that she would have had sufficient influence over a total stranger. I understand you have charged someone?''

'Thomas Truelove. He has confessed to the Osborne murder,' said Sam.

'Oh that preposterous, stereotypical Irishman.'

'You've met him?'

'Once. He came to the house to see Amélie. He did not come inside; he seemed most reluctant to be here. He reminded me of a scolded dog, downcast and shaking. They spoke in the garden. I did not overhear their conversation but I could tell that Amélie was incandescent. She did not suffer fools gladly.'

'Did you ask her about it afterwards?

'Why no of course not.'

'Thomas Truelove is a longstanding member of staff at Netherholt, the family home of Julia Osborne.'

'Ah well, the devoted manservant acting from devotion to his mistress perhaps? I see no need for Amélie's involvement. She may have been a friend of Mrs Osborne, but surely that's insufficient to condemn her.'

'Where is she now Dr Brookes?' asked Treloar sternly.

'Gone, alas gone. Taken from me by my brother. Nate and I, sometimes I think of us as living The Picture of Dorian Gray with me being the painting aging in the attic whilst Nate walks on in beauty. My brother is one of the golden ones. They pass through life untouched, untrammelled by the vicissitudes of pain and fear and strife as if their feet do not touch the sullying earth. And Amélie, la belle amie,' Brookes laughed, 'marvellous creature don't you find? Pure energy, pure spirit and such magnetism. An animal force, essential raw and untamed. They make a formidable couple don't you think? And how typical of Nate to steal her from me. All my precious things, since childhood; toys, friends, lovers, all stolen by my precious brother. I shall miss her enormously. "They who go feel not the pain of parting". Henry Wadsworth Longellow; The Song of Hiawatha, as I recall. They left yesterday. I believe they are travelling under the name of Bellamy; French for beautiful friend; Nate always had a sense of humour. But I doubt you'll find them.'

'We believe she has killed four people this summer!' Sam's voice rose in outrage.

'Ah, you mean the local murders. Well yes. And then of course the earlier deaths when she was a child. I don't know how many she has killed. I have always thought that killing is an absolute not a matter of degree. Once you've killed one why not one hundred? It's the ultimate control. But here there is a method, a perverse logic: hurting the hurters. The killer as Nemesis, exacting justice. Therein lays the justification in her eyes. And, if you were to ask people, on a visceral level, most would agree that her victims are no loss to the world. Here we are in a world of instinct not intellect, an older, primal world beyond civilisation.'

'Why did you say nothing of this?' Sam found herself speaking like her host and determined to stop it.

'Sergeant, these were childhood incidents and Ms Bonnard was punished by society for them. Who am I, I of all people to dredge up dark matters of the past, to cast aspersions and level blame?'

'Well tell us now,' said Treloar with vehemence.

'Fine, when she was five she killed two children, family friends I believe, drowned them because they were chasing flamingos. She has an abhorrence of cruelty to animals and an amazing affinity with them, birds in particular. She was incarcerated in some avant-garde institution in the south of France, very progressive, very experimental, and that is where she met Julia Honor, as I understand, although obviously they were not held under their real names. I think Julia was a Natalie. Anyway, some of the treatment was exceedingly dubious, bordering on, if not actual, abuse, with a reprehensible concentration on the sexual psyche. Natalie, or Julia in effect, being psychologically weaker, her nature as victim was compounded but, well Amélie, she truly proved Nietzsche right; she grew stronger. She has the most powerful personality I have ever encountered. I gather from allusions she has made to that time that she killed at least another two men, including a particularly heinous doctor, but these deaths were attributed to accident.'

'So, you're saying that to your knowledge she has killed at least eight people?' asked Sam incredulously.

'No, to my knowledge she has killed the two children. These others are inference and supposition. Can you prove she killed the four visitors this summer?'

'What about your brother's role in these deaths?' asked Treloar.

'Oh, none whatsoever. Nate would not involve himself in anything so visceral. For the Osborne fellow I would imagine some malleable brute devoted to Julia. This Truelove fellow would fit the bill perfectly. I understand she has that effect on some men; the inspiration of a powerful urge to protect and defend. As for the others... well sexual domination, physical overpowering of that sort would be child's play to Amélie. No I think with the others, should she have indeed acted, it would have been alone.'

'You sound as if you admire her' said Sam.

'Oh yes I do. Not for her violence but for her splendour. And after all what was the true nature of those she killed this summer, what type of creature were they Sergeant? From what I understand of the German couple they had, unusual leisure tastes shall we say? Of course such pastimes were no more or less perverse to Amélie than model railways or needlepoint. Really Sergeant for someone of your age you do strike me as rather judgmental and unenlightened. Did you have a fundamentalist religious upbringing? There is a distinct whiff of Plymouth Rock about you. But I digress. Come, see her rooms.'

Brookes led the way through into the hall and along to a back staircase. Followed by Treloar and Sam he climbed three floors and opened a door. A tremendous brightness flooded out of the room causing them to stand their ground as Brookes entered.

'Come through, come through,' he said.

They walked into a vast space running the length of the house with French windows entirely covering one wall offering unbroken views out to sea.

'Wow,' said Sam involuntarily.

As their eyes adjusted to the light they could see that the walls were covered with paintings and tapestries. There were easels and painting paraphernalia everywhere, and at the far end of the room an old brass bed and several large bookcases. An old dusty decorative Chinese screen obscured half of the bed. The wooden floor was partially strewn with dirty Chinese rugs and sheets of newspaper. To her right on the wall facing the windows Sam noticed the same painted flowers creeping up onto the ceiling, the same as in the small sitting room they had just left.

'This is Amélie's space,' said Brookes in a hushed tone as if she were still there somewhere. 'This is where she works and sometimes sleeps and sometimes with my brother. She has tremendous talent, both original and in pastiche of others. Let me show you.' He walked further into the room beckoning to them to follow. 'I saw you admiring the wall painting downstairs Sergeant. Yes, indeed Amélie's hand,' he pointed to the creeping flowers. 'And here, look, what do you see Inspector?' Treloar followed Brookes' gaze towards a triptych resembling a medieval altarpiece. 'Look closely,' Brookes spoke slowly. Treloar approached the work and gasped audibly. In an Italianate rural background reminiscent of da Vinci sat three separate naked women in openly sexual poses, smiling seductively. All three were images of Julia Osborne.

As Treloar and Brookes stood gazing at the triptych Sam moved further into the room scrutinising the paintings. Some were modern abstracts in vivid primary colours, others were obvious pastiches; a Magritte depicting a string of dancing children emerging from a fireplace, a Seurat of Julia with Jack sitting by a river with bathers.

'She painted the portraits hanging in the hall at Polgwynn,' Sam murmured.

'Oh yes indeed,' chortled Brookes, 'are they not great fun? Millie loves them and they are very popular with the visitors. I believe they sell many postcard copies to the tourists.'

'What about these?' asked Treloar, 'there is one like this in her room at the pub. These are not her work.' He pointed to a series of posters, rather battered and faded. A ghostly figure stood before a table by a window overlooking a garden; an elongated white cat with marmalade touches stood back arched; a naked female figure lay deathlike in an enamel bath; a solitary girl child sat reading at a table with a cream shaded lamp in the foreground; a ghostly figure stood beneath a palm frond with a Mediterranean village in the background.

'Ah no' said Brookes, 'those are by her chosen namesake Pierre Bonnard. I don't know her true name. She named herself after her favourite artist. There are no pastiche versions of his work. Just poster copies of the originals.'

'She has also been calling herself Marthe,' said Treloar.

'Ha. Marthe was the name of Bonnard's wife,' Brookes chortled.

'Look at this!' called Sam, 'it's 'Saturn devouring his Son' by Francisco Goya, except it's Oliver Osborne devouring Jack. It's chilling but brilliant.'

'An excellent appraisal Sergeant,' said Brookes.

But the most striking and beautiful painting in the room stood on an easel by the windows. At five foot by six it was the largest in the room and was painted in vibrant acrylic. A lone flamingo stood in the foreground. Behind it stretched a large coastal lagoon fading into distant mountains. No other bird or creature was depicted; no road or building; no other sign of life. Brookes watched as Sam gazed at the canvas.

'Ah yes,' he said quietly, 'exquisite is it not?'

'Indeed.'

'She calls it Rogue Flamingo. I rather think it is a figurative self-portrait.'

Treloar was now looking at photographs and books piled on an old oak table at the far end of the room by the Chinese screen. 'Here Sam,' he called, 'photos of the Osbornes and the Cavendishes, the students from Point End House and various locals. Here's one of you outside the pub. Here's 'Birds of Southern Africa' by Kenneth Newman with Julia Honor handwritten in the flyleaf. She used the Kynsna lourie for the pastiche of Audubon at Polgwynn. Here's L'Education Sentimentale by Flaubert and several Proust and Baudelaire editions. We'll need to go through all this but I don't think we'll find anything to help find her.' He pointed to a cleared space where a laptop had been and a small photograph printer lay on its side amongst a tangle of cables and extension blocks.

'Indeed not. They will have left no clues. They are in the wind,' said Brookes sadly.

Downstairs again Brookes made tea and they sat solemnly in the garden, each lost in their own thoughts.

'What I don't understand,' said Treloar, 'is why here? If the primary victim was Oliver Osborne, why not London? I can see that the others were just the wrong people in the wrong place at the wrong time but why bring Osborne here?'

'Well, I think that was to punish Helen Cavendish by implicating her, if only briefly, it did make her suffer to a degree and Julia wanted that,' suggested Sam.

'Oh no,' said Brookes, 'I believe this was Amélie's choice not Julia's. Yes, Julia was responsible for bringing the families here but at Amélie's behest. Amélie is a Pentreath. She believes that Polgwynn is her ancestral home, stolen from her great grandfather by the evil bankers, Oliver Osborne's mother's family, you say. If she is behind the murder of Osborne I believe that her affection for Julia would have been exceeded by her hatred of what Osborne represented. Love and hate, love and hate.'

'I still cannot believe that you knew all this, that you had this background information and you said nothing when Osborne was killed,' said Sam.

'What was I to say? That a young French artist and part-time barmaid, known for her love of animals and birds and of whom I am extremely fond is probably a criminal mastermind? You forget I did not know of her connection to Julia or of Osborne's family connection to Polgwynn until long after the event. The only thing I knew before his death was that she had family connections with the area. And are we not all agreed that she did not actually commit the deed? As for the other deaths, again we are all just speculating are we not? There is no substantive evidence. I can believe that the others were murdered by the same hand but I do not see the link to Osborne. As for fleeing the area she has no ties here other than a seasonal part-time employment in a public house. Given the chance of an adventure with a charismatic older man what would you do Sergeant? You've met my brother.'

'I don't know that I'd be as phlegmatic if I were you Dr Brookes,' said Sam tetchily. 'If this is primarily about revenge, Osborne's family may have taken Polgwynn but your family, your grandfather, took Penmol. Why wouldn't you or your brother be next?'

'Ah but Sergeant, look around you. She has already reclaimed Penmol.'

'So that painting of the house and grounds in the hall wasn't just another pastiche, it pictures Amélie in her rightful home,' said Treloar glumly sipping his pint. He and Sam had called in at The Harbour Lights on leaving Penmol.

'Yeah. The lady of the manor. Some lady. Still you can see what devotion she inspires in people; Julia, Jack, Hugo even the self-centred cynical Nathaniel. Not to mention Toby and Ben almost coming to blows over her, and them the very best of pals. Amazing. What about you, didn't you fall for her charms, even a little? You certainly fitted the bill when it came to Hugo's description of Julia's effect on some men. Brookes said his brother travels doing deals around the world. Perhaps he's some kind of spook, looks the sort to me. All that ... smooth charm, very dodgy. He'd have contacts and channels to get them out of the country avoiding border checks and controls. I think Hugo's right, they're in the wind and we'll never find them...... Who was that on the phone by the way, when we got to Penmol?'

'Christ, sorry Sam. It was Col. They found Jack Osborne.'

'Where?' she cried.

He'd pitched a tent in the private enclosed garden at the centre of the Georgian square in London where his paternal grandparents live. They only found him because he'd lit a fire, otherwise he could have gone unnoticed for days! He was living on bags of crisps and chocolate and drinking from the tap the gardeners use to water the plants. When they asked him how he got there, he said he was dropped off by Thomas Truelove who helped him climb over the fence and left him there.'

'So where's the lovely Julia?'

'Jack says he has no idea. He last saw Julia when she left their London house. She gave him a hug, told him to wait for Truelove and said she'd see him at Christmas. Then she left with an overnight bag and got in a taxi. Apparently, Truelove turned up later that evening and took him across to the grandparents' square on his Gull Wing. Jack thought it was brilliant.'

'So do you think she'll get rid of Julia?' asked Sam.

'No Julia's safe. She loves Amélie; she's devoted to her like she was with David Cavendish, like a dumb animal, a pet dog. That's probably how Amélie sees her. No I think their shared past and that devotion will save her,' said Treloar glumly. 'No in the end, after all this, I think we'll get Truelove for Osborne, Hanbury for the attack on you, and Anderson for conspiracy to pervert the course of justice. Annabelle Hanbury will skate and so will the others.

'What have we actually got?' Treloar ticked the points off on his raised fingers. 'Osborne. We've got Truelove's accusation. But he admits he assaulted Osborne, gave him the drugs, staked him out on the beach and left him to drown. Bond. We've got absolutely nothing. The German couple. We've got the CCTV coverage of her leaving The Gig that afternoon. You Sam. We've got the photograph on Hanbury's phone and his story that he thought she wanted you out of his life and he somehow thought that meant dead. A jury would probably find that preposterous. Then we have her apparently walking out on a casual summer job without giving notice. Wow. Do I think she did any or all of it? You bet. Can we prove any or all of it? No way. Christ, we don't even know her real name and we have no idea where she is. We'll never get her.'

And not for the first or last time Treloar was absolutely right. Truelove went down for Oliver Osborne. The charge of Attempted Murder against Adam Hanbury was dropped by the CPS; the insulin was his, prescribed and of insufficient quantity to kill, and he had back tracked on his fears that Sam would identify him as a motive.

Annabelle Hanbury would walk away from all charges on the word of Tobias Anderson. His claim that she was merely investing in his company could not be refuted. No doubt he would serve his sentence looking forward to a further hefty investment in the future. He was convicted of Perverting the Course of Justice. But in an ironic twist Annabelle's name would appear in the papers some six months after her son's imprisonment for Grievous Bodily Harm when she was divorced by her husband on the grounds of unreasonable behaviour.

They tried to track Julia Osborne by following her money trail but it led nowhere; her accounts, those they knew about, remained untouched.

And in the late autumn, Jack Osborne was back at Eton, his popularity and standing much enhanced by the lurid details of the death of his father and the salacious stories about his stepmother.

Nathaniel Brookes parted from Amélie on amicable terms in Paris and returned to his London flat and to his work in defence of Queen and country. Hugo Brookes remained in his isolation at Penmol reflecting on the summer that had passed. He often found himself in the attic rooms smiling wistfully at the paintings.

Treloar and Sam continued to work together and to skirt around their personal feelings.

As for Amélie and Julia ....

She remembered being surprised at how surprised she had been. She had flown quite a lot but never first class; it had been luxurious. Her eyes had widened when she saw the amount of space around the seats and the quality of carpet on the floor. At first the seats had looked like armchairs; they were covered in soft beige leather, and looked to be hand-stitched. Even before they were seated the hostess had asked if they would like champagne, and when they said yes they were asked if they wanted rosé or white. It had been a warm late summer day and they had both had the rosé. She had smiled to herself when she noticed that it was Dom that was being poured.

She was surprised at the amount of leg room, and the fact there were two hostesses for just seventeen passengers. When they were taking off she had worried for a second before realising what it was when she felt the front wheel retracting into the plane and heard the creaking and clanking as it folded up and back into the body and the fairing moving into place. When they were airborne she had been surprised at how muted the sound of the flight was, then she had realised the noise from the engines would be low because they were so far behind her, and there was probably extra sound proofing in the cabin.

She wasn't a foodie and never would be but, for some reason she still didn't get, the food had been an incredible and indelible revelation; she hadn't had an amuse-bouche before, and she remembered thinking, with a corny smile, that their mouths had been extremely amused at the time, by the seared scallops in seaweed salad and the raw halibut with red beets and goats cheese that they had shared.

They had skipped the soup course, it had been creamed broccoli with roasted walnuts and didn't seem right for a warm day, and both had gone straight to the fresh salad leaves with green beans and blue cheese. Then, for starters they had swapped and shared their portions of organic Madagascan king prawns with citrus fruit salad and beef carpaccio with mustard mayonnaise sauce.

For their mains they had had the Seville orange marmalade glazed breast of Gressingham duck with a galette of parsnip, braised red cabbage and celeriac and the poached Kingclip with lime and ginger sauce, blanched early season Eastern Free State asparagus and boiled baby potatoes. The kingclip had been sublime. They had swapped and shared again, although she had been reluctant to pass the kingclip across. For pudding they had shared a single portion of roast plum crumble with minted crème Anglaise.

After dinner they had chosen and watched "The Lincoln Lawyer" DVD, and had had three glasses of Chablis each while they watched, the cabin lights had already been dimmed for the night. Then they had had two large, warmed, bubbles of Armagnac each, before pressing the buttons to fold the middle seat arms back and extending their seats and flattening them into adjacent beds and covering themselves with the fluffy light blue blankets. Before sleeping she had thought again that it was unfortunate that Thomas Truelove had had to be sacrificed but soon she had been distracted from such troubling thoughts as she had felt a hand move under the blanket, up her thigh under her dress, then between her legs.

They had both slept well, and woken to the captain telling them it was going to be a perfect early spring day in Cape Town and that he'd been given permission to make a detour on the approach to see the spectacular flower display at Langebaan close up. This year because of the unusually mild winter it was even more incredible than usual.

They had made themselves as presentable as possible with their freshen-up bags, and had actually enjoyed the breakfast. There hadn't been a lot of it but the smoked salmon with scrambled eggs had been exceptional. It had been the warm brown bread that had made it; tasting every bit as good as the aroma it had created when it had been baking earlier. Before that, the Granadilla juice had been new to both of them and it had gone down so well that they had had another with the salmon.

The plane had seemed to be really slow and only just above the sea when the captain came back on and told everyone on the left to look out their windows. They had laughed as they had run to the front windows, knelt on the floor and looked out and seen an incredible bright purple, yellow, white, and orange patchwork set against the bright sparkling blue green of what she knew was Langebaan lagoon.

The plane banked and turned and all she could see was the bright blue of the sky and the captain told those on the right to look out and they'd laughed and hurried to the other side and knelt again. The sun was behind a cloud now, the flowers weren't so bright and her eyes were drawn towards the blue green of the lagoon, not sparkling now..........to the tightly grouped familiar pink shapes she knew were clumsily flapping as they came in to land like a cloud setting down.

The plane banked and turned again and they rushed back to the left as the plane resumed its long low approach and she was smiling as she watched the 'flamboyance' of flamingos until it disappeared from view.

They had been third and fourth off the plane and were quickly inside the arrivals hall, and they had been surprised yet again when their luggage appeared on the carousel after just a few minutes. Walking through to the arrivals hall the Cape Grace chauffeur, there to meet them, was immediately obvious because the sign with their names showing was bigger and held higher than the all the others. He had welcomed them to Cape Town, stowed their luggage in the boot and they set off for the thirty minute journey to one of the two penthouse suites at the Cape Grace hotel at the Victoria and Alfred Waterfront. It would be their base for the next two weeks; while they made up their minds what to do next.

As the courtesy car had driven towards town, along the slopes at the bottom of Table Mountain, she remembered looking up at it and being curious about the tiny square at the far end on the top. Later she would know it was the upper cable car garage and restaurant. As they rounded yet another sweeping bend they had looked down at the stunning view across the city to the docks, and the green-blue sea beyond in the vast open bay. They smiled, and Julia had said 'Wow, welcome to the Cape, Amélie, I think we might just enjoy it'. 'Oh yes, oh yes!' she replied.

If you enjoyed Rogue Flamingo, read on for the beginning of

BROKEN DOVE

by

LA KENT

Number 2 in the DI Treloar series - available in December 2014.

The Island Park - St Ives ** *NEW* **

New this year, The Island Park offers great facilities and accommodation for the family looking for an upmarket self-catering holiday in individual seaside chalet style cabins. A splendid water complex with three swimming pools, climbing wall, trampolining, fully equipped gym, tennis and basketball. Two bars and a bistro plus a well-stocked shop with an excellent deli counter. Just 4 miles from St Ives with its abundance of shops and restaurants and its safe, sandy beaches.

A great new addition to our guide.

www.summeringincornwall.co.uk

May 1

'It started as an ordinary day. It was busy, yeah, and hellish noisy; everybody was amped, but what do you expect?' Harry Stokes told the dude from BBC Spotlight.

It was May 1st, half term and a gloriously sunny early summer's day, busiest of the year so far at The Island Park 'holiday haven' near St Ives in Cornwall, where Harry was in his second week as a lifeguard. And it had been a normal afternoon until that one piercing scream cut through the cacophony of yelling and laughter, whooping and squealing which echoed around the heaving swimming pool complex, and then those words:

'There's blood in the water!'

Harry reacted. He blew lengthily on his whistle and slid down from his ladder seat, shouting at the top of his voice, 'OUT OF THE WATER! NOW!' as if that were necessary as the water churned with thrashing bodies dragging themselves to the steps at the shallow end, the more athletic hauling themselves out at the sides. In no time the pool was deserted. Nobody was drowned, nobody was injured. Harry sighed with relief; he had done his job.

Everyone relaxed: a hoax, a prank. Among the detritus floating in the abandoned pool they found a deflated rubber ring oozing red. As Harry said, it wasn't very big, but hell you don't need a lot of blood in water, just some prat having a joke with red dye or pigs' blood.

But then they discovered that two little girls had gone missing; and then they discovered that the blood was human.

The owners of The Island Park were devastated. They'd done everything right, everything. They'd passed all the inspections; they had lifeguards trained with the RNLI at the Leisure Centre in St Ives; they had 'swim-minders' and they were getting CCTV coverage of the entire pool complex, it would be in place for the season, and nobody had expected this weather in May, nobody had expected all these people, nobody!

♫♫ Summer is a-coming in
Loudly sing cuckoo
Groweth seed and bloweth mead
and springs the wood anew
Sing cuckoo! ♫♫

Detective Sergeant Sam Scott of Devon & Cornwall Police sang along with the car radio as she navigated the narrow lanes on a glorious afternoon. She smiled as she remembered the song from school. It was 1st of May, an early summer's day full of promise, she was in love, and all was right with the world.

She had left her home in Truro and travelled west down the A30 turning off towards Lelant then bearing left up Mill Hill passing through dappled woodland to join the B3311 which runs between St Ives on the north coast and Penzance on the south. Here she turned left towards Cripplesease and Nancledra. As she crested a hill she indicated right and turned onto a narrow lane with passing places where a newly erected sign on the grass verge read 'Lower Farm Holiday Cottages and Camping' and beside it an older brick and slate sign read 'Lost Farm Farm Shop'. After 50 yards a whitewashed farmhouse with roses around the trellised entrance appeared on her left with an old sign on its wall – Lower Farm. Outside the gate, draped along the hedge, was a hand-painted banner reading 'For cottages and camping pitches apply at Farm Shop - 50 yards on your right', and indeed shortly she passed a purpose built rustic building with a gravelled car park where a small refrigerated truck sporting 'Roskilly's' distinctive playful livery was reversing. She was looking forward to the evening.

After another couple of minutes she passed a rough track leading uphill to her right with a worn sign indicating Lost Farm and Higher Farm but she continued on. She opened the front windows of the car to a dusty airflow with the slight scent of cow manure and a stronger vegetal smell. A city girl born and bred, she quickly closed them again, laughing. Finally she came to a gap in the hedgerow where a brightly coloured garland of paper flowers was strung across the opening: Lost Farm Barn, home to her boss, the object of her secret affections, Detective Inspector Félipe Treloar, and today the venue for the annual May Day Treloar family party.

Samantha Scott was on a fast track with Devon & Cornwall Police having joined from Bristol University where she had attained a 2:1 in History. This had earned her the nickname 'Samba' –Sam B. A. - with some of her colleagues which she took in good spirit. For the past few years she had been working on major crimes in a small team led by Treloar which included D S Colin Matthews and a new member, D C Luke Callaway. She was expecting to see them at the party.

Sam turned in under the garland and drove onto a field where a large number of cars were already parked. She pulled up alongside a beautiful old golden Mercedes and climbed out of her Brilliant Red VW Beetle. The boot of the Mercedes was open and a portly balding man with a bushy grey beard was rooting about inside muttering to himself.

'Hi Doc,' Sam called out pulling two bottles of wine from the rear seat.

'Good afternoon my dear,' replied Dr. Anthony Tremayne, police doctor and Treloar family friend, 'somewhere in here Molly has secreted a bumper box of my cheese and pea pasties, but I can't for the life of me... ah, yes here they are.'

He lifted out a cardboard box and closed the boot. Just then a buxom middle aged woman with thick chestnut hair and a broad gap-toothed smile, dressed in bright floral shorts and a white man's linen shirt, emerged from the side of a dilapidated stable block.

'Jesus Christ Tremayne what are you doing?' asked Molly Rackham, Tremayne's wife good-naturedly. 'Hello Sam, lovely to see you again. What is my idiot husband up to?'

'God Almighty woman, why did you hide these pasties under all that rubbish?' he huffed. 'Well, I have them now so we can all go join the fun!'

'Come along then, follow me,' Molly said, 'Oh and watch your step Sam. Phil's done wonders but the going's still rather uneven underfoot.

The wonders Molly was referring to were a major refurbishment and conversion of a group of old farm buildings. The son of a Cornish farming father and a Spanish mother, Félipe Treloar had grown up in west Cornwall on the family farm near Zennor. Four years previously, he had acquired the Lost Farm Barn site from old family friend Edmund Maddox, owner of the Lost Farm estate which consisted of three separate farms: Lost Farm, Lower Farm and Higher Farm. The sale had not however been without the fierce opposition of Edmund's elder son, Dylan, who managed Lower Farm with his wife,

Hope. Dylan was intent upon the redevelopment of the Lost Farm holdings as tourist accommodation and a major entertainment complex. However, younger son, Rees, and daughter, Megan, had sided with their father in selling Lost Farm Barn and the surrounding buildings along with twelve acres of woodland, moorland and sloping pasture to Treloar. Further to Dylan's disgust, this had been at a below market price. Since the sale Treloar has spent all of his spare time and leave on the conversion, doing the majority of the work himself. As Sam and the Tremaynes rounded the corner of the stable block they surveyed the fruits of his labours.

'Wow!' exclaimed Sam, 'he's done so much since I was last here.'

They had emerged into a cobbled courtyard flanked by the stable block and two long sheds, one open on one side. Making up the square was the main building: Lost Farm Barn. This was in fact two barns connected by a pitch-roofed glass atrium. Today the yard was lined with huge coloured flags, depicting fish, flowers and wildlife, on extensible poles, and a mismatch of wooden and plastic picnic tables with bright umbrellas was ranged across the cobbles. There was the noise of laughter and soft music, clusters of people were eating and drinking and gangs of children chased about, shrieking.

'I see Ochre's been having a field day,' Dr. Tremayne said.

'Who?' asked Sam.

'No slacking, follow me with the goodies,' Molly interjected. 'This way,' and she strode on through the crowds, heading for the barn.

As they progressed through the throng, Dr. Tremayne pointed out a couple deep in animated conversation. The two women were of a similar age but very different in appearance. One was statuesque with masses of blonde hair piled and somehow secured on top of her head. She was dressed in a multicolour kaftan with rope upon rope of beads around her neck. The other could not have made a sharper contrast, being small and slight with cropped steel grey hair and dressed in a plain black shift dress.

'The Amazon is Ochre Pengelly, local artist, writer and entrepreneur and the other, well that's Phil's eldest sister, Eva.'

'I'd never have guessed; she's nothing like Phil.'

'No she takes after their mother, Inés, the two are very alike. You'll see when you meet her,' said Molly steaming ahead.

'Look there's John and Priss over there with Colin,' she added waving at a tall thin man standing closely beside a beautiful black woman talking with a taller younger man who stood at a slight distance from them. John was Dr. John Forbes, local pathologist; Priss, his psychiatrist wife, Dr. Priscilla Forbes and Colin was Sam's colleague D S Colin Matthews.

'Well the gang's all here,' said Dr. Tremayne.

'Give me that box Tremayne and I'll take it through,' said Molly. 'You join John and the others. Come on Sam let's deliver our gifts and find our hosts.'

With that she grabbed the box from her husband and sailed on towards the barn with Sam in her wake suppressing a grin. Molly Rackham was indeed something to behold.

Detective Sergeant Tom Grigg was depressed. He hated child abductions, hated them. It was clear, at least to him, after the girls had disappeared, that they hadn't just wandered off, run away, got lost or trapped or shut in. No, some bastard had them.

The two girls were nine years old and had met for the first time that day at the pool. One was local, daughter of a friend of a manager at The Island Park, one a visitor from Ludlow. They had both been at the Splash Pool adjacent to the main swimming pool without any parental supervision. It always amazed Grigg how people on holiday behave in ways they would never dream of when at home; leaving their children alone or with strangers, getting drunk, wandering about at night, driving under the influence. He hated the summer: too many people being stupid, too many cars, too much of everything. God he was turning into a curmudgeon. His wife Lizzie said he had forgotten that when their children were young he allowed them out to play for hours on end, especially in the summer and when they were away on holiday. He pointed out to her in return, that that was then and this was now, a point she conceded without really understanding its relevance; sometimes, it definitely wasn't worth the argument.

The local girl was Lily Warren, the girl from Ludlow, Tamsin Thomas and they were both going to turn up dead, Grigg knew it, the parents knew it, the press knew it.

8

Sam and Molly crossed the courtyard to an open stable door which led directly into the barn's kitchen. Every work surface, table, cupboard and shelf in the large sunlit room was covered with plates of food. There were huge bowls of salads, quiches, tortillas, empanadas, plates of cold meats, patés, cold salmon, various breads, nuts, olives, pickles, trays of fruit and cheeses and three large flat cakes. Ranks of wine bottles were lined up beneath a large wooden table. Ahead of them glass doors were open onto a patio where Sam could see Félipe Treloar standing with two women, one small and wiry, dressed in a black calf-length cotton dress, her long silver- streaked black hair swept up into a loose bun at the back of her head, the other simply stunning; a tall lithe beauty, her long black hair falling in a single plait over her left shoulder.

'We come bearing gifts,' Molly called out.

The smaller woman broke away from her companions and hurried into the kitchen smiling, leaving Treloar with the other woman. Sam watched in dismay as he pulled her towards him, his hands on her shoulders and kissed her on the forehead.

'Molly! How wonderful for you to come,' the smaller woman said taking the box of food Molly held out to her.

'Inés, this is Phil's colleague, Samantha Scott, Sam meet Phil's mother, Inés de Santangel.'

Seeing no alternative Sam put the bottles of wine down on the floor at her feet and took the woman's hand, 'I'm so pleased to meet you Ms de Santangel.'

'Oh Sam, please this is such a mouthful, call me Inés.'

Sam smiled distractedly trying to keep one eye on the couple on the patio.

'Félipe, Lucia, come in to greet our new guests!' Treloar's mother called out.

Treloar and the beauty walked in to meet them. Sam was transfixed by the woman. She was about Sam's height but in her black stiletto heels stood almost as tall as Treloar. Her hair was lustrous and her eyes large, the deepest brown and expertly made up. She wore a knee length black linen pencil skirt and a sleeveless red silk shirt and Sam hated her on sight. Treloar took his arm from her shoulder and crossed to kiss Molly on the cheek.

'Molly, great to see you,' he turned and smiled at Sam.

'Molly Rackham, how wonderful to see you,' the beauty said in a deep sonorous voice that made Sam think of molten chocolate. She crossed to join Treloar and kissed Molly on both cheeks, then turned to face Sam, 'and who have we here?' she asked.

Treloar draped his arm back across her shoulder and smiled at Sam whose heart sank. She felt horribly as if she were about to burst into tears.

'Sam Scott, meet Lucia Lo Verde,' he said beaming as the two women shook hands, 'Lucia, Sam works with me, she's my right hand woman so to speak.'

'Delighted to meet you Sam. I hope you keep Flip in order, he needs a firm hand I imagine,' she added with a deep chuckle.

As Sam stood speechless, rooted to the spot whilst the beauty turned and said something to Inés and the two of them walked over to one of the food-laden cupboards, Treloar spoke.

'Let me get you a drink ladies; what will you have? How about a glass of Asti? Lucia brought it. It's wonderful, nothing like the sweet stuff,' he walked away towards a huge American fridge.

Sam heard Molly chuckle at her side.

'Sam sweetheart, don't look so crestfallen. Lucia Lo Verde is an exceptionally beautiful and accomplished woman, she is a brilliant photographer and expert swordswoman, but she also happens to be one of Phil's three sisters.'

Sam felt her cheeks burn and a wave of warmth flood through her body: relief.

The public and press were responding rapidly to the alert. Radio appeals were going out, twitter and Facebook alerts. Posters with the girls' photographs were being printed, everybody was being asked to search everywhere: cars, caravans, tents, boats, sheds, garages, outbuildings, farm buildings, shops, beaches. There had even been a light plane trailing a banner along the coast, sponsored by a local building firm, calling for people to be on the lookout. Grigg had to admit that he was impressed with the speed and the extent of the response, but the stats were all too bleak. What was it, 80% of abducted children dead within the first 24 hours? Still, he could always be pleasantly surprised.

D S Grigg and a female constable, who was acting as family liaison, were standing in the conservatory at the back of Rebecca and Guy Warren's Victorian terrace house in St Ives. Rebecca and Kate Thomas were sitting together on an over-stuffed cream sofa. Their husbands were out searching.

'People say it's like an endless screaming in your head, but it isn't,' said Rebecca Warren in a tear-strained voice. She was a small plump thirty something with dirty blonde tousled hair, barefoot and dressed in jeans and a baggy Weird Fish T shirt. As she spoke she was unconsciously wringing the neck of an old teddy bear clutched in her hands. 'It's like an endless panic attack. I feel like I'll never breathe normally again. I feel like I'm drowning. The doctor came but I can't take anything, not now, not yet. I just can't stop thinking about what's happening to them. I just cannot bear that,' tears rolled down her face as she spoke. 'Guy and Sebastian are out looking for them but we all thought I should stay here, we should be here, in case Lily can find her way home.' She looked at Grigg with pleading eyes.

'I think that's a very good idea,' he said softly, dropping to one knee before her.

Kate Thomas had said nothing. A tall thin woman with long dark red hair, wearing a denim dress and red tennis shoes, she sat staring fixedly at a basket of dried flowers in the corner, showing no emotion, her hands folded calmly in her lap.

As PC Fiona Cameron walked Grigg through the hallway to the front porch she spoke quietly.

'There's something not quite right here Sir.'

'I know. The Warren woman is behaving exactly as I would expect, but the other woman... well she's just too calm.'

'I know. She's been like that since I arrived. I'm wondering if she's taken something?'

'Possibly, but it's more than that. She's concerned, worried even, but she's not frightened, she's not frantic like Rebecca. She's anxious but she's not terrified. It's odd. Keep a close eye on her in particular.'

We do hope you enjoyed these first pages of Broken Dove; look out for the book in December 2014, when it will be first published.